AMERICAN SCHOOL TEXTBOOK

VOCABULARY KEY

GRADE 5

Michael A. Putlack

FÜN學美國英語課本

各學科關鍵英單 二版＋ Workbook

MP3

寂天雲 APP

如何下載 MP3 音檔

❶ 寂天雲 APP 聆聽：掃描書上 QR Code 下載「寂天雲－英日語學習隨身聽」APP。加入會員後，用 APP 內建掃描器再次掃描書上 QR Code，即可使用 APP 聆聽音檔。

❷ 官網下載音檔：請上「寂天閱讀網」（www.icosmos.com.tw），註冊會員／登入後，搜尋本書，進入本書頁面，點選「MP3 下載」下載音檔，存於電腦等其他播放器聆聽使用。

FÜN學美國英語課本
各學科關鍵英單
GRADE 5

AMERICAN SCHOOL TEXTBOOK
VOCABULARY KEY

二版

作者簡介

Michael A. Putlack

專攻歷史與英文，擁有美國麻州 Tufts University 碩士學位。

作　　者　Michael A. Putlack
　　　　　Zachary Fillingham / Shara Dupuis (Workbook B 大題）
編　　輯　丁宥榆／歐寶妮
翻　　譯　歐寶妮
校　　對　丁宥暄
封面設計　林書玉
內頁排版　丁宥榆／林書玉
製程管理　洪巧玲
出 版 者　寂天文化事業股份有限公司
電　　話　+886-(0)2-2365-9739
傳　　真　+886-(0)2-2365-9835
網　　址　www.icosmos.com.tw
讀者服務　onlineservice@icosmos.com.tw
出版日期　2023 年 10 月　二版二刷　（寂天雲隨身聽 APP 版）

郵 撥 帳 號　1998620-0 寂天文化事業股份有限公司
訂書金額未滿 1000 元，請外加運費 100 元。
〔若有破損，請寄回更換，謝謝。〕

國家圖書館出版品預行編目資料

FUN 學美國英語課本：各學科關鍵英單 . Grade 5（寂天隨
身聽 APP 版）/ Michael A. Putlack 著；歐寶妮譯 . -- 二版 . --
[臺北市]：寂天文化 , 2023.10
　面；　公分

ISBN 978-626-300-215-9（平裝附光碟片）

1.CST: 英語 2.CST: 詞彙
805.12　　　　　　　　　　　　　　112016206

FUN學美國英語課本：各學科關鍵英單

進入明星學校必備的英文單字

用美國教科書學英文是最道地的學習方式，有越來越多的學校選擇以美國教科書作為教材，用全英語授課（immersion）的方式教學，讓學生把英語當成母語學習。在一些語言學校裡，也掀起了一波「用美國教科書學英文」的風潮。另外，還有越來越多的父母優先考慮讓子女用美國教科書來學習英文，讓孩子將來能夠進入明星學校或國際學校就讀。

為什麼要使用美國教科書呢？TOEFL 等國際英語能力測驗都是以各學科知識為基礎，使用美國教科書不但能大幅提升英文能力，也可以增加數學、社會、科學等方面的知識，因此非常適合用來準備考試。即使不到國外留學，也可以像在美國上課一樣，而這也是使用美國教科書最吸引人的地方。

以多樣化的照片、插圖和例句來熟悉跨科學習中的英文單字

到底該使用何種美國教科書呢？還有如何才能讀懂美國教科書呢？美國各州、各學校的課程都不盡相同，而學生也有選擇教科書的權利，所以單單是教科書的種類就多達數十種。若不小心選擇到程度不適合的教科書，就很容易造成孩子對學英語的興趣大減。

因此，正確的作法應該要先累積字彙和相關知識背景。我國學生的學習能力很強，只需要培養對不熟悉的用語和跨科學習（Cross-Curricular Study）的適應能力。

本系列網羅了在以全英語教授社會、科學、數學、語言、藝術、音樂等學科時，所有會出現的必備英文單字。只要搭配書中真實的照片、插圖和例句，就能夠把這些在美國小學課本中會出現的各學科核心單字記起來，同時還可以熟悉相關的背景知識。

四種使用頻率最高的美國教科書的字彙分析

本系列套書規畫了 6 個階段的字彙學習課程，搜羅了 McGraw Hill、Harcourt、Pearson 和 Core Knowledge 等四大教科書中的主要字彙，並且整理出各科目、各主題的核心單字，然後依照學年分為 Grade 1 到 Grade 6。

本套書的適讀對象為「準備大學學測指考的學生」和「準備參加 TOEFL 等國際英語能力測驗的學生」。對於「準備赴美唸高中的學生」和「想要看懂美國教科書的學生」，本套書亦是最佳的先修教材。

《FUN學美國英語課本：各學科關鍵英單》系列的結構與特色

1. 本套書中所收錄的英文單字都是美國學生在上課時會學到的字彙和用法。

2. 將美國小學教科書中會出現的各學科核心單字，搭配多樣化照片、插圖和例句，讓讀者更容易熟記。

3. 藉由閱讀教科書式的題目，來強化讀、聽、寫的能力。透過各式各樣的練習與題目，不僅能夠全盤吸收與各主題有關的字彙，也能夠熟悉相關的知識背景。

4. 每一冊的教學大綱（syllabus）皆涵蓋了社會、歷史、地理、科學、數學、語言、美術和音樂等學科，以循序漸進的方式，學習從基礎到高級的各科核心字彙，不僅能夠擴增各科目的字彙量，同時還提升了運用句子的能力。（教學大綱請參考第 8 頁）

5. 可學到社會、科學等的相關背景知識和用語，也有助於準備 TOEFL 等國際英語能力測驗。

6. 對於「英語程度有限，但想看懂美國教科書的學生」來說，本套書是很好的先修教材。

7. 全系列 6 階段共分為 6 冊，可依照個人英語程度，選擇合適的分冊。

   Grade 1 美國小學 1 年級課程　　**Grade 2** 美國小學 2 年級課程

   Grade 3 美國小學 3 年級課程　　**Grade 4** 美國小學 4 年級課程

   Grade 5 美國小學 5 年級課程　　**Grade 6** 美國小學 6 年級課程

8. 書末附有關鍵字彙的中英文索引，方便讀者搜尋與查照（請參考第 141 頁）。

強烈建議下列學生使用本套書：

1.「準備大學學測指考」的學生

2.「準備參加以全英語授課的課程，想熟悉美國學生上課時會用到的各科核心字彙」的學生

3.「對美國小學各科必備英文字彙已相當熟悉，想朝高級單字邁進」美國學校的七年級生

4.「準備赴美唸高中」的學生

MP3

收錄了本書的「Key Words」、「Power Verbs」、「Word Families」單元中的所有單字和例句，和「Checkup」中 E 大題的文章，以及 Workbook 中 A 大題聽寫練習文章。

How to Use This Book

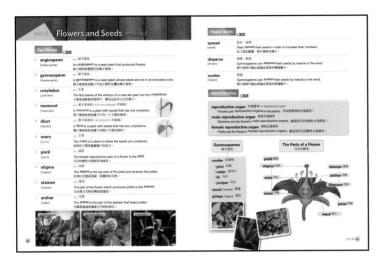

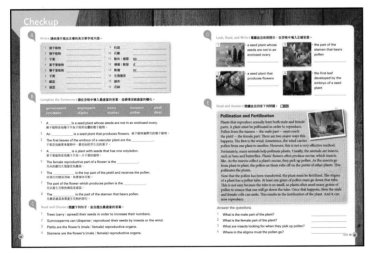

Checkup

A Write｜練習寫出本書所學到的字彙，一方面能夠熟悉單字的拼法，一方面也能夠幫助記憶。

B Complete the Sentences｜將本書所學到的字彙和例句，確實背熟。

C Read and Choose｜透過多樣化的練習，熟悉本書所學到的字彙用法。

D Look, Read, and Write｜透過照片、插畫和提示，加深對所學到的字彙的印象。

E Read and Answer｜透過與各單元主題有關的「文章閱讀理解測驗」，來熟悉教科書的出題模式，並培養與各學科相關的背景知識和適應各種考試的能力。

Review Test 每 5 個單元結束會有一回總複習測驗，有助於回想起沒有辦法一次就記起來或忘記的單字，並且再次複習。

Table of Contents

Workbook 聽力閱讀試題本

Syllabus Vol.5

Subject	Topic & Area	Title
Social Studies ● **History and Geography**	Geography and Culture	A Nation of Diversity
	Social Studies	The American Electoral System
	History and Culture	History and Culture
	American History	The Native People of North America
	World History	The Age of Exploration
	World History	The Spanish Conquerors
	American History	Colonial America
	American History	The Declaration of Independence
	American History	Post-Civil War
	American History	The United States in the Modern Age
Science	Life Science	Classifying Living Things
	Life Science	Plant Structure
	Life Science	Plants Without Seeds
	Life Science	Flowers and Seeds
	Life Science	Adaptations
	Life Science	The Human Body
	Life Science	Ecosystems
	Earth Science	Earth and Resources
	Physical Science	Matter
	Earth Science	The Universe
Mathematics	Numbers and Number Sense	Numbers
	Computation	Computation
	Fractions and Decimals	Decimals, Fractions, and Ratios
	Geometry	Geometry
Language and Literature	Mythology	Stories, Myths, and Legends
	Language Arts	Learning About Literature
	Language Arts	Learning About Language
Visual Arts	Visual Arts	Renaissance Art
	Visual Arts	American Art
Music	A World of Music	A World of Music

CHAPTER 1

Social Studies • History and Geography ①

A Nation of Diversity 多樣性的民族

Key Words
🔊 001

01 diversity
[daɪ`vɝsətɪ]

(n.) 多樣性；差異　　*a great diversity of 各種各樣的；多方面的
*biological diversity 生物多樣性

The United States is a nation of **diversity** where people of different races and ethnicities live together.
美國是一個多元化國家，有各個不同民族和種族的人聚居在這裡。

02 ethnic group
[`ɛθnɪk grup]

(n.) 族群　　*ethnic minorities 少數民族　　*ethnic background 民族文化背景

An **ethnic group** is a group of people who have the same customs, language, and history.　族群是指擁有相同習俗、語言和歷史的一群人。

03 melting pot
[`mɛltɪŋ pɑt]

(n.) 文化熔爐

The United States is called a **melting pot** because people from different countries go there and all become Americans.
美國被稱為文化熔爐，因為不同國家的人民來到美國，並成為美國人。

04 national identity
[`næʃənḷ aɪ`dɛntətɪ]

(n.) 國家認同　　*national pride 民族自尊　　*racial identity 種族認同

National identity is important to many immigrants.
國家認同對許多移民來說很重要。

05 authority
[ə`θɔrətɪ]

(n.) 權力；權威人士　　*under the authority of sb. 受某人支配
*have the authority to V. / over sth. 有權做某事／對某事有決定權

The government's **authority** comes from the people.　政府的權力來自人民。

06 democratic republic
[ˌdɛmə`krætɪk rɪ`pʌblɪk]

(n.) 民主共和國　　*democratic election 民主選舉　　*Democratic Party【美】民主黨

The United States is called a **democratic republic**.
美國被稱為民主共和國。

07 constitution
[ˌkɑnstə`tjuʃən]

(n.) 憲法　　*the Constitution 美國憲法　　*democratic constitution 民主憲法

The United States **Constitution** is the supreme law of the land.
《美國憲法》是國家的最高法律。

08 amendment
[ə`mɛndmənt]

(n.) 修正案；修訂　　*an amendment to 議案等的修正案
*constitutional amendments 憲法修正案

An **amendment** is an addition to the constitution in order to change a law or to make a new one.　修正案是用來更改法條或制訂新法的憲法增補條款。

09 party
[`pɑrtɪ]

(n.) 政黨　　*ruling party 執政黨　　*party leader 政黨領袖；黨魁

There are two main political **parties** in the United States: the Democratic Party and the Republican Party.　美國有兩個主要政黨：民主黨與共和黨。

10 compromise
[`kɑmprə,maɪz]

(n.) 妥協；讓步　　*come to / reach a compromise 達成妥協
*a compromise plan 折衷計畫

The two main parties often reach a **compromise** on bills they want to pass.
兩個主要政黨常對他們想通過的法案達成妥協。

melting pot

U.S. Constitution

national identity

ratify
['rætə,faɪ]
正式生效
The Bill of Rights was **ratified** in 1791. 《權利法案》於 1791 年正式生效。

establish
[ə'stæblɪʃ]
制定;建立
The Constitution of the United States was **established** in 1789. 《美國憲法》制訂於 1789 年。

amend
[ə'mɛnd]
修訂;修改
Sometimes it is necessary to **amend** a constitution. 有時候必須修憲。

change
更正;改變
Sometimes it is necessary to **change** a constitution. 有時候必須改憲。

bear
[bɛr]
攜帶
The Constitution gives Americans the right to **bear** arms.
《美國憲法》賦予美國人攜帶武器的權利。

carry
攜帶
The Constitution gives Americans the right to **carry** arms.
《美國憲法》賦予美國人攜帶武器的權利。

Declaration of Independence

compromise
['kɑmprə,maɪz]
妥協;讓步
When two parties **compromise**, they find some middle ground.
當兩個政黨達成妥協,表示他們找到了折衷點。

reach a compromise
達成妥協 (= come to a compromise)
When two parties **reach a compromise**, they find some middle ground.
當兩個政黨達成妥協,表示他們找到了折衷點。

Declaration of Independence　獨立宣言
The Declaration of Independence was signed on July 4, 1776.
《獨立宣言》簽署於 1776 年 7 月 4 日。

Articles of Confederation　聯邦條例
The Articles of Confederation were used by the states after the
Revolutionary War ended. 美國於獨立戰爭後開始採行《聯邦條例》。

Constitution
[,kɑnstə'tjuʃən]
美國憲法
The Constitution divides the government into three branches.
《美國憲法》將政府區分為三個部門。

Bill of Rights
權利法案
The Bill of Rights gives many rights to both the people and the states.
《權利法案》賦予人民和國家許多權利。

Rights Granted by the Bill of Rights 《權利法案》賦予的權利

freedom of speech 言論自由	**the right to bear arms** 攜帶武器權
freedom of religion 宗教自由	**the right to a swift trial** 迅速審判權
freedom of the press 新聞自由	**the right to a trial by jury** 陪審團審判權

Checkup

A

Write l 請依提示寫出正確的英文單字或片語。

1	多樣性；差異	9	政黨
2	族群	10	妥協；讓步
3	文化熔爐	11	正式生效
4	國家認同	12	制定；建立
5	權力；權威人士	13	修訂；修改 a
6	民主共和國	14	攜帶
7	憲法	15	達成妥協
8	修正案；修訂	16	權利法案

B

Complete the Sentences l 請在空格中填入最適當的答案，並視情況做適當的變化。

diversity	democratic republic	ethnic group	authority	amendment
constitution	national identity	melting pot	party	compromise

1 The United States is a nation of _____ where people of different races and ethnicities live together.
美國是一個多元化國家，有各個不同民族和種族的人聚居在這裡。

2 An _____ is a group of people who have the same customs, language, and history. 族群是指擁有相同習俗、語言和歷史的一群人。

3 _____ is important to many immigrants.
國家認同對許多移民來說很重要。

4 The United States is called a _____. 美國被稱為民主共和國。

5 The United States _____ is the supreme law of the land.
《美國憲法》是國家的最高法律。

6 The government's _____ comes from the people. 政府的權力來自人民。

7 An _____ is an addition to the constitution in order to change a law or to make a new one. 修正案是用來更改法條或制訂新法的憲法增補條款。

8 There are two main political _____ in the United States: the Democratic Party and the Republican Party. 美國有兩個主要政黨：民主黨與共和黨。

C

Read and Choose l 閱讀下列句子，並且選出最適當的答案。

1 The Bill of Rights was (established | ratified) in 1791.

2 Sometimes it is necessary to (compromise | amend) a constitution.

3 The Constitution gives Americans the right to (bear | pass) arms.

4 When two parties (reach | compromise), they find some middle ground.

D Look, Read, and Write | 看圖並且依照提示，在空格中填入正確答案。

1 ▸ a place where people from different races, countries, or social classes go and live together
_____

3 ▸ an addition to a constitution
_____

2 ▸ the state of having different people or things in a group or place
_____

4 ▸ the legal right to express one's opinions freely
_____

E Read and Answer | 閱讀並且回答下列問題。 🔊 004

The Bill of Rights

In 1787, the states' leaders started to write the Constitution. The Constitution is the supreme law of the land. But many Americans were not happy. They were worried about the strength of the national government. They knew a strong government could take away their rights. So they wanted to add some amendments to the Constitution. These would give specific rights to the people and the states. So they wrote 10 amendments to the Constitution. Together, they were called the Bill of Rights. The Bill of Rights was ratified in 1791 and then became law.

The First Amendment is about freedom. People have freedom of speech, religion, and the press and the right to assemble peacefully. The Second Amendment gives people the right to have guns. The Third Amendment says the government cannot put soldiers in people's houses. The Fourth Amendment protects people from illegal searches and arrests. The Fifth Amendment says a person cannot be tried twice for the same crime. The Sixth Amendment gives people the right to a speedy trial. The Seventh Amendment gives people the right to a jury trial. The Eighth Amendment protects people from high bail. The Ninth and Tenth amendments protect the people and states by giving them all rights not mentioned in the Constitution.

What is true? Write T(true) or F(false).

1 The American people wanted a strong national government. _____

2 The Bill of Rights became law in 1787. _____

3 The first 10 amendments are the Bill of Rights. _____

4 The First Amendment gives people freedom of speech. _____

Key Words 🔊 005

01 primary
['praɪˌmɛrɪ]

(n.) 初選　　*(a.)* 主要的；原始的　　*presidential primary 總統初選
*primary goal 首要目標

Residents vote for their favorite presidential candidate in their state's **primary**. 居民在州內初選投票給他們喜愛的總統候選人。

02 caucus
['kɔkəs]

(n.) 黨代表大會；黨團會議　　*presidential caucus 總統大選黨團會議
*legislative caucus 立法院黨團

State residents choose delegates to vote for a presidential nominee at a **caucus**. 州民選出黨代表，負責在黨代表大會上投票決定總統提名人選。

03 candidate
['kændədet]

(n.) 候選人　　*presidential candidate 總統候選人　　*a candidate for …… 的候選人

A **candidate** is a person running for a political office.
候選人是競選政治職務的人。

04 delegate
['dɛləgɪt]

(n.) 代表；會議代表　　*a delegate to …… 的代表　　*convention delegate 大會代表

A **delegate** is a representative of a political party. 黨代表是一個政黨的代表。

05 nominee
[ˌnɑməˈni]

(n.) 被提名人　　*nominator 提名者；任命者；推薦者
*the nominee for (Best Actress, etc.) 被提名 ……（最佳女主角等）的人

A **nominee** is a party's official candidate for a political office.
提名人是代表一個政黨參選政治職務的正式候選人。

06 nomination
[ˌnɑməˈneʃən]

(n.) 提名；任命　　*a nomination for sth. 提名做某事、某榮耀
*approve one's nomination 同意任命、提名某人

A candidate must win the **nomination** from his or her party to be able to run for a political office. 候選人要獲得所屬政黨的提名，才能參選政治職務。

07 convention
[kənˈvɛnʃən]

(n.) 大會；協定；公約；習俗　　*by / according to convention 按習俗
*Geneva Convention 日內瓦公約

Political parties hold **conventions** to determine their presidential nominee.
政黨舉行大會來決定總統提名人選。

08 ballot
['bælət]

(n.) 選票；投票　　*cast a ballot for sb. 投某人一票
*(by) secret ballot（採取）不記名投票

A voter casts a **ballot** on Election Day. 投票人於大選日投票。

09 voting station
['votɪŋ ˈsteʃən]

(n.) 投票所（= polling station）

Citizens go to a **voting station** to vote on Election Day.
公民於大選日前往投票所投票。

10 electoral college
[ɪˈlɛktərəl ˈkɑlɪdʒ]

(n.) 選舉人團　　*electoral district 選區　　*electoral system 選舉制度

The **electoral college** is the group of people who cast the final vote for president. 選舉人團是負責執行總統選舉最終投票的一群人。

Election Day

the Democratic Party mascot

the Republican Party mascot

voting/polling station

voting booth

ballot

nominate
['nɑmə,net]

提名；任命
A party **nominates** someone for president at its convention.
政黨於大會上提名總統參選人。

select

挑選；選擇
A party **selects** its presidential nominee at its convention.
政黨於大會上選擇總統提名人。

run

競選
Many candidates **run** for office each year. 每年都有許多候選人競選公職。

vie
[vaɪ]

競爭
Many candidates **vie** for office each year. 每年都有許多候選人競選公職。

raise

籌集
Politicians need to **raise** money to run for office. 從政者需要籌措資金來競選公職。

donate
['donet]

捐獻；捐贈
Many people **donate** money to the politicians they support.
許多人捐錢給他們支持的從政者。

cast a ballot
[kæst ə 'bælət]

投票 (= cast a vote)
Voters **cast** their **ballots** on Election Day. 投票人於大選日投票。

raise money

cast a ballot

Word Families ● 007

survey [sə've]	調查；測量 Journalists often take **surveys** of potential voters. 新聞工作者常對潛在選民進行調查。	
poll	民意調查；投票 **Polls** tell people which candidates are favored to win. 民意調查告知人們哪些候選人當選的呼聲較高。	
voting booth	投票間 (= polling booth) Voters cast their votes from inside a **voting booth**. 投票人於投票間內投票。	

Famous Primaries and Caucuses 著名的初選與黨代表大會

New Hampshire Primary 新罕布夏初選
[nju 'hæmpʃə 'praɪ,mɛrɪ] The New Hampshire Primary is the first primary in the country.
新罕布夏初選是全美國第一個進行的初選。

Iowa Caucus 愛荷華州黨團會議
['aɪəwə 'kɔkəs] The Iowa Caucus is the first caucus in the country.
愛荷華州黨團會議是全美國第一個進行的黨團會議。

Super Tuesday 超級星期二
Many states hold their presidential primaries and caucuses on Super Tuesday.
許多州在超級星期二舉行總統初選和黨代表大會。

Checkup

A

Write | 請依提示寫出正確的英文單字或片語。

1	初選	_____	9	投票所	_____
2	黨代表大會	_____	10	選舉人團	_____
3	候選人	_____	11	提名；任命 (v.)	_____
4	代表；會議代表	_____	12	競爭	_____
5	被提名人	_____	13	籌集	_____
6	提名；任命 (n.)	_____	14	捐獻；捐贈	_____
7	大會；協定	_____	15	投票	_____
8	選票；投票	_____	16	投票間	_____

B

Complete the Sentences | 請在空格中填入最適當的答案，並視情況做適當的變化。

candidate	voting station	caucus	nominee	delegate
nomination	electoral college	ballot	convention	primary

1 Residents vote for their favorite presidential candidate in their state's _____.
居民在州內初選投票給他們喜愛的總統候選人。

2 A _____ is a person running for a political office. 候選人是競選政治職務的人。

3 A _____ is a representative of a political party. 黨代表是一個政黨的代表。

4 State residents choose delegates to vote for a presidential nominee at a
_____. 州民選出黨代表，負責在黨代表大會上投票決定總統提名人選。

5 A candidate must win the _____ from his or her party to be able to run
for a political office.
候選人要獲得所屬政黨的提名，才能參選政治職務。

6 Political parties hold _____ to determine their presidential nominee.
政黨舉行大會來決定總統提名人選。

7 The _____ is the group of people who cast the final vote for
president. 選舉人團是負責執行總統選舉最終投票的一群人。

8 Citizens go to a _____ to vote on Election Day.
公民於大選日前往投票所投票。

C

Read and Choose | 閱讀下列句子，並且選出最適當的答案。

1 A party (nominates | votes) someone for president at its convention.

2 Many candidates (run | select) for office each year.

3 Politicians need to (donate | raise) money to run for office.

4 Voters (vote | cast) their ballots on Election Day.

D

Look, Read, and Write | 看圖並且依照提示，在空格中填入正確答案。

 ▸ a party's official candidate for a political office

_____

 ▸ an activity in which many people are asked what they think about something

_____

 ▸ to give something such as money or goods to a person or an organization

_____

 ▸ a piece of paper that you use to vote

_____

E

Read and Answer | 閱讀並且回答下列問題。 008

The American Presidential Election System

In the United States, there are many political parties. But two are very powerful. They are the Republican Party and the Democratic Party. About two years before the presidential election, members of both parts start running for president. They want to be their party's presidential nominee. They raise money and travel around the country giving speeches.

Every four years, the U.S. elects a president. In an election year, every state has either a primary or a caucus. This is where they elect delegates. The candidates want to get as many delegates as possible. New Hampshire has the first primary in the country. Iowa has the first caucus. As the states hold their primaries and caucuses, unpopular politicians drop out of the race. When one candidate has enough delegates, he or she becomes the party's nominee. In July or August, both parties have conventions. They officially nominate their presidential and vice presidential candidates there. Then, the race for president really begins. The candidates for both parties visit many states. They give speeches. They try to win voters. On the first Tuesday in November, the American voters decide who the next president will be.

Fill in the blanks.

1 The _____ Party and the Democratic Party are the most powerful parties.

2 The U.S. elects a new president every _____ years.

3 New Hampshire has the first _____ in the country.

4 Election Day is on the first _____ in November.

History and Culture 歷史與文化

Key Words 🔊 009

01 historian
[hɪsˈtorɪən]
(n.) 歷史學家　*military historian 軍事歷史學家　*make history 名留青史
Historians study events and people from the past.
歷史學家研究過去的事件與人物。

02 archaeologist
[ˌɑrkɪˈɑlədʒɪst]
(n.) 考古學家　*archaeology 考古學　*archaeological site 考古遺址
Archaeologists study ancient human cultures.
考古學家研究古人類文化。

03 timeline
[ˈtaɪmˌlaɪn]
(n.) 時間表；時間軸；大事記　*timetable 時間表（作此義時為同義詞）
A timeline lists a sequence of events in history.
大事記列出一連串的歷史事件。

04 interpretation
[ɪnˌtɝprɪˈteʃən]
(n.) 詮釋；解釋　*be open to interpretation 可作各種解釋
*further interpretation 進一步說明
The interpretation of an event is important to historians.
事件的解釋對歷史學家來說很重要。

05 primary source
[ˈpraɪˌmɛrɪ sors]
(n.) 第一手資料；原始資料（= original source）
A primary source is material written by a person who witnessed an event.
第一手資料是由事件目擊者所寫的資料。

06 secondary source
[ˈsɛkənˌdɛrɪ sors]
(n.) 第二手資料　*from a reliable source 來自可靠消息來源
A secondary source is a work based on primary sources.
第二手資料是根據第一手資料而來的作品。

07 artifact
[ˈɑrtɪˌfækt]
(n.) 工藝品；手工藝品　*prehistoric artifact 史前手工藝品
Historians study artifacts — things made by humans long ago — to learn how people lived in the past.
歷史學家研究手工藝品——古人製作的東西——來得知古人的生活。

08 chronology
[krəˈnɑlədʒɪ]
(n.) 年表；年代學；按時間排列的大事記
*reconstruct the chronology 還原事件發生順序
*in chronological/historical order 依照時間先後順序
The sequence in which something happened is its chronology.
事情發生的順序稱為該事件的年表。

09 historical figure
[hɪsˈtɔrɪkḷ ˈfɪgjɚ]
(n.) 歷史人物　*historical research 史學研究　*historical background 歷史背景
Important people in history are known as historical figures.
歷史上的重要人物稱為歷史人物。

10 oral history
[ˈorəl ˈhɪstərɪ]
(n.) 口述歷史　*oral historian 口述歷史學家
Some historians study oral history, such as spoken memories, stories, and songs. 有些歷史學家研究口述歷史，例如口傳的記憶、故事以及歌曲。

Artifacts

historical figure

interpret
[ɪnˋtɝprɪt]

解釋；說明
Historians try to **interpret** events from the past.
歷史學家設法解釋過去的事件。

examine
[ɪgˋzæmɪn]

調查；檢查
Archaeologists **examine** artifacts to learn about ancient cultures.
考古學家仔細檢查手工藝品來了解古代文化。

translate
[trænsˋlet]

翻譯；解釋
Many historians must **translate** writings from different languages.
許多歷史學家必須翻譯不同語言的著作。

utilize
[ˋjutḷͺaɪz]

利用
Historians **utilize** many different sources when they do research.
歷史學家做研究時，會利用許多不同的原始資料。

take place

發生
Important historical events **take place** all the time. 重大歷史事件不斷在發生。

occur
[əˋkɝ]

發生 (= happen)
Important historical events **occur** all the time. 重大歷史事件不斷在發生。

B.C.	西元前 B.C. stands for "before Christ." B.C. 代表「耶穌出生前」。 Rome was founded in the year 753 **B.C.** 羅馬建立於西元前 753 年。
A.D.	西元年 A.D. stands for "anno domini." A.D. 代表「主的年」。 Nero became emperor in 54 **A.D.** 尼祿於西元 54 年成為君王。
century	世紀 A **century** is a period that lasts 100 years. 世紀是為期一百年的時間。
decade [ˋdɛked]	年代 A **decade** is a period of 10 years. 年代是為期十年的時間。
historic	歷史上著名的；具有重大歷史意義的 **Historic** sites are where important events occurred. 歷史古蹟是重大事件發生的地方。
historical	歷史的；史學的 **Historical** events are events that made an impact on history. 歷史事件是對歷史有重大影響的事件。

historic site

Checkup

A

Write | 請依提示寫出正確的英文單字或片語。

1	歷史學家	_____	9	歷史人物	_____
2	考古學家	_____	10	口述歷史	_____
3	時間表；時間軸	_____	11	解釋；說明 (v.)	_____
4	詮釋；解釋 (n.)	_____	12	翻譯；解釋	_____
5	第一手資料	_____	13	利用	_____
6	第二手資料	_____	14	西元前	_____
7	工藝品；手工藝品	_____	15	西元年	_____
8	年表；年代學	_____	16	歷史上著名的	_____

B

Complete the Sentences | 請在空格中填入最適當的答案，並視情況做適當的變化。

historical figure	interpretation	oral history	historian	archaeologist
primary source	secondary source	chronology	timeline	artifact

1 _____ study ancient human cultures. 考古學家研究古人類文化。

2 _____ study events and people from the past.
歷史學家研究過去的事件與人物。

3 The _____ of an event is important to historians.
事件的解釋對歷史學家來說很重要。

4 Historians study _____ to learn how people lived in the past.
歷史學家研究手工藝品來得知古人的生活。

5 A _____ is material written by a person who witnessed an event. 第一手資料是由事件目擊者所寫的資料。

6 The sequence in which something happened is its _____.
事情發生的順序稱為該事件的年表。

7 Important people in history are known as _____.
歷史上的重要人物稱為歷史人物。

8 Some historians study _____, such as spoken memories,
stories, and songs. 有些歷史學家研究口述歷史，例如口傳的記憶、故事以及歌曲。

C

Read and Choose | 閱讀下列句子，並且選出最適當的答案。

1 Historians try to (translate | interpret) events from the past.

2 Historians (utilize | make) many different sources when they do research.

3 Important historical events (take | occur) place all the time.

4 B.C. (shows | stands) for "before Christ."

Look, Read, and Write ┃ 看圖並且依照提示，在空格中填入正確答案。

1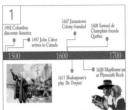
▸ a diagram showing
a sequence of
events in history
_____

3
▸ a period of 10 years
_____

2
▸ an object made by
humans long ago
_____

4
▸ someone who
studies archaeology
_____

E

Read and Answer ┃ 閱讀並且回答下列問題。 012

What Do Historians Do?

Historians study the past. They are concerned about past events and people who lived in the past. But historians do not just learn names, dates, and places. Instead, they try to interpret past events. They want to know why an event happened. They want to know why a person acted in a certain way. And they want to know how one event caused another to occur.

To do this, historians must study many sources. First, they use primary sources. These are sources that were recorded at the same time an event occurred. They could be journals. They could be books. They could be newspaper articles or photographs. In modern times, they could even be videotaped recordings. Historians use primary sources to get the opinions of eyewitnesses to important events. They also use secondary sources. These are works written by people who did not witness an event. Good historians use both primary and secondary sources in their work.

There are many kinds of history. Some historians like political history. Others study military history. Some focus on economics. And others prefer social or cultural history. All of them are important. And all of them help us understand the past better.

What is NOT true?

1 Historians want to know about the past.
2 Historians often use primary sources.
3 Good historians only use primary sources.
4 Some people study political or military history.

The Native People of North America

北美原住民

Key Words 🔊 013

01	**ancestral**	*(a.)* 祖先的；祖傳的 *ancestral home 祖居 *ancestral custom 祖傳習俗
	[æn`sɛstrəl]	Many Native American tribes still live in their ancestral lands. 許多美洲印地安部落仍住在祖先的土地上。

02	**hunter-gatherer**	*(n.)* 採獵者 *a tribe of hunter-gatherers 採獵者部落
	[`hʌntə`gæðrə]	Many archaeologists believe that the first Native Americans were hunter-gatherers from Asia. 許多考古學家相信，第一批印地安人是來自亞洲的採獵者。

03	**mound**	*(n.)* 土石堆 *burial mound 墳塚 *pitcher's mound（棒球）投手丘
	[maʊnd]	Some tribes are called mound builders because they buried their dead in large mounds. 有些部落被稱為築墩人，因為他們將亡者埋於巨大的土石堆中。

04	**totem pole**	*(n.)* 圖騰柱
	[`totəm pol]	Many tribes in the Northwest erected totem poles. 許多美國西北部的部落會設立圖騰柱。

05	**potlatch**	*(n.)* 炫富宴
	[`pɑt,lætʃ]	A potlatch was a special feast held by Native Americans in the Northwest at which guests received gifts. 炫富宴是美國西北部印地安人所舉辦的特殊盛宴，參與的賓客會收到禮物。

06	**craft**	*(n.)* 工藝品；（需要手藝的）行業 *(v.)* 精巧地製作 *arts and crafts 手工藝 *mason's/potter's/photographer's craft 泥水匠／陶藝／攝影（行業）
	[kræft]	The Tlingit used tree bark and other materials to make colorful crafts. 特林基特族利用樹皮和其他材料來製作色彩鮮豔的工藝品。

07	**dwelling**	*(n.)* 住處；住宅 *cave dwelling 穴居 *my humble dwelling 寒舍
	[`dwɛlɪŋ]	The Anasazi lived in dwellings that looked like apartment buildings built into the cliffs. 阿納薩齊人的住宅看起來像是嵌進懸崖壁的公寓大樓。

08	**remains**	*(n.)* 遺跡；遺體；遺骨 *fossil remains 化石遺骸 *mortal remains（人的）屍體
	[rɪ`menz]	Archaeologists have found the remains of many Native American cultures. 考古學家已經發現許多美洲印地安文化的遺跡。

09	**wampum**	*(n.)* 貝殼串珠
	[`wɑmpəm]	Wampum was polished beads made from shells and was used in ceremonies or as gifts. 貝殼串珠是用貝殼做成的拋光珠子，被用於儀式或作為贈禮。

10	**clan**	*(n.)* 部族；家族；氏族 *the Sparrow clan 史派洛家族 *rival clan 敵對部族
	[klæn]	A clan is a group of families that share the same ancestor. 家族是指來自於相同祖先的一些家庭。

Native American Dwellings

hogan

teepee

pueblo

🔊 014

igloo

impact
[ɪmˋpækt]

影響；衝擊

How did the environment **impact** Native Americans' lives?
環境如何影響印地安人的生活？

affect
[əˋfɛkt]

影響 (= influence)

How did the environment **affect** Native Americans?
環境如何影響印地安人的生活？

be urged to

被迫

Native Americans **were urged to** drop their traditions.
印地安人被迫放棄他們的傳統。

be forced to

被迫

Native Americans **were forced to** live on reservations. 印地安人被迫住在保留區。

be compelled to

被迫

Native Americans **were compelled to** live on reservations.
印地安人被迫住在保留區。

set aside

留出；撥出

A reservation is land **set aside** by the government for Native Americans.
保留區是政府為印地安人保留的土地。

Word Families

🔊 015

Native American Homes 美洲印地安人的住所

teepee
[ˋtipi]

圓錐形帳篷

Teepees were like tents that Native Americans slept in and could move from place to place. 圓錐形帳篷是印地安人睡覺用的帳篷，可以四處移動。

Pueblo
[ˋpwɛblo]

普韋布洛（普韋布洛人的村莊）

Pueblos are made of adobe bricks, which are made of mud and straw.
普埃布羅是用泥漿和稻草製成的泥磚所建造。

hogan
[ˋhogən]

泥蓋木屋

The Navajo lived in a hogan, a dome-shaped home for one family.
納瓦霍族住在泥蓋木屋裡，是供給一戶人家居住的圓頂房屋。

longhouse
[ˋlɔŋhaʊs]

長屋

The Iroquois lived in large communal homes called longhouses.
易洛魁族住在稱為長屋的大型共用住宅裡。

longhouse

igloo
[ˋiglu]

冰屋

The Inuit built dome-shaped igloos, which were temporary shelters of ice blocks.
因紐特人建造圓頂的冰屋，是一種用冰磚搭建的臨時住所。

North American Tribes 北美部落

Pueblo 普韋布洛族 [ˋpwɛblo]	**Navajo** 納瓦霍族 [ˋnævə‚ho]	**Apache** 阿帕契族 [əˋpɑʃ]	**Hopi** 霍皮族 [ˋhopɪ]
Cherokee 卻洛奇族 [ˋtʃɛrə‚ki]	**Creek** 克里克族 [krik]	**Iroquois** 易洛魁族 [ˋɪrə‚kwɔɪ]	**Sioux** 蘇族 [su]
Lakota 拉科塔族 [ləˋkotə]	**Shoshone** 休休尼族 [ʃoˋʃon]		

Checkup

A

Write | 請依提示寫出正確的英文單字或片語。

1. 祖先的；祖傳的 _____
2. 採獵者 _____
3. 土石堆 _____
4. 圖騰柱 _____
5. 炫富宴 _____
6. 工藝品 _____
7. 住處；住宅 _____
8. 遺跡；遺體；遺骨 _____
9. 貝殼串珠 _____
10. 部族；家族 _____
11. 影響；衝擊 i_____
12. 影響 a_____
13. 被迫 be u_____
14. 被迫 be f_____
15. 留出；撥出 _____
16. 圓錐形帳篷 _____

B

Complete the Sentences | 請在空格中填入最適當的答案，並視情況做適當的變化。

| hunter-gatherer | totem pole | ancestral | potlatch | clan |
| mound builder | wampum | dwelling | remains | craft |

1. Many Native American tribes still live in their _____ lands.
   許多美洲印地安部落仍住在祖先的土地上。

2. Many archaeologists believe that the first Native Americans were _____ from Asia. 許多考古學家相信，第一批印地安人是來自亞洲的採獵者。

3. The Tlingit used tree bark and other materials to make colorful _____.
   特林基特族利用樹皮和其他材料來製作色彩鮮豔的工藝品。

4. Some tribes are called _____ because they buried their dead in large mounds. 有些部落被稱為築墩人，因為他們將亡者埋於巨大的土石堆中。

5. The Anasazi lived in _____ that looked like apartment buildings built into the cliffs. 阿納薩齊人的住宅看起來像是嵌進懸崖壁的公寓大樓。

6. _____ was polished beads made from shells and was used in ceremonies or as gifts. 貝殼串珠是用貝殼做成的拋光珠子，被用於儀式或作為贈禮。

7. A _____ is a group of families that share the same ancestor.
   家族是指來自於相同祖先的一些家庭。

8. Archaeologists have found the _____ of many Native American cultures.
   考古學家已經發現許多美洲印地安文化的遺跡。

C

Read and Choose | 請選出與鋪底字意思相近的答案。

1. How did the environment impact Native Americans' lives?
   a. influence   b. find   c. urge

2. Native Americans were forced to live on reservations.
   a. set aside   b. compelled   c. moved

3. Many tribes in the Northwest erected totem poles.
   a. made   b. carved   c. built

D

Look, Read, and Write I 看圖並且依照提示，在空格中填入正確答案。

1  ▸ the parts of something that are left when the other parts are gone, used, or destroyed

_____

3  ▸ a dome-shaped home for one family which the Navajo lived in

_____

2  ▸ a building made from snow or ice

_____

4  ▸ beads or shells on strings that Native Americans used as money or decoration in the past

_____

E

Read and Answer I 閱讀並且回答下列問題。 ⊙ 016

The Anasazi

Today, there are many Native American tribes in North America. In the past, there were many more. However, some of them, like the Maya and Aztecs, disappeared. This happened to another tribe of Native Americans many centuries ago. They were the Anasazi.

The Anasazi lived in the area that is the Southwest today. They lived in that area more than a thousand years ago. They had an impressive culture. They made their own unique pottery. And some of them even lived in homes built into cliffs. However, around 1200, they suddenly disappeared. No one is sure what happened. Some people believe another tribe defeated the Anasazi in war. Others believe that a disease killed them. But most archaeologists think there was a drought. The area in the Southwest where they lived gets very little rain. The Anasazi had a lot of people in their tribes. If it did not rain for a while, they would have quickly run out of water. Perhaps a drought caused them to move to another area. Today, only artifacts and the ruins of Anasazi buildings remain. No one knows where the people went, though.

Answer the questions.

1 What happened to some Native American tribes? _____

2 Where did the Anasazi use to live? _____

3 When did the Anasazi disappear? _____

4 Why did the Anasazi disappear? _____

Key Words 🔊 017

01	**trader** [ˈtredɚ]	(n.) 經商者；商人　　*stock/bond trader 股票／債券交易商 *horse/fur trader 從事馬匹／皮草交易的人 Many **traders** traveled on the Silk Road connecting Europe and China. 許多商人往來於連接歐洲與中國的絲路上。
02	**raider** [ˈredɚ]	(n.) 劫掠者；突擊者　　*corporate raider 大量購買股票以控制某公司的人或機構 The Vikings were **raiders** who sailed on the ocean and attacked coastal villages.　維京人是航行於大海並襲擊沿海村莊的劫掠者。
03	**pirate** [ˈpaɪrət]	(n.) 海盜　　*pirate ship 海盜船　　*pirate book/software 盜版書／軟體 **Pirates** sailed on the ocean and raided ships to steal their treasures. 海盜航行於大海，並襲擊船隻以偷取金銀財寶。
04	**merchant** [ˈmɝtʃənt]	(n.) 商人　　*wine merchant 酒商　　*merchant ship/vessel 商船 **Merchants** sell various goods to people.　商人販賣各式各樣的商品給人們。
05	**barter** [ˈbɑrtɚ]	(n.) 易貨貿易　　*barter system 以貨易貨制度 **Barter** is a form of trade where people exchange goods for other goods rather than for money.　易貨貿易是一種以物易物而非換取金錢的貿易形式。
06	**navigation** [ˌnævəˈgeʃən]	(n.) 航行；航海　　*an onboard navigation system 車內導航系統 *satellite navigation 衛星導航 **Navigation** on the ocean was difficult for ships in the fifteenth century. 十五世紀時，船隻在海上航行十分艱難。
07	**Age of Exploration** [edʒ ɑv ˌɛkspləˈreʃən]	(n.) 地理大發現；大航海時代 (= Age of Discovery) The **Age of Exploration** led Europeans to sail to Asia and the Americas. 地理大發現帶領歐洲人航行至亞洲與美洲。
08	**caravel** [ˈkærəˌvɛl]	(n.) 輕快帆船；卡拉維爾帆船 The Portuguese developed a new ship, the **caravel**, which could sail farther and faster than others. 葡萄牙人發展出一種稱為卡拉維爾帆船的新船，能夠航行得更遠更快。
09	**Cape of Good Hope** [kep ɑv gʊd hop]	(n.) 好望角　　*cape 岬；海角　　*Cape Cod 科德角；鱈魚角 Bartolomeu Dias was the first European to sail around the southernmost point of Africa, the **Cape of Good Hope**. 巴爾托洛梅烏・迪亞士是第一個航行至非洲最南端好望角的歐洲人。
10	**expedition** [ˌɛkspɪˈdɪʃən]	(n.) 遠征隊　　*go on/organize/launch an expedition 進行／計畫／發起探險活動 *an expedition to 去……的探險 Christopher Columbus led an **expedition** across the Atlantic Ocean. 克里斯多福・哥倫布帶領一支遠征隊橫跨大西洋。

pirate

Christopher Columbus' expedition

caravel

🔊 018

raid
[red]
襲擊；突襲
The Vikings often **raided** towns and villages. 維京人常襲擊城鎮和村莊。

invade
[ɪn`ved]
侵入；侵略
The Vikings often **invaded** towns and villages. 維京人常侵入城鎮和村莊。

attack
[ə`tæk]
攻擊
Pirates often **attacked** people sailing on ships. 海盜常攻擊乘船航行的人。

navigate
[`nævə,get]
駕駛；操縱
A good captain can **navigate** his ship well on the ocean.
一名優秀的船長能在海上順利駕駛船隻。

barter
[`bɑrtɚ]
進行易貨貿易
Some merchants **bartered** gold for salt. 有些商人以黃金換鹽。

exchange
[ɪks`tʃendʒ]
交換；交易
Some merchants **exchanged** goods for other goods.
有些商人以貨物交換其他貨物。

dominate
[`dɑmə,net]
控制；支配
In medieval Europe, trade with the East had been **dominated** by merchants from Italian cities. 在中世紀的歐洲，與東方的貿易一直由義大利城市的商人掌控。

Word Families

🔊 019

vessel
[`vɛsl]
船
Many sailors traveled around the world in merchant **vessels**.
許多船員搭乘商船環遊世界。

ship
船
Columbus captained his **ships** across the Atlantic Ocean.
哥倫布率領他的船艦橫跨大西洋。

sail (n.)
帆
The caravel had square **sails** and triangle-shaped sails.
輕快帆船使用橫帆和三角帆。

sail (v.)
航行
Portuguese explorers **sailed** across the Indian Ocean and landed in India.
葡萄牙探險家航行橫越印度洋，並於印度登陸。

Cape of Good Hope

Early Portuguese Explorers
早期葡萄牙探險家

Gil Eanes 吉爾‧埃亞內斯

Bartolomeu Dias 巴爾托洛梅烏‧迪亞士

Vasco da Gama 瓦斯科‧達伽馬

Ferdinand Magellan 斐迪南‧麥哲倫

Checkup

A

Write | 請依提示寫出正確的英文單字或片語。

1	經商者；商人	t_____	
2	劫掠者；挖取者	_____	
3	海盜	_____	
4	商人	m_____	
5	易貨貿易	_____	
6	航行；航海	_____	
7	輕快帆船	_____	
8	遠征隊	_____	
9	地理大發現	_____	
10	好望角	_____	
11	襲擊；突襲	_____	
12	侵入；侵略	_____	
13	攻擊	_____	
14	駕駛；操縱	_____	
15	進行易貨貿易	_____	
16	控制；支配	_____	

B

Complete the Sentences | 請在空格中填入最適當的答案，並視情況做適當的變化。

merchant	trader	raider	expedition	pirate
navigation	sail	barter	Age of Exploration	caravel

1 Many _____ traveled on the Silk Road connecting Europe and China.
許多商人往來於連接歐洲與中國的絲路上。

2 The Vikings were _____ who sailed on the ocean and attacked coastal villages. 維京人是航行於大海並襲擊沿海村莊的劫掠者。

3 _____ sell various goods to people. 商人販賣各式各樣的商品給人們。

4 _____ on the ocean was difficult for ships in the fifteenth century.
十五世紀時，船隻在海上航行十分艱難。

5 The Portuguese developed a new ship, the _____, which could sail farther and faster than others. 葡萄牙人發展出一種稱為卡拉維爾帆船的新船，能夠航行得更遠更快。

6 Christopher Columbus led an _____ across the Atlantic Ocean.
克里斯多福・哥倫布帶領一支遠征隊橫跨大西洋。

7 _____ is a form of trade where people exchange goods for other goods rather than for money. 易貨貿易是一種以物易物而非換取金錢的貿易形式。

8 The _____ led Europeans to sail to Asia and the Americas.
地理大發現帶領歐洲人航行至亞洲與美洲。

C

Read and Choose | 閱讀下列句子，並且選出最適當的答案。

1 The Vikings often (traveled | raided) towns and villages.

2 Some merchants (sailed | bartered) gold for salt.

3 A good captain can (navigate | invade) his ship well on the ocean.

4 In medieval Europe, trade with the East had been (bartered | dominated) by merchants from Italian cities.

D Look, Read, and Write | 看圖並且依照提示，在空格中填入正確答案。

1 ▸ someone who sails on the ocean and raids ships to steal their treasures

_____

3 ▸ the movement of a ship or an aircraft along a planned path

_____

2 ▸ a group of people who travel together to a distant place

_____

4 ▸ a ship developed by the Portuguese which had square sails and triangle-shaped sails

_____

E Read and Answer | 閱讀並且回答下列問題。　⊙ 020

Bartolomeu Dias

Ferdinand Magellan

The Age of Exploration

In 1453, the Ottoman Turks defeated the Byzantine Empire. They captured its capital city Constantinople. Suddenly, the land route from Europe to Asia became more dangerous. At that time, many Europeans purchased spices from China and other Asian countries. But now they could not get them from land. So they tried to get their spices by sea.

This began the Age of Exploration. Many Europeans began sailing south around Africa. At first, the Portuguese and Spanish started sailing south. But then other Europeans started to follow them.

In 1488, Bartolomeu Dias became the first European to sail to the Cape of Good Hope in Africa. This was the southernmost point of Africa. He had discovered the way to India by water. In 1498, Vasco da Gama sailed across the Indian Ocean and landed in India. He returned to Portugal in 1499.

By this time, the Americas had been discovered. But people did not know how big the earth was. Finally, in 1519, Ferdinand Magellan set sail from Spain. He sailed past the southern part of South America and into the Pacific Ocean. Magellan was later killed during a fight with the native people of the Philippines. But, in 1522, his crew returned to Spain. They had sailed around the world!

What is NOT true?

1 The Europeans defeated the Byzantine Empire in 1453.

2 The Age of Exploration began in the fifteenth century.

3 Bartolomeu Dias sailed around the southern part of Africa.

4 Magellan's crew was the first to sail around the world.

A

Write | 請依提示寫出正確的英文單字或片語。

1	文化熔爐	_____	11	正式生效 _____
2	國家認同	_____	12	修訂；修改 (v.) _____
3	初選	_____	13	選舉人團 _____
4	黨代表大會	_____	14	提名；任命 (v.) _____
5	考古學家	_____	15	西元前 _____
6	工藝品；手工藝品	a _____	16	西元年 _____
7	工藝品	c _____	17	部族；家族 _____
8	住處；住宅	_____	18	被迫 be f _____
9	劫掠者；挖取者	_____	19	進行易貨貿易 _____
10	遠征隊	_____	20	控制；支配 _____

B

Choose the Correct Word | 請選出與鋪底字意思相近的答案。

1 The Vikings often **invaded** towns and villages.

  a. attacked   b. raided   c. sailed

2 Sometimes it is necessary to **amend** a constitution.

  a. make   b. ratify   c. change

3 How did the environment **impact** Native Americans' lives?

  a. influence   b. find   c. urge

4 Native Americans were **forced** to live on reservations.

  a. set aside   b. compelled   c. moved

C

Complete the Sentences | 請在空格中填入最適當的答案，並視情況做適當的變化。

convention	diversity	remains	chronology

1 The United States is a nation of _____ where people of different races and ethnicities live together.
美國是一個多元化國家，有各個不同民族和種族的人聚居在這裡。

2 Political parties hold _____ to determine their presidential nominee.
政黨舉行大會來決定總統提名人選。

3 The sequence in which something happened is its _____.
事情發生的順序稱為該事件的年表。

4 Archaeologists have found the _____ of many Native American cultures.
考古學家已經發現許多印地安文化的遺跡。

CHAPTER 2

Social Studies •
History and
Geography ②

The Spanish Conquerors 西班牙征服者

Key Words 🔊 021

01 Spaniard
[ˈspænjəd]

(n.) 西班牙人　*Spain 西班牙　*Spanish 西班牙語；西班牙的

The arrival of the **Spaniards** in the Americas changed the Native American empires. 西班牙人抵達美洲改變了印地安人的帝國。

02 conquistador
[kɑnˈkwɪstəˌdɔr]

(n.)【西】征服者　*conquest 征服；佔領

The **conquistadors** were Spanish warriors who went to the New World to fight the Native Americans.
征服者是指前往新大陸與印地安人戰鬥的西班牙戰士。

03 smallpox
[ˈsmɔlˌpɑks]

(n.) 天花

Smallpox was a deadly disease that killed millions of Native Americans.
天花是一種致命的疾病，奪走了無數印地安人的性命。

04 downfall
[ˈdaʊnˌfɔl]

(n.) 沒落；垮臺；墮落的原因　*sth. be sb.'s downfall 某事物是某人墮落的原因

The Spanish conqueror Hernando Cortés caused the **downfall** of the Aztec Empire. 西班牙征服者赫爾南多‧科特斯，造成阿茲提克帝國的沒落。

05 Machu Picchu
[ˈmɑtʃu ˈpɪktʃu]

(n.) 馬丘比丘

Machu Picchu was an Incan city hidden high in the Andes Mountains.
馬丘比丘是一個高隱於安地斯山脈的印加城市。

06 quipus
[ˈkipuz]

(n.)（古印加人的）結繩記事法

The Incas used the **quipus** to keep records and to make calculations.
印加人利用結繩法來記錄和計算。

07 missionary
[ˈmɪʃənˌɛrɪ]

(n.) 傳教士　*Christian missionary 基督教傳教士

The Spanish brought **missionaries** to convert the Native Americans to Christianity. 西班牙人帶來傳教士，使印地安人改信基督教。

08 mestizo
[mɛsˈtizo]

(n.) 麥士蒂索人（歐洲人與美洲印地安人混血）

Mestizos were people of mixed Spanish and Native American ancestry.
麥士蒂索人是指西班牙人與美洲印地安人祖先混血所生的人。

09 enslave
[ɪnˈslev]

(v.) 奴役　*be enslaved 遭到奴役　*enslaver 奴役他人者

The Spanish **enslaved** many Native Americans and Africans.
西班牙人奴役許多美洲印地安人和非洲人。

10 El Dorado
[ˌɛl dəˈrɑdo]

(n.) 黃金國；寶山

Many adventurers searched for **El Dorado**, a legendary city made of gold.
許多探險家都在尋找黃金國，一座傳說中由黃金打造的城市。

Spanish conquistador Hernando Cortés

the ruins of Machu Picchu

quipus

cd by Claus Ableiter

🔊 022

demand
[dɪˈmænd]

需要；要求

The Spanish demanded gold and silver from the Native Americans.
西班牙人向印地安人索討黃金和白銀。

break out

爆發；突然發生

Fights often broke out between the Spanish and the natives.
西班牙人經常與原住民爆發戰役。

drive away

趕走；驅趕

The Aztecs tried to drive away the Spanish conquistadors.
阿茲提克人試圖趕走西班牙征服者。

drive out

驅趕

The Aztecs tried to drive out the Spanish conquistadors.
阿茲提克人試圖驅趕西班牙征服者。

Aztec warriors defending Tenochtitlan

retreat
[rɪˈtrit]

撤退

The Spaniards retreated but left behind diseases.
西班牙人撤退了，卻留下疾病。

move away

離去

The Spaniards moved away but left behind diseases.
西班牙人離去了，卻留下疾病。

infect
[ɪnˈfɛkt]

傳染；感染

The Europeans infected many Native Americans with smallpox and other diseases.
歐洲人傳染天花和其他疾病給印地安人。

collapse
[kəˈlæps]

瓦解；垮掉 (= fall)

The Aztec and Incan empires both collapsed because of the Spanish.
西班牙人導致阿茲提克和印加帝國雙雙瓦解。

🔊 023

Tenochtitlan [tɛˌnɔtʃtɪtˈlɑn]	特諾奇提特蘭	The capital of the Aztec Empire was Tenochtitlan. 阿茲提克帝國的首都是特諾奇提特蘭。
Cuzco [ˈkuzko]	庫斯科	The capital of the Inca Empire was Cuzco. 印加帝國的首都是庫斯科。
ruins	遺跡；廢墟	The ruins of Machu Picchu are high in the Andes of Peru. 馬丘比丘的遺址位於秘魯的安地斯山脈高處。
remains	遺跡；遺體	The remains of the Inca Empire are still in the Andes Mountains. 印加帝國的遺跡仍保留於安地斯山脈。
deadly	致命的	The Spaniards left behind a deadly disease, smallpox. 西班牙人留下了一種名為天花的致命疾病。
fatal	致命的	Many European diseases were fatal to the Native Americans. 許多歐洲的疾病對印地安人來說足以致命。

Checkup

A

Write | 請依提示寫出正確的英文單字或片語。

1	天花	_____	9	西班牙人	_____
2	沒落；垮臺	_____	10	征服者	_____
3	馬丘比丘	_____	11	需要；要求	_____
4	結繩記事法	_____	12	爆發；突然發生	_____
5	傳教士	_____	13	趕走；驅趕	_____
6	麥士蒂索人	_____	14	撤退	_____
7	奴役	_____	15	傳染；感染	_____
8	黃金國；寶山	_____	16	瓦解；垮掉	_____

B

Complete the Sentences | 請在空格中填入最適當的答案，並視情況做適當的變化。

Machu Picchu	Spaniard	downfall	quipus	El Dorado
conquistador	smallpox	enslave	missionary	Mestizo

1 The arrival of the _____ in the Americas changed the Native American empires. 西班牙人抵達美洲改變了印地安人的帝國。

2 The _____ were Spanish warriors who went to the New World to fight the Native Americans. 征服者是指前往新大陸與印地安人戰鬥的西班牙戰士。

3 The Spanish conqueror Hernando Cortés caused the _____ of the Aztec Empire. 西班牙征服者赫爾南多・科特斯，造成阿茲提克帝國的沒落。

4 _____ was an Incan city hidden high in the Andes Mountains. 馬丘比丘是一個高隱於安地斯山脈的印加城市。

5 The Spanish _____ many Native Americans and Africans. 西班牙奴役許多美洲印地安人和非洲人。

6 The Incas used the _____ to keep records and to make calculations. 印加人利用結繩法來記錄和計算。

7 _____ were people of mixed Spanish and Native American ancestry. 麥士蒂索人是指西班牙人與美洲印地安人祖先混血所生的人。

8 The Spanish brought _____ to convert the Native Americans to Christianity. 西班牙人帶來傳教士，使印地安人改信基督教

C

Read and Choose | 請選出與鋪底字意思相近的答案。

1 The Spaniards retreated but left behind diseases.
   a. moved away   b. drove away   c. broke out

2 The ruins of Machu Picchu are high in the Andes of Peru.
   a. sites   b. remains   c. artifacts

3 The Spaniards left behind a deadly disease, smallpox.
   a. serious   b. deep   c. fatal

D

Look, Read, and Write | 看圖並且依照提示，在空格中填入正確答案。

▸ someone who is sent to a place to teach people about a particular religion

_____

▸ one that conquers, especially a Spanish conqueror during the 16th century

_____

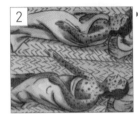
▸ a serious disease in which your skin becomes covered in spots that can leave permanent marks

_____

▸ a legendary city made of gold

_____

E

Read and Answer | 閱讀並且回答下列問題。　🔊 024

The Spanish Conquer the New World

When Christopher Columbus discovered America in 1492, there were already millions of people living in the Americas. Some of them had formed great empires. Two of these were the Aztecs and the Incas. However, after a few years, the Spanish defeated both of them.

The Aztec Empire was in the area of modern-day Mexico. The Aztecs were very warlike. They had conquered many of their neighbors. But they did not have modern weapons like guns and cannons. In 1519, Hernando Cortés invaded the Aztec Empire. He only had about 500 soldiers. But many neighboring tribes allied with him. They disliked the Aztecs very much. There were several battles as Cortés and his men marched to Tenochtitlan, the Aztec capital. In 1521, Cortés captured the city and conquered the empire.

The Inca Empire was in South America in the Andes Mountains. In 1531, Francisco Pizarro arrived there with 182 soldiers. At that time, the Inca Empire was already weak. There had just been a civil war in the empire. By 1532, Pizarro and his men had captured the Incan emperor. The next year, they put their own emperor on the throne. They had succeeded in defeating the Incas.

Fill in the blanks.

1　Two great empires in the Americas were the _____ and Inca empires.

2　The Aztecs did not have modern _____ like cannons.

3　The capital of the Aztec Empire was _____.

4　Francisco _____ conquered the Inca Empire.

Key Words 🔊 025

01 fur trade
[fɝ tred]
(n.) 毛皮貿易　*slave trade 奴隸買賣　*good trade 好生意
The French made a lot of money in the fur trade with Native Americans.
法國人透過與印地安人的毛皮貿易賺了很多錢。

02 trapper
['træpɚ]
(n.) 設陷阱捕獸者　*fur trapper 為取毛皮而捕獸者　*trap 設陷阱捕捉
Trappers hunted animals like beavers for their skins.
捕獸者獵取海狸之類的動物以獲取毛皮。

03 ally
[ə'laɪ]
(n.) 盟友　*the Allies 一次世界大戰的協約國；二次世界大戰的同盟國
*a powerful ally 強而有力的助手
The French often became allies with Native American tribes in order to strengthen the colony.　法國人常與印地安部落結盟以鞏固殖民地。

04 charter
['tʃɑrtɚ]
(n.) 特許狀；許可證　*be granted a charter 獲准取得執照
*the United Nations Charter 聯合國憲章
In 1585, England's Queen Elizabeth granted a charter to start a colony in North America.
英國女王伊莉莎白於 1585 年授予特許狀，開啟了在北美的殖民地。

05 cash crop
[kæʃ krɑp]
(n.) 經濟作物　*crop production 農產量　*corn crops 玉米作物
Tobacco became an important cash crop in the American colonies.
菸草成為美國殖民地的重要經濟作物。

06 indentured servant
[ɪn'dɛntʃɚd 'sɝvənt]
(n.) 契約勞工　*indentured 受契約束縛而須為人工作的　*indenture 契約
Many indentured servants from Europe worked in tobacco fields.
許多來自歐洲的契約勞工在菸草田裡工作。

07 apprentice
[ə'prɛntɪs]
(n.) 學徒；見習生　*an apprentice to sb./sth. 某人或某行業的學徒
*an apprentice carpenter/mechanic 木匠／技工學徒
An apprentice is someone who works for a skilled person in order to learn that person's skills.　學徒是指跟隨師傅學習技藝的人。

08 House of Burgesses
[haʊs ɑv 'bɝdʒɪsɪz]
(n.) 美殖民議會的下議院　*burgess（美殖民地時期維吉尼亞或馬里蘭的）下院議員
The Virginia House of Burgesses, a colonial assembly, made laws for the colony.　維吉尼亞州下議院是一個殖民議會，負責為殖民地立法。

09 Mayflower Compact
['me,flaʊɚ 'kɑmpækt]
(n.) 五月花號公約
The Pilgrims were governed by the Mayflower Compact.
英國清教徒受《五月花號公約》的制約。

10 triangular trade
[traɪ'æŋgjəlɚ tred]
(n.) 三角貿易
There was triangular trade between the colonies, England, and the islands in the Caribbean Sea.　殖民地、英國與加勒比海群島之間存在著三角貿易。

fur trade

signing the Mayflower Compact

skilled baker　apprentice

cash crop

coffee

tobacco

sugarcane

cotton

ally [əˋlaɪ]	結盟；聯合 The French and Native Americans **allied** against the British. 法國人與印地安人結盟，一起對抗英國人。
tolerate [ˋtɑləˏret]	容忍；容許 Some Native American tribes **tolerated** the colonists. 有些印地安部落能夠容忍殖民者。
issue [ˋɪʃju]	核發；發給 The French government **issued** permits to trappers. 法國政府核發許可證給捕獸者。
be engaged in	從事 Many Frenchmen **were engaged in** the fur trade in North America. 許多法國人在北美從事毛皮貿易。
grant [grænt]	授予；准予 King Charles II **granted** a large piece of land to William Penn. 國王查理二世授予威廉・佩恩一大片土地。
bestow [bɪˋsto]	授予；給予 King Charles II **bestowed** a large piece of land to William Penn. 國王查理二世授予威廉・佩恩一大片土地。
apprentice [əˋprɛntɪs]	當學徒　*be apprenticed to 當學徒 The young man was **apprenticed** to the blacksmith for five years. 這名年輕人當了五年的鐵匠學徒。

Word Families 🔊 027

sachem [ˋsetʃəm]	酋長 The **sachem** was the chief of a tribe.　酋長是部落的首領。
chief	首領；頭目 The **chief** of a Native American tribe was the most powerful individual. 印地安部落的首領是最有權力的人。
Quebec [kwɪˋbɛk]	魁北克 **Quebec** was an early French colony in North America. 魁北克是早期法國在北美的殖民地。
Montreal [ˏmɑntrɪˋɔl]	蒙特婁 The French built a city at **Montreal** on the St. Lawrence River. 法國人在聖勞倫斯河畔的蒙特婁建立了一個都市。
La Salle [ləˋsæl]	拉薩爾 Robert de **La Salle** was a French explorer who sailed from the Great Lakes down the Mississippi River to the Gulf of Mexico. 法國探險家羅伯・德・拉薩爾曾由五大湖出發，沿著密西西比河航行至墨西哥灣。
Champlain [ˏʃæmˋplen]	尚普蘭 Samuel de **Champlain** founded Quebec in 1608. 薩繆爾・德・尚普蘭於 1608 年發現魁北克。

statue of Samuel de Champlain

Checkup

A

Write | 請依提示寫出正確的英文單字或片語。

1	毛皮貿易	_____	
2	設陷阱捕獸者	_____	
3	盟友	_____	
4	特許狀；許可證	_____	
5	經濟作物	_____	
6	學徒；見習生	_____	
7	五月花號公約	_____	
8	三角貿易	_____	

9	契約勞工	_____
10	美殖民議會的下議院	_____
11	結盟；聯合	_____
12	容忍；容許	_____
13	核發；發給	_____
14	從事	_____
15	授予；准予	g_____
16	授予；給予	b_____

B

Complete the Sentences | 請在空格中填入最適當的答案，並視情況做適當的變化。

ally	fur trade	indentured servant	House of Burgesses	trapper
charter	cash crop	Mayflower Compact	triangular trade	apprentice

1 The French made a lot of money in the _____ with Native Americans.
法國人透過與印地安人的毛皮貿易賺了很多錢。

2 The French often became _____ with Native American tribes in order to strengthen the colony. 法國人常與印地安部落結盟以鞏固殖民地。

3 In 1585, England's Queen Elizabeth granted a _____ to start a colony in North America. 英國女王伊莉莎白於 1585 年授予特許狀，開啟了在北美的殖民地。

4 Tobacco became an important _____ in the American colonies.
菸草成為美國殖民地的重要經濟作物。

5 Many _____ from Europe worked in tobacco fields.
許多來自歐洲的契約勞工在菸草田裡工作。

6 There was _____ between the colonies, England, and the islands in the Caribbean Sea. 殖民地、英國與加勒比海群島之間存在著三角貿易。

7 The Pilgrims were governed by the _____.
英國清教徒受《五月花號公約》的制約。

8 The Virginia _____, a colonial assembly, made laws for the colony. 維吉尼亞州下議院是一個殖民議會，負責為殖民地立法。

C

Read and Choose | 閱讀下列句子，並且選出最適當的答案。

1 The French and Native Americans (engaged | allied) against the British.

2 Some Native American tribes (tolerated | apprenticed) the colonists.

3 King Charles II (granted | issued) a large piece of land to William Penn.

4 The French government (issued | traded) permits to trappers.

D

Look, Read, and Write | 看圖並且依照提示，在空格中填入正確答案。

1 ▸ a person who traps animals, especially for their fur

_____

3 ▸ someone who works for a skilled person in order to learn that person's skills

_____

2 ▸ a crop grown for sale rather than for use by the grower

_____

4 ▸ the colonial assembly of Virginia

_____

E

Read and Answer | 閱讀並且回答下列問題。 🔊 028

The *Mayflower*

In Britain, there was a group of people called Pilgrims. They were different from most people there. They had certain religious beliefs that others did not share. So they wanted to leave Britain and go to the New World. They hired a ship called the *Mayflower* to take them to America.

They left in 1620 and landed in America after two months of sailing. They were supposed to go to the Hudson River area. But they landed at a place called Plymouth Rock. It was in modern-day Massachusetts on Cape Cod. Still, the Pilgrims decided to settle there.

The first winter was hard. Many Pilgrims died. But the Native Americans there made peace with them. Their leader was Samoset. He brought Squanto to stay with the Pilgrims. Squanto and other Native Americans taught the Pilgrims how to farm the land properly. That year, the Pilgrims harvested many crops. They had a big three-day festival with the Native Americans. That was the first Thanksgiving.

Every year, the Pilgrim colony became stronger and stronger. More colonists came from Britain. So the colony became very successful.

What is NOT true?

1 The Pilgrims sailed to America on the *Mayflower*.
2 The Pilgrims landed at Plymouth Rock.
3 Squanto was the leader of the Pilgrims.
4 The first Thanksgiving was held in 1621.

The Declaration of Independence 獨立宣言

Key Words 🔊 029

01 territory
[ˈtɛrəˌtorɪ]
(n.) 領土　*lost territory 失地　*disputed territory 有爭議的領土
The French and British both had huge **territories** in North America.
法國和英國都在北美擁有大片的領土。

02 intolerable
[ɪnˈtɑlərəb̩l]
(a.) 無法忍受的 (= unbearable)　*tolerable 可忍受的
*intolerable pain/behavior 無法忍受的痛苦／行為
The colonists thought many of the new taxes were **intolerable**.
殖民地居民認為許多新稅法都令人無法忍受。

03 militia
[mɪˈlɪʃə]
(n.) 民兵部隊；國民軍　*militiaman 民兵
The colonists formed groups of soldiers called **militias**.
殖民地居民組成稱為「民兵」的兵團。

04 minuteman
[ˈmɪnɪtˌmæn]
(n.)（美國獨立戰爭期間）後備民兵
The **minutemen** were American militiamen ready to fight "at a minute's notice." 後備民兵是指「一接到徵召」隨時可戰鬥的民兵。

05 troop
[trup]
(n.) 部隊　*enemy troops 敵軍　*withdraw troops 撤軍
British **troops** went to Boston to stop the colonists' protests.
英國部隊前去波士頓阻止殖民地居民的抗議。

06 patriot
[ˈpetrɪət]
(n.) 愛國者　*Patriot 愛國者，美國獨立戰爭期間反抗英國統治的人
A **patriot** is a person who loves his or her country.
愛國者是指熱愛祖國的人。

07 mercenary
[ˈmɜsn̩ˌɛrɪ]
(n.)（外國人的）傭兵
The British hired German **mercenaries** to fight for them.
英國雇用德國傭兵來為他們打仗。

08 Loyalist
[ˈlɔɪəlɪst]
(n.) 效忠者；反對獨立者（美國獨立戰爭期間支持英國繼續統治，反對獨立的人）
A **Loyalist** was an American who stayed loyal to England.
效忠者是指對英國忠誠的美國人。

09 profiteering
[ˌprɑfəˈtɪrɪŋ]
(n.) 牟取暴利　*profiteer（趁物資匱乏）牟取暴利的人
Some merchants became rich by **profiteering**.
有些商人靠牟取暴利致富。

10 turning point
[ˈtɜnɪŋ pɔɪnt]
(n.) 轉捩點
The Boston Massacre was the **turning point** that led to the Revolutionary War. 波士頓慘案是導致獨立戰爭的轉捩點。

Revolutionary War

Battle of Guilford Court House

Wyoming Massacre

the British surrendering at Yorktown, Virginia, 1781

enact	制定（法律）；頒佈（法案）
[ɪnˈækt]	The British Parliament **enacted** many taxes. 英國國會制訂許多稅法。
repeal	廢除；撤銷
[rɪˈpil]	The British Parliament **repealed** some taxes. 英國國會廢除一些稅法。
repay	償還；報答
[rɪˈpe]	Many colonists struggled to **repay** their debts. 許多殖民地居民努力償還債務。
enlist	從軍；入伍
[ɪnˈlɪst]	Many men **enlisted** in the colonial militias. 許多男人加入殖民地民兵。
desert	逃跑
[dɪˈzɝt]	Some soldiers **deserted** and left the army. 有些士兵逃離軍隊。
run away	逃跑
	Some soldiers **ran away** and left the army. 有些士兵逃離軍隊。

dispute	爭執；爭論
[dɪˈspjut]	The colonists had many **disputes** with Britain. 殖民地居民與英國起過許多爭執。
conflict	衝突
[ˈkɑnflɪkt]	The American Revolution was a **conflict** between America and Britain. 美國獨立戰爭是美國與英國之間的衝突。
Sons of Liberty	自由之子（反抗英國統治的秘密民間組織）
	The Sons of Liberty protested the Tea Act in Boston. 自由之子抗議波士頓的《茶稅法》。
Boston Massacre	波士頓慘案（英國殖民當局屠殺北美殖民地人民）
[ˈbɔstn̩ ˈmæsəkɚ]	British troops killed five American civilians in the Boston Massacre. 英國軍隊在波士頓慘案中殺害了五名美國平民。

Sons of Liberty

The Intolerable Acts
不可容忍的法令

Stamp Act《印花稅法》

Tea Act《茶稅法》

Boston Port Act《波士頓港口法》

Quartering Act《駐營法案》

Boston Massacre

Checkup

A

Write | 請依提示寫出正確的英文單字或片語。

1 領土	_____	9 效忠派	_____
2 無法忍受的	_____	10 後備民兵	_____
3 民兵部隊；國民軍	_____	11 制定（法律）；頒布（法案）	_____
4 部隊	_____	12 廢除；撤銷	_____
5 愛國者	_____	13 償還；報答	_____
6 （外國人的）傭兵	_____	14 從軍；入伍	_____
7 牟取暴利	_____	15 逃跑 d_____
8 轉捩點	_____	16 衝突	_____

B

Complete the Sentences | 請在空格中填入最適當的答案，並視情況做適當的變化。

mercenary	intolerable	militia	minuteman	profiteering
troop	Loyalist	territory	patriot	Boston Massacre

1 The French and British both had huge _____ in North America.
法國和英國都在北美擁有大片的領土。

2 The colonists thought many of the new taxes were _____.
殖民地居民認為許多新稅法都令人無法忍受。

3 The colonists formed groups of soldiers called _____.
殖民地居民組成稱為「民兵」的兵團。

4 The _____ were American militiamen ready to fight "at a minute's notice."
後備民兵是指「一接到徵召」隨時可戰鬥的民兵。

5 British _____ went to Boston to stop the colonists' protests.
英國部隊前去波士頓阻止殖民地居民的抗議。

6 A _____ was an American who stayed loyal to England.
效忠派是指對英國忠誠的美國人。

7 Some merchants became rich by _____. 有些商人靠牟取暴利致富。

8 The _____ was the turning point that led to the Revolutionary War. 波士頓慘案是導致獨立戰爭的轉捩點。

C

Read and Choose | 閱讀下列句子，並且選出最適當的答案。

1 The British Parliament (enacted | repaid) many taxes.

2 Many men (deserted | enlisted) in the colonial militias.

3 Some soldiers (deserted | repealed) and left the army.

4 The colonists had many (disputes | territories) with Britain.

D

1
▸ making large profits by charging high prices for goods that are hard to get

_____

2
▸ a person who loves his or her country

_____

3
▸ a soldier who fights for any country that pays him or her

_____

4
▸ fighting between countries or groups

_____

E

Read and Answer | 閱讀並且回答下列問題。   ⊙ 032

Boston Tea Party

The French and Indian War Leads to Revolution

In the eighteenth century, countries in Europe often fought wars against each other. They usually fought in Europe. But sometimes they fought in other places. One of these other places was in America. In the 1750s and 1760s, the British and French fought a war in North America. Some people called it the French and Indian War. Others called it the Seven Years' War. Basically, the British and American colonists were on one side. The French and Native Americans were on the other side.

The British won the war. So the French left most of North America. They had to give many of their colonies to the British. But the war was very expensive for the British. So King George III of Britain wanted to raise taxes in the colonies. He said the British had protected the colonies. So they should pay higher taxes.

The British passed many taxes. These included the Stamp Act and the Tea Act. There were many others, though. The Americans hated the taxes and thought they were unfair. They called them the Intolerable Acts. Eventually, Britain's actions led to war in the colonies. The Americans revolted. And then they gained their freedom from Britain.

Answer the questions.

1   What was the other name of the French and Indian War?   _____

2   Who won the French and Indian War?   _____

3   Who was the king of England during the French and Indian War?   _____

4   What did the Americans call the Stamp Act and the Tea Act?   _____

Key Words 🔊 033

01 Jim Crow Laws
[dʒɪm kro lɔz]

(n.) 種族隔離法律（美國重建時期結束直至 1965 年，美國南部各州對有色人種所實行種族隔離的法律。）

Jim Crow Laws discriminated against black people in the South.
《種族隔離法律》歧視南方黑人。

02 abolition
[,æbə`lɪʃən]

(n.) 廢除；廢止　*abolition 可專指美國奴隸制度的廢止　*abolitionist 廢奴主義者

The abolition of slavery happened during the Civil War.
奴隸的廢除發生在南北戰爭期間。

03 Reconstruction
[,rikən`strʌkʃən]

(n.) 美國重建時期　*reconstruction 重建；復原

Reconstruction was the period when the South was trying to rebuild after the Civil War. 美國重建時期是南方在南北戰爭後努力重建的時期。

04 industrialization
[ɪn,dʌstrɪələ`zeʃən]

(n.) 工業化　*Industrial Revolution 工業革命

Industrialization and urbanization started the age of industry.
工業化與都市化開啟了工業時代。

05 monopoly
[mə`napḷɪ]

(n.) 壟斷；獨佔　*have a monopoly on/of/over sth. 壟斷某事物
　　　　　　　　*break up monopolies 打破壟斷事業

A monopoly happens when one company controls an entire market.
當一個企業掌控了整個市場，就稱為壟斷。

06 regulation
[,rɛgjə`leʃən]

(n.) 管理；規章　*the regulation of sth. 管理某物　*rules and regulations 規章制度

The government often gets involved in the regulation of businesses.
政府經常干涉企業管理。

07 isolationism
[,aɪsḷ`eʃənɪzm]

(n.)（一國在政治上或經濟上的）孤立主義
*isolationist（反對本國參與國際政治或經濟盟約的）孤立主義者

Isolationism happens when a country stops dealing with other countries.
當一個國家停止和其他國家交涉，就稱為孤立主義。

08 stock market
[stak `markɪt]

(n.) 股票市場　*stock exchange 證券交易所　*stock certificate 股票；證券

People can buy and sell stock on a stock market.
人們可以在股票市場上買賣股票。

09 depression
[dɪ`prɛʃən]

(n.) 蕭條；不景氣　*the (Great) Depression（1930 年代）經濟大蕭條時期
*depression 沮喪；意志消沈；憂鬱症（suffer from depression 患憂鬱症）

Many Americans lost their jobs in the Great Depression.
許多美國人在經濟大蕭條的時候失業。

10 unemployment
[,ʌnɪm`plɔɪmənt]

(n.) 失業　*employment 雇用；受雇　*face unemployment 面臨失業

In a depression, unemployment is high because there are no jobs.
不景氣時，缺乏工作機會導致高失業率。

industrialization

unemployment line during the Great Depression

segregation

the transcontinental railroad

🔊 034

abolish
[ə`bɑlɪʃ]

廢除；廢止

Northern abolitionists tried to abolish slavery.
北部的廢奴主義者努力廢除奴隸制度。

get rid of

去除；擺脫

Northern abolitionists tried to get rid of slavery.
北部的廢奴主義者努力廢除奴隸制度。

reconstruct
[ˌrɪkən`strʌkt]

重建；再建

The South had to reconstruct itself after the Civil War.
南北戰爭後，南方必須重建。

rebuild
[ri`bɪld]

重建；改建

The South had to rebuild itself after the Civil War.
南北戰爭後，南方必須重建。

industrialize
[ɪn`dʌstrɪəlˌaɪz]

工業化

The United States industrialized very much during the post-Civil War period. 後內戰時期，美國高度工業化。

regulate
[`rɛgjəˌlet]

控制；管理

Many monopolies were regulated by the government.
許多壟斷企業受到政府的控管。

Attack on Pearl Harbor

World War I

World War II

Word Families

🔊 035

Southerner 南方人
Most Southerners joined the Confederacy. 多數南方人加入邦聯。

Northerner 北方人
Most Northerners stayed in the Union. 多數北方人留在聯邦。

Famous Events in American History 美國著名歷史事件

the transcontinental railroad 橫貫大陸鐵路
The transcontinental railroad connected the east and west. 橫貫大陸鐵路接通東部與西部。

World War I 第一次世界大戰
America joined World War I in 1917. 美國於 1917 年加入第一次世界大戰。

the Roaring Twenties 咆哮的20年代
The Roaring Twenties was a great time in U.S. history. 咆哮的 20 年代是美國史上一段美好的時期。

the Great Depression 經濟大蕭條
The Great Depression lasted all through the 1930s. 經濟大蕭條持續了整個 1930 年代。

Attack on Pearl Harbor 珍珠港事件
The attack on Pearl Harbor was a sneak attack conducted by the Japanese navy on December 7, 1941. 珍珠港事件是日本海軍於 1941 年 12 月 7 日所發動的偷襲行動。

World War II 第二次世界大戰
World War II began in 1939 and ended in 1945. 第二次世界大戰始於 1939 年，終於 1945 年。

Checkup

A

Write | 請依提示寫出正確的英文單字或片語。

1	種族隔離法律	_____	9	蕭條;不景氣 _____
2	廢除;廢止 (n.)	_____	10	失業 _____
3	美國重建時期	_____	11	廢除;廢止 (v.) a_____
4	工業化 (n.)	_____	12	去除;擺脫 g_____
5	壟斷;獨佔	_____	13	重建;再建 _____
6	管理;規章	_____	14	工業化 (v.) _____
7	孤立主義	_____	15	控制;管理 (v.) _____
8	股票市場	_____	16	南方人 _____

B

Complete the Sentences | 請在空格中填入最適當的答案,並視情況做適當的變化。

abolition	stock market	regulation	Jim Crow Laws	isolationism
monopoly	Great Depression	unemployment	industrialization	Reconstruction

1 _____ discriminated against black people in the South.
《種族隔離法律》歧視南方黑人。

2 The _____ of slavery happened during the Civil War.
奴隸的廢除發生在南北戰爭期間。

3 _____ and urbanization started the age of industry.
工業化與都市化開始於工業時期。

4 A _____ happens when one company controls an entire market.
當一個企業掌控了整個市場,就稱為壟斷。

5 The government often gets involved in the _____ of businesses.
政府經常干涉企業管理。

6 _____ happens when a country stops dealing with other countries.
當一個國家停止和其他國家交涉,就稱為孤立主義。

7 Many Americans lost their jobs in the _____.
許多美國人在經濟大蕭條的時候失業。

8 In a depression, _____ is high because there are no jobs.
不景氣時,缺乏工作機會導致高失業率。

C

Read and Choose | 閱讀下列句子,並且選出最適當的答案。

1 Northern abolitionists tried to (rebuild | abolish) slavery.

2 The South had to (construct | reconstruct) itself after the Civil War.

3 Many monopolies were (conducted | regulated) by the government.

4 The United States (industrialized | declined) very much during the post-Civil War period.

D Look, Read, and Write l 看圖並且依照提示，在空格中填入正確答案。

1

▸ the period when the South was trying to rebuild after the Civil War

_____

3

▸ the state of not having a job

_____

2

▸ a long period of economic decline

_____

4

▸ the development of industry on an extensive scale

_____

E Read and Answer l 閱讀並且回答下列問題。 ⊙ 036

The Roaring Twenties and the Great Depression

Franklin Roosevelt

In the 1920s, the American economy was very strong, and life was good. World War I had just ended. So people were interested in peace, not war. They had jobs and were making a lot of money. There were new technologies being created, and people could afford to buy them. They began moving to the suburbs and living in houses. People had leisure time, so they could go out and enjoy themselves.

Then, on October 24, 1929, the stock market crashed. Suddenly, life changed for millions of people. Instantly, people lost billions of dollars in stock. Companies went bankrupt. As they went out of business, millions of people lost their jobs. The unemployment rate climbed. The president at the time, Herbert Hoover, was blamed for the economic problems. In 1932, Franklin Roosevelt was elected the new president of the United States.

Roosevelt had a plan to end the Great Depression. His plan was called the New Deal. He increased the influence of the government on the economy. He tried to have the government give people jobs. During the 1930s, life in the U.S. was very difficult. It was only when World War II began in 1941 that the Great Depression ended. Then, the U.S. economy began to recover.

What is NOT true?

1   The American economy was good in the 1920s.

2   The stock market crashed in 1929.

3   Franklin Roosevelt was president when the stock market crashed.

4   The Great Depression ended in World War II.

Key Words 🎧 037

01	**surprise attack** [səˈpraɪz əˈtæk]	(n.) 突襲　*air/ground attack 空襲／地面攻擊　*suicide attack 自殺攻擊 The Japanese **surprise attack** on Pearl Harbor made the U.S. enter World War II. 日本突襲珍珠港的行為，促使美國加入第二次世界大戰。
02	**atomic bomb** [əˈtɑmɪk bɑm]	(n.) 原子彈　*atomic [= nuclear] energy 原子能；核能 　　　　　　　　*atomic [= nuclear] reactor 原子爐；核子反應爐 The **atomic bomb** uses the power of the atom to cause great destruction. 原子彈利用原子的威力造成巨大的破壞。
03	**nuclear weapon** [ˈnjuklɪə ˈwɛpən]	(n.) 核子武器（ = atomic weapon）　*nonnuclear 非核武的；不使用核能的 **Nuclear weapons** have tremendous destructive power. 核武有毀滅性的威力。
04	**Cold War** [kold wɔr]	(n.) 冷戰（二次大戰後美國與蘇聯之間的對峙局面） *the Cold-War era = the era of the Cold War 冷戰時期 The **Cold War** was between the United States and the Soviet Union after World War II. 冷戰發生於第二次世界大戰後的美國與蘇聯之間。
05	**desegregation** [di,sɛgrəˈgeʃən]	(n.) 廢除種族隔離 The **desegregation** of American schools meant that blacks and whites went to school together. 美國學校的廢除種族隔離，意味著黑人與白人可以在同一所學校受教育。
06	**union** [ˈjunjən]	(n.) 工會；聯盟　*union member 工會成員　*join the union 加入工會 Laborers organized themselves into **unions** to fight for better working conditions. 工人自組工會來爭取更好的工作環境。
07	**corrupt** [kəˈrʌpt]	(a.) 腐敗的；貪污的　*corrupt judge/politician 腐敗的法官／政客 　　　　　　　　　*corrupt values 敗壞的價值觀 There were many **corrupt** politicians in East Coast cities where many immigrants arrived. 大量移民抵達的東岸城市有許多腐敗的政客。
08	**demonstration** [,dɛmənˈstreʃən]	(n.) 示威；示威運動　*demonstration against/for sth. 反對／支持某事的示威遊行 　　　　　　　　　　　*nonviolent demonstration 和平示威 People hold **demonstrations** to protest or support something. 人們舉行示威來抗議或支持某事。
09	**suffrage** [ˈsʌfrɪdʒ]	(n.) 選舉權；投票權　*universal suffrage 公民普選權 　　　　　　　　　*woman suffrage 婦女投票權 Women struggled for equal rights such as **suffrage**, educational rights, and property rights. 婦女努力爭取平等的選舉權、教育權以及財產權等。
10	**superpower** [,supəˈpauə]	(n.) 超級強國　*economic/military superpower 經濟／軍事強國 The U.S. is called the world's only **superpower** today. 美國被稱為是當今世界唯一的超級強國。

atomic bomb

Cold War symbol

desegregation

Berlin Airlift

GIVE WOMEN THE VOTE

demonstration for female suffrage

declare
[dɪˈklɛr]
宣布;宣告
The U.S. declared war on Japan on December 7, 1941.
美國在 1941 年 12 月 7 日向日本宣戰。

embark
[ɪmˈbɑrk]
上船(或飛機等)
Many immigrants embarked from ports in Europe to go to America.
許多移民自歐洲的港口登船,以前往美國。

disembark
[ˌdɪsɪmˈbɑrk]
登陸;上岸
Ellis Island in New York Harbor was where many immigrants disembarked from 1892 until 1954.
在 1892 年到 1954 年期間,紐約港的埃利斯島是許多移民登陸的地方。

encounter
[ɪnˈkaʊntə]
遭遇;偶遇
Immigrants sometimes encountered discrimination. 移民有時會遭受歧視。

strike
[straɪk]
罷工
Labor unions sometimes stop working and strike instead.
工會有時會停止工作並舉行罷工。

demonstrate
[ˈdɛmənˌstret]
示威
Some labor unions demonstrate in front of their companies.
有些工會在他們的公司前面示威。

confront
[kənˈfrʌnt]
面臨;遭遇
Labor unions often confront companies' management. 工會常與企業的管理部門對抗。

protest
[prəˈtɛst]
抗議;反對
Many blacks protested for civil rights in the 1960s.
許多黑人於 1960 年代為民權而抗議。

Word Families 🔊 039

industrialist
[ɪnˈdʌstrɪəlɪst]
企業家;實業家
Industrialists help the economy by hiring people and creating wealth.
企業家雇用員工和創造財富來提升經濟。

capitalist
[ˈkæpətlɪst]
資本家;資本主義者
Capitalists support free market economies.
資本家擁護自由市場經濟。

reformer
[rɪˈfɔrmə]
改革者;革新者
Reformers want to change the way something is done.
改革者想去改變事情原有的作法。

statues of Vietnam War veterans

Important Cold War Events
冷戰重要事件

the Berlin Airlift 柏林空中補給
the Korean War 韓戰
the Berlin Wall 柏林圍牆
the Vietnam War 越戰

Checkup

A

Write | 請依提示寫出正確的英文單字或片語。

1	突襲	_____	
2	原子彈	_____	
3	核子武器	_____	
4	冷戰	_____	
5	廢除種族隔離	_____	
6	工會；聯盟	_____	
7	腐敗的；貪污的	_____	
8	示威 (n.)	_____	
9	選舉權；投票權	_____	
10	超級強國	_____	
11	宣布；宣告	_____	
12	上船（或飛機等）	_____	
13	登陸；上岸	_____	
14	遭遇；偶遇	e_____	
15	罷工	_____	
16	面臨；遭遇	c_____	

B

Complete the Sentences | 請在空格中填入最適當的答案，並視情況做適當的變化。

nuclear weapon	union	suffrage	demonstration	Cold War
surprise attack	corrupt	superpower	desegregation	atomic bomb

1 The Japanese _____ on Pearl Harbor made the U.S. enter World War II. 日本突襲珍珠港的行為，促使美國加入第二次世界大戰。

2 _____ have tremendous destructive power.
核子武器擁有毀滅性的威力。

3 The _____ was between the United States and the Soviet Union after World War II. 冷戰發生於第二次世界大戰後的美國與蘇聯之間。

4 The _____ of American schools meant that blacks and whites went to school together. 美國學校的廢除種族隔離，意味著黑人與白人可以在同一所學校受教育。

5 There were many _____ politicians in East Coast cities where many immigrants arrived. 大量移民抵達的東岸城市有許多腐敗的政客。

6 Laborers organized themselves into _____ to fight for better working conditions. 工人自組工會來爭取更好的工作環境。

7 Women struggled for equal rights such as _____, educational rights, and property rights. 婦女努力爭取平等的選舉權、教育權以及財產權等。

8 The U.S. is called the world's only _____ today.
美國被稱為是當今世界唯一的超級強國。

C

Read and Choose | 閱讀下列句子，並且選出最適當的答案。

1 The U.S. (declared | confronted) war on Japan on December 7, 1941.

2 Ellis Island in New York Harbor was where many immigrants (embarked | disembarked) from 1892 until 1954.

3 Many immigrants (embarked | disembarked) from ports in Europe to go to America.

4 Many blacks (protested | encountered) for civil rights in the 1960s.

D

Look, Read, and Write | 看圖並且依照提示，在空格中填入正確答案。

 ▸ a person who supports free market economies
_____

 ▸ the right to vote
_____

 ▸ doing dishonest, illegal, or immoral things in order to gain money or power
_____

 ▸ the period of hostility and tension between the United States and the Soviet Union after World War II
_____

E

Read and Answer | 閱讀並且回答下列問題。 🔊 040

The Cold War

Berlin Wall

World War II lasted from 1939 to 1945. When it ended, another war immediately began. It was between the United States and the Soviet Union. But this was a different kind of war. It was called the Cold War. The U.S. was for freedom and democracy. The Soviet Union was for tyranny and communism. So they battled around the world in different places.

There were many events in the Cold War, but few involved actual fighting. The Berlin Blockade of 1948 and 1949 was one incident. So was the construction of the Berlin Wall in 1961. Of course, there were some wars. Both the Korean War and the Vietnam War were part of the Cold War since the U.S. and the Soviet Union both supported opposite sides. Even the Space Race in the 1950s and 1960s was part of the Cold War. And so was the nuclear race. Both countries had thousands of nuclear weapons, but they never used them.

Eventually, the Cold War ended in the 1980s. Thanks to U.S. President Ronald Reagan, the Soviet Union began to collapse. In 1989, the Berlin Wall came down. The countries of Eastern Europe started becoming free. And, in 1991, the Soviet Union ended. The Cold War was over.

Fill in the blanks.

1 The United States supported _____ and democracy.

2 The _____ Blockade was in 1948 and 1949.

3 The Space Race was a part of the _____.

4 American President _____ helped end the Cold War and defeated the Soviet Union.

A

Write | 請依提示寫出正確的英文單字或片語。

1 天花	_____	11 爆發；突然發生	_____
2 沒落；垮臺	_____	12 趕走；驅趕	_____
3 毛皮貿易	_____	13 核發；發給	_____
4 特許狀；許可證	_____	14 授予；准予	g _____
5 領土	_____	15 制定（法律）；頒佈（法案）	_____
6 無法容忍的	_____	16 廢除；撤銷	r _____
7 廢除；廢止 (n.)	_____	17 蕭條；不景氣	_____
8 美國重建時期	_____	18 失業	_____
9 突襲	_____	19 選舉權；投票權	_____
10 原子彈	_____	20 超級強國	_____

B

Choose the Correct Word | 請選出與鋪底字意思相近的答案。

1 The Spaniards retreated but left behind diseases.
a. broke out　　b. moved away　　c. drove out

2 Northern abolitionists tried to abolish slavery.
a. regulate　　b. get rid of　　c. reconstruct

3 Some soldiers deserted and left the army.
a. ran away　　b. enlisted　　c. disputed

4 King Charles II granted a large piece of land to William Penn.
a. bestowed　　b. issued　　c. engaged

C

Complete the Sentences | 請在空格中填入最適當的答案，並視情況做適當的變化。

conquistador	monopoly	indentured servant	militia

1 The _____ were Spanish warriors who went to the New World to fight the Native Americans.
征服者是指前往新大陸與印地安人戰鬥的西班牙戰士。

2 Many _____ from Europe worked in tobacco fields.
許多來自歐洲的契約勞工在菸草田裡工作。

3 The colonists formed groups of soldiers called _____.
殖民地居民組成稱為「民兵」的兵團。

4 A _____ happens when one company controls an entire market.
當一個企業掌控了整個市場，就稱為壟斷。

CHAPTER 3

Science ①

Classifying Living Things 生物的分類

Key Words 🔘 041

| 01 | **classification** [ˌklæsəfəˈkeʃən] | *(n.)* 分類;【生】分類法　*biological classification 生物分類法 |

The way to group organisms according to certain characteristics is called **classification**. 將有機體根據某些特徵歸類的方法稱做分類法。

02 kingdom [ˈkɪŋdəm]
(n.)【生】界　*the animal/plant/mineral kingdom 動物／植物／礦物界

All living things are classified into large groups called **kingdoms**.
所有的生物可被歸入稱為「界」的大群體。

03 phylum [ˈfaɪləm]
(n.)【動物】門 *pl. phyla*　*superphylum 總門　*subphylum 亞門

A **phylum** is one of the large groups in the animal kingdom.
「門」是動物界的大群體之一。

04 division [dəˈvɪʒən]
(n.)【植物】門 *pl. divisions*　*subdivision 亞門

Divisions in the plant kingdom are like phyla in the animal kingdom.
植物界的「divisions」等同於動物界的「phyla」。

05 class [klæs]
(n.) 綱　*superclass 總綱　*subclass 亞綱

A **class** is a subdivision of a phylum. 「綱」是「門」下面細分的級別。

06 genus [ˈdʒinəs]
(n.) 屬　*subgenus 亞屬

A **genus** is a group of animals and plants that has several closely related species. 「屬」是指具有許多關係相近品種的一群動植物。

07 species [ˈspiʃiz]
(n.)（物）種　*subspecies 亞種　*variety 變種

There are more than 1.5 million different **species** on Earth.
地球上有超過一百五十萬種不同的物種。

08 bacterium [bækˈtɪrɪəm]
(n.) 細菌 *pl. bacteria*

A **bacterium** is a kind of one-celled organism. 細菌是一種單細胞有機體。

09 prokaryote [ˌproˈkærɪɑt]
(n.) 原核生物

Prokaryotes are small, one-celled organisms like bacteria.
原核生物是如細菌之類的微小單細胞有機體。

10 biodiversity [baɪoˌdaɪˈvɝsətɪ]
(n.) 生物多樣性　*biological diversity 生物多樣性

The wide variety of life living on Earth is called **biodiversity**.
地球上各式各樣的生物稱為生物多樣性。

54

categorize
[ˋkætəgə͵raɪz]

分類

Scientists categorize all life into five separate kingdoms.
科學家把所有的生物分為五個不同的「界」。

classify
[ˋklæsə͵faɪ]

分類;分等級

Scientists classify all life into five separate kingdoms.
科學家把所有的分物分為五個不同的「界」。

divide
[dəˋvaɪd]

分;分開

Scientists divide all life into five separate kingdoms.
科學家把所有的生物分為五個不同的「界」。

contain
[kənˋten]

包含

Each kingdom can contain several phyla, and each phylum can contain several classes. 每個「界」包含數個「門」,每個「門」包含數個「綱」。

contribute
[kənˋtrɪbjut]

貢獻;捐獻

Each member of each of the kingdoms contributes to its ecosystem.
每個「界」的成員都對自己的生態系統有所貢獻。

nonvascular plants

vascular plants
[ˋvæskjələ plænts]

維管束植物

Vascular plants are divided into seedless plants and seed plants.
維管束植物可分為孢子植物和種子植物。

nonvascular plants
[nʌnˋvæskjələ plænts]

無維管束植物

A moss is a nonvascular plant. 苔蘚屬於無維管束植物。

vertebrate
[ˋvɝtə͵bret]

脊椎動物

An animal that has a backbone is a vertebrate. 有脊椎的動物稱為脊椎動物。

invertebrate
[ɪnˋvɝtəbrɪt]

無脊椎動物

An animal that doesn't have a backbone is an invertebrate.
無脊椎的動物稱為無脊椎動物。

Kingdoms
界

| animal kingdom 動物界 | plant kingdom 植物界 | fungi kingdom 真菌界 | protist kingdom 原生生物界 | bacteria/ prokaryote kingdom 原核生物界 |

Checkup

A

Write I 請依提示寫出正確的英文單字或片語。

1	分類;【生】分類法	_____	9	細菌 _____
2	界	_____	10	生物多樣性 _____
3	【動物】門	_____	11	分類 (v.) ca _____
4	【植物】門	_____	12	分類;分等級 cl _____
5	綱	_____	13	分;分開 d _____
6	屬	_____	14	包含 _____
7	(物)種	_____	15	貢獻;捐獻 _____
8	原核生物	_____	16	真菌界 _____

B

Complete the Sentences I 請在空格中填入最適當的答案,並視情況做適當的變化。

division	phylum	class	biodiversity	classification
species	kingdom	genus	prokaryote	bacterium

1 All living things are classified into large groups called _____.
所有的生物可被歸入稱為「界」的大群體。

2 The way to group organisms according to certain characteristics is called
_____. 將有機體根據某些特徵歸類的方法稱做分類。

3 A _____ is one of the large groups in the animal kingdom.
「門」是動物界的大群體之一。

4 _____ in the plant kingdom are like phyla in the animal kingdom.
植物界的「divisions」等同於動物界的「phyla」。

5 A _____ is a subdivision of a phylum. 「綱」就是「門」的附屬級別「亞門」。

6 There are more than 1.5 million different _____ on Earth.
地球上有超過一百五十萬種不同的物種。

7 _____ are small, one-celled organisms like bacteria.
原核生物是如細菌之類的微小單細胞有機體。

8 The wide variety of life living on Earth is called _____.
地球上各式各樣的生物稱為生物多樣性。

C

Read and Choose I 閱讀下列句子,並且選出最適當的答案。

1 Scientists (classify | provide) all life into five separate kingdoms.

2 Each member of each of the kingdoms (contains | contributes) to its ecosystem.

3 Each kingdom can (contain | contribute) several phyla.

4 (Nonvascular | Vascular) plants are divided into seedless plants and seed plants.

D Look, Read, and Write | 看圖並且依照提示，在空格中填入正確答案。

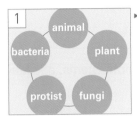

▸ the largest group of living things in a classification

_____

▸ a group of animals and plants that has several closely related species

_____

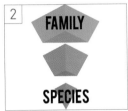

▸ the variety of different types of plant and animal life in an environment

_____

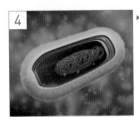

▸ small, one-celled organisms like bacteria

_____

E Read and Answer | 閱讀並且回答下列問題。 🔊 044

Kingdoms

There are many organic creatures on Earth. Some are very different from others. But many have some similarities. So scientists have divided organisms into five separate kingdoms. These kingdoms are animals, plants, protists, fungi, and bacteria. All of the creatures in each kingdom are similar in some way.

The animal kingdom is the biggest. It has over 800,000 species. Most animals are either vertebrates or invertebrates. Animals include mammals, reptiles, birds, amphibians, and insects.

The second largest kingdom is the plant kingdom. Plants include trees, bushes, flowers, vines, and grasses. The third kingdom is the protists. They are animals that have only one cell. They include protozoans, algae, and diatoms. The fourth kingdom is the fungi. Most fungi are mushrooms. But there are also certain molds, yeasts, and lichen, too. The final kingdom is the bacteria. These are some kinds of bacteria and various pathogens, such as viruses.

What is true? Write T(true) or F(false).

1 There are five different kingdoms of organisms. _____

2 The biggest kingdom is the plant kingdom. _____

3 Insects and algae belong to the protist kingdom. _____

4 Fungi are mushrooms and yeasts. _____

Key Words 🔊 045

01	**epidermis** [ˌɛpəˈdɝmɪs]	*(n.)* 表皮 The **epidermis** is the outermost layer of the roots, stems, and leaves. 表皮是根、莖和葉的最外層。
02	**root hair** [rut hɛr]	*(n.)* 根毛 *root vegetable 根菜類 **Root hairs** help plants absorb water and minerals. 根毛幫助植物吸收水分和礦物質。
03	**taproot** [ˈtæpˌrut]	*(n.)* 主根 *take root 生根 *have deep/shallow roots 根長得深／淺 The **taproot** is the main root of a plant. 主根是植物最主要的根。
04	**xylem** [ˈzaɪlɛm]	*(n.)* 木質部 The **xylem** moves water and minerals from the roots to all of the parts of the plant. 木質部將水分和礦物質由根部輸送到植物的各部位。
05	**phloem** [ˈfloɛm]	*(n.)* 韌皮部 The **phloem** moves food from the leaves to all of the parts of the plant. 韌皮部將養分由葉子輸送到植物的各部位。
06	**cambium** [ˈkæmbɪəm]	*(n.)* 形成層 The **cambium** is the layer of cells that separates the xylem and phloem. 形成層是分隔木質部和韌皮部的一層細胞。
07	**cortex** [ˈkɔrtɛks]	*(n.)* 皮質；皮層 *cerebral cortex = brain's cortex 腦皮層 The **cortex** is a layer just inside the epidermis of roots and stems. 皮質是位於植物根莖表皮內側的皮層。
08	**chloroplast** [ˈklorəˌplæst]	*(n.)* 葉綠體 *chlorophyll 葉綠素 **Chloroplasts** make plants green and enable photosynthesis to occur. 葉綠體讓植物變綠，並能行使光合作用。
09	**transpiration** [ˌtrænspəˈreʃən]	*(n.)* 蒸散作用 **Transpiration** is the process by which water moves from inside a plant out to the air. 蒸散作用是水分從植物內部排到空氣中的過程。
10	**respiration** [ˌrɛspəˈreʃən]	*(n.)* 呼吸作用；呼吸 *artificial respiration 人工呼吸 **Respiration** occurs in both plants and animals. 動物和植物都會進行呼吸作用。

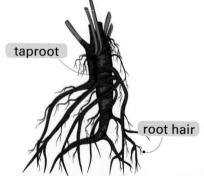

taproot

root hair

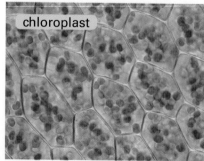

chloroplast

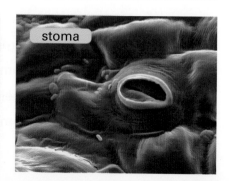

stoma

● 046

transpire
[træn`spaɪr]

蒸散
Plants **transpire** through the leaf's stomata. 植物透過葉孔來進行蒸散。

respire
[rɪ`spaɪr]

呼吸
Plants **respire** by breaking down nutrients into sugar, carbon dioxide, and water.
植物透過將養分分解為糖、二氧化碳和水來進行呼吸。

function
[`fʌŋkʃən]

運行；起作用
Roots **function** to supply plants with nutrients. 根部的作用是供給植物養分。

operate
[`ɑpə,ret]

運作；工作；起作用
Roots **operate** to supply plants with nutrients. 根部的工作是供給植物養分。

hold

支撐；抓住
All stems **hold** the transportation system for plants.
莖部支撐植物的運輸系統。

support
[sə`port]

支撐；支持
All stems **support** the transportation system for plants.
莖部支撐植物的運輸系統。

Word Families

● 047

simple leaf

單葉
Single leaves like a maple's leaves are called **simple leaves**.
像楓葉這樣的單一葉片稱為單葉。

compound leaf
[`kɑmpaʊnd lif]

複葉
Leaves that come in clusters like an acacia's are called
compound leaves. 像金合歡葉這樣叢生的葉片稱為複葉。

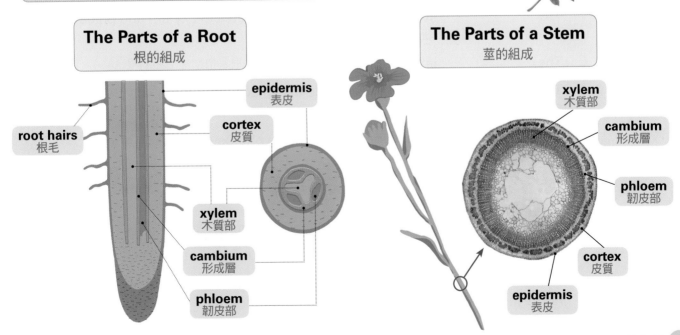

The Parts of a Root
根的組成

epidermis 表皮
cortex 皮質
root hairs 根毛
xylem 木質部
cambium 形成層
phloem 韌皮部

The Parts of a Stem
莖的組成

xylem 木質部
cambium 形成層
phloem 韌皮部
cortex 皮質
epidermis 表皮

Checkup

A

Write | 請依提示寫出正確的英文單字或片語。

1	表皮	_____	9	皮質；皮層	_____
2	根毛	_____	10	葉綠體	_____
3	主根	_____	11	蒸散 (v.)	_____
4	木質部	_____	12	呼吸 (v.)	_____
5	韌皮部	_____	13	運行；起作用 f _____
6	形成層	_____	14	運作；起作用 o _____
7	蒸散作用	_____	15	支撐；抓住 h _____
8	呼吸作用	_____	16	單葉	_____

B

Complete the Sentences | 請在空格中填入最適當的答案，並視情況做適當的變化。

cortex	respiration	root hair	taproot	phloem
chloroplast	transpiration	cambium	epidermis	xylem

1 _____ occurs in both plants and animals.
動物和植物都會進行呼吸作用。

2 _____ is the process by which water moves from inside a plant out to the air. 蒸散作用是水分從植物內部排到空氣中的過程。

3 _____ help plants absorb water and minerals. 根毛幫助植物吸收水分和礦物質。

4 The _____ moves food from the leaves to all of the parts of the plant.
韌皮部將養分由葉子輸送到植物的各部位。

5 The _____ is the layer of cells that separates the xylem and phloem.
形成層是分隔木質部和韌皮部的一層細胞。

6 The _____ is the main root of a plant. 主根是植物最主要的根。

7 The _____ is a layer just inside the epidermis of roots and stems.
皮質是位於植物根莖表皮內側的皮層。

8 _____ make plants green and enable photosynthesis to occur.
葉綠體使植物變綠，並讓光合作用發生。

C

Read and Choose | 閱讀下列句子，並且選出最適當的答案。

1 Plants (respire | transpire) through the leaf's stomata.

2 Plants (respire | transpire) by breaking down nutrients into sugar, carbon dioxide, and water.

3 Roots (hold | function) to supply plants with nutrients.

4 Leaves that come in clusters like an acacia's are called (simple | compound) leaves.

Look, Read, and Write | 看圖並且依照提示，在空格中填入正確答案。

 1 ▶ the outermost layer of the roots, stems, and leaves

_____

 3 ▶ a single leaf like a maple's leaf

_____

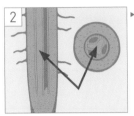 2 ▶ the part that moves water and minerals from the roots to all of the parts of the plant

_____

 4 ▶ a part of a plant cell that makes plants green and enables photosynthesis to occur

_____

E

Read and Answer | 閱讀並且回答下列問題。　● 048

Roots, Stems, and Leaves

Plants are made up of many parts. Three of the most important are their roots, stems, and leaves. All three of them have various functions.

The roots are found at the bottom of the plant. Roots grow underground. They help anchor the plant to the ground. This keeps the plant from being washed away by rain or blown away by the wind. Also, a plant's roots help it extract nutrients from the ground. These nutrients include water and various minerals.

The stems have several important responsibilities. First, they move water and nutrients from the roots to the leaves. They also store some nutrients and water if the plant has too much of them. And they transport food, such as sap, down from the leaves to the roots. Finally, they provide support for the leaves.

The leaves have a very important role. They contain chloroplasts. These let photosynthesis take place. Because of this, plants can create sugar, which they use for food. And they also take carbon dioxide and turn it into oxygen. This lets all of the other animals on Earth breathe.

Fill in the blanks.

1   The three most important parts of plants are the roots, _____, and leaves.

2   Roots help extract water and _____ from the ground.

3   A plant's _____ stores nutrients and water.

4   _____ are what allow photosynthesis to take place.

Key Words 🔊 049

01	**seedless** [ˋsidlɪs]	(a.) 無核的；無籽的　　*seedless grapes 無籽葡萄　　*seed 種子；籽 Mosses and liverworts are **seedless** plants.　苔蘚與地錢屬於孢子植物。
02	**spore** [spor]	(n.) 孢子 A **spore** is a reproductive cell of seedless plants that can grow into new life. 孢子是可以長成新生命的孢子植物生殖細胞。
03	**rhizoid** [ˋraɪzɔɪd]	(n.) 假根 Mosses have root-like fibers called **rhizoids**. 苔蘚擁有類似根的纖維，稱作假根。
04	**frond** [frɑnd]	(n.) （蕨類、棕櫚類的）葉　　*palm fronds 棕櫚葉 The divided leaves of some plants, such as ferns, are **fronds**. 某些植物如蕨類的分裂葉片稱為 frond。
05	**fertilization** [ˏfɝtḷəˏzeʃən]	(n.) 受精作用　　*cross-fertilization【生】異體受精；【植】異花受粉 　　　　　　　　　*self-fertilization【植】自花受粉 **Fertilization** occurs when a plant is pollinated. 植物在授粉時會發生受精作用。
06	**fertilized egg** [ˋfɝtḷˏaɪzd ɛg]	(n.) 受精卵 When a male sex cell meets a female sex cell, they make a **fertilized egg**. 雄性生殖細胞與雌性生殖細胞結合時，會形成受精卵。
07	**asexual reproduction** [eˋsɛkʃʊəl ˏriprəˋdʌkʃən]	(n.) 無性生殖 **Asexual reproduction** is reproduction which does not involve fertilization. 無性生殖是指不需要受精作用的生殖方式。
08	**sexual reproduction** [ˋsɛkʃʊəl ˏriprəˋdʌkʃən]	(n.) 有性生殖 The reproduction from the joining of a male sex cell and a female sex cell is called **sexual reproduction**. 雄性生殖細胞與雌性生殖細胞結合的生殖方式，稱為有性生殖。
09	**asexually** [eˋsɛkʃʊəlɪ]	(adv.) 無性地 Some plants reproduce **asexually**.　有些植物為無性生殖。
10	**gamete** [ˋgæmit]	(n.) 配子 In sexual reproduction, a male **gamete** and a female **gamete** join to form a fertilized egg.　在有性生殖中，雄配子與雌配子結合形成受精卵。

frond

spore

fertilize
[ˈfɝtḷˌaɪz]
使受精;使受粉
A plant must be **fertilized** before it can reproduce. 植物必須受粉才能繁殖。

pollinate
[ˈpɑləˌnet]
授粉;傳粉
Bees and other insects help **pollinate** flowers and other plants.
蜜蜂和其他昆蟲幫忙授粉到花朵和別的植物上。

reproduce
[ˌriprəˈdjus]
繁殖;生育
Mosses and ferns use spores to **reproduce**. 苔蘚和蕨類利用孢子繁殖。

regenerate
[rɪˈdʒɛnərɪt]
使再生;再生
Many organisms have the ability to **regenerate** their lost cells.
許多有機體有能力使失去的細胞再生。

pop
[pɑp]
爆開
When the spore cases **pop** open, they scatter spores all around.
當孢子囊爆開時,孢子就會四散。

branch out
長出枝芽
The roots of ferns **branch out** from the rhizome. 蕨類的根從地下莖長出來。

rhizome
[ˈraɪzom]
根莖;地下莖
The underground stems of ferns are called **rhizomes**.
蕨類埋於地底下的莖稱為地下莖。

fiddlehead
[ˈfɪdəlhɛd]
捲形嫩葉
Young fern fronds are called **fiddleheads**.
幼小的蕨葉稱為捲形嫩葉。

fiddlehead

Seedless Nonvascular Plants
無維管束孢子植物

mosses
[ˈmɔsɪz]
苔蘚

liverworts
[ˈlɪvəˌwɝts]
地錢

Seedless Vascular Plants
維管束孢子植物

ferns
[fɝnz]
蕨類

horsetails
[ˈhɔrsˌtelz]
木賊

club mosses
[klʌb ˈmɔsɪz]
石松

Checkup

A

Write | 請依提示寫出正確的英文單字或片語。

1	無核的;無籽的 _____	9	無性地 _____
2	孢子 _____	10	配子 _____
3	假根 _____	11	使受精;使受粉 _____
4	(蕨類、棕櫚類的)葉 _____	12	授粉;傳粉 _____
5	受精作用 _____	13	繁殖;生育 _____
6	受精卵 _____	14	使再生;再生 _____
7	無性生殖 _____	15	長出枝芽 _____
8	有性生殖 _____	16	根莖;地下莖 _____

B

Complete the Sentences | 請在空格中填入最適當的答案,並視情況做適當的變化。

asexual reproduction	fertilized egg	seedless	frond	rhizoid
sexual reproduction	fertilization	gamete	spore	asexually

1 Mosses and liverworts are _____ plants. 苔蘚和地錢屬於孢子植物。

2 A _____ is a reproductive cell of seedless plants that can grow into new life.
孢子是可以長成新生命的孢子植物生殖細胞。

3 Mosses have root-like fibers called _____.
苔蘚擁有類似根的纖維,稱作假根。

4 _____ occurs when a plant is pollinated. 植物在授粉時會發生受精作用。

5 When a male sex cell meets a female sex cell, they make a _____.
雄性生殖細胞與雌性生殖細胞結合時,會形成受精卵。

6 The reproduction from the joining of a male sex cell and a female sex cell is called
_____.
雄性生殖細胞與雌性生殖細胞結合的生殖方式,稱為有性生殖。

7 Some plants reproduce _____. 有些植物為無性生殖。

8 In sexual reproduction, a male _____ and a female gamete join to form a
fertilized egg.
在有性生殖中,雄配子與雌配子結合,並形成受精卵。

C

Read and Choose | 閱讀下列句子,並且選出最適當的答案。

1 Bees and other insects help (pollinate | carry) flowers and other plants.

2 A plant must be (fertilized | regenerated) before it can reproduce.

3 Mosses and ferns use spores to (pollinate | reproduce).

4 The roots of ferns (pop | branch) out from the rhizome.

D

Look, Read, and Write | 看圖並且依照提示，在空格中填入正確答案。

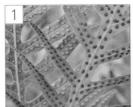 1 ▸ a reproductive cell of seedless plants

_____

3  ▸ to place pollen from one flower on another flower

_____

 2 ▸ a thick plant stem that grows along the ground and produces roots and new plant growth

_____

4  ▸ reproduction which does not involve fertilization

_____

E

Read and Answer | 閱讀並且回答下列問題。 🔘 052

Sexual and Asexual Reproduction

All plants need to reproduce in order to create new plants. There are two ways they can reproduce. The first is sexual reproduction. The second is asexual reproduction.

Sexual reproduction involves a male and female of the same species. Plants that reproduce this way have flowers. Flowers are where their reproductive organs and seeds are. The male reproductive organ is the stamen. It has pollen that needs to be carried to the female part of the plant. The female part is the pistil. When the pollen gets transferred, the plant has been pollinated. This causes seeds to grow in the flower. Soon, the seeds germinate, which means they are growing into young plants.

The second method is asexual reproduction. In this method, there is only one parent plant. Asexual reproduction can happen in many ways. For example, a new plant may simply start growing from an old plant. Other plants reproduce from bulbs. Onions and potatoes are both bulbs. Parts of these plants can simply begin growing roots, and thus they become new plants. In the case of asexual reproduction, there is no pollen, and there are no male and female plants. New plants simply grow from old ones.

What is NOT true?

1   Plants can reproduce in two different ways.

2   The reproductive organs of plants are in their flowers.

3   When seeds germinate, they can grow into new plants.

4   Asexual reproduction requires male and female parts.

Key Words 🔘 053

01	**angiosperm**	*(n.)* 被子植物
	[ˈændʒɪoˌspɝm]	An **angiosperm** is a seed plant that produces flowers. 被子植物是會開花的種子植物。

02	**gymnosperm**	*(n.)* 裸子植物
	[ˈdʒɪmnəˌspɝm]	A **gymnosperm** is a seed plant whose seeds are not in an enclosed ovary. 裸子植物是指種子不為子房所包覆的種子植物。

03	**cotyledon**	*(n.)* 子葉
	[ˌkɑtlˈidən]	The first leaves of the embryo of a vascular plant are the **cotyledons**. 子葉是指維管束植物中，最初由胚芽生出的葉子。

04	**monocot**	*(n.)* 單子葉植物（monocotyledon 的縮寫）
	[ˈmɑnəˌkɑt]	A **monocot** is a plant with seeds that has one cotyledon. 單子葉植物是指種子只有一片子葉的植物。

05	**dicot**	*(n.)* 雙子葉植物（dicotyledon 的縮寫）
	[ˈdaɪˌkɑt]	A **dicot** is a plant with seeds that has two cotyledons. 雙子葉植物是指種子有兩片子葉的植物。

06	**ovary**	*(n.)* 子房
	[ˈovərɪ]	The **ovary** of a plant is where the seeds are contained. 植物的子房是蘊藏種子的地方。

07	**pistil**	*(n.)* 雌蕊
	[ˈpɪstɪl]	The female reproductive part of a flower is the **pistil**. 花朵的雌性生殖器官為雌蕊。

08	**stigma**	*(n.)* 柱頭
	[ˈstɪgmə]	The **stigma** is the top part of the pistil and receives the pollen. 柱頭位於雌蕊頂端，負責接收花粉。

09	**stamen**	*(n.)* 雄蕊
	[ˈstemən]	The part of the flower which produces pollen is the **stamen**. 花朵產生花粉的構造是雄蕊。

10	**anther**	*(n.)* 花藥
	[ˈænθɚ]	The **anther** is the part of the stamen that bears pollen. 花藥是雄蕊負責產生花粉的部位。

angiosperm

gymnosperm

cotyledon

spread [sprɛd]	散布；展開 Trees **spread** their seeds in order to increase their numbers. 為了增加數量，樹木會散布種子。
disperse [dɪˋspɝs]	傳播；散發 Gymnosperms can **disperse** their seeds by insects or the wind. 裸子植物可藉由昆蟲或是風來傳播種子。
scatter [ˋskætɚ]	散播 Gymnosperms can **scatter** their seeds by insects or the wind. 裸子植物可藉由昆蟲或是風來散播種子。

Word Families ● 055

reproductive organ 生殖器官 (= reproductive part)
　Flowers are reproductive organs in the plants.　花朵是植物的生殖器官。

male reproductive organ 雄性生殖器官
　Stamens are the flower's male reproductive organs.　雄蕊是花朵的雄性生殖器官。

female reproductive organ 雌性生殖器官
　Pistils are the flower's female reproductive organs.　雌蕊是花朵的雌性生殖器官。

Gymnosperms 裸子植物

conifer 針葉樹
- **pine** 松樹
- **cedar** 西洋杉
- **fir** 冷杉
- **juniper** 杜松

cycad [ˋsaɪkæd] 蘇鐵

ginkgo [ˋgɪŋko] 銀杏

The Parts of a Flower 花朵的構造

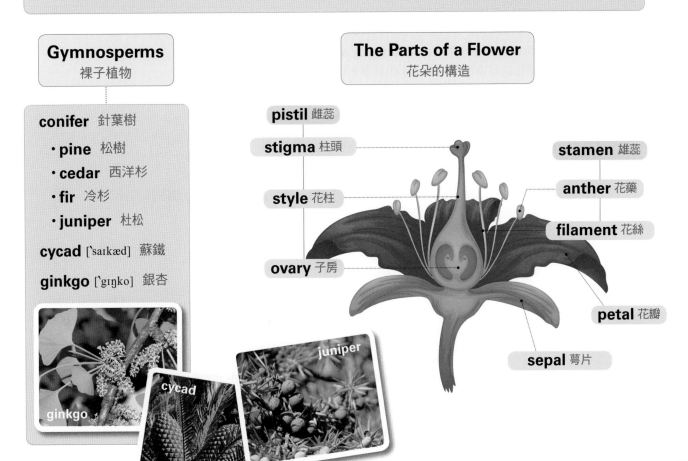

pistil 雌蕊
stigma 柱頭
style 花柱
ovary 子房
stamen 雄蕊
anther 花藥
filament 花絲
petal 花瓣
sepal 萼片

ginkgo
cycad
juniper

Checkup

Write | 請依提示寫出正確的英文單字或片語。

1	被子植物	_____	9	柱頭	_____
2	裸子植物	_____	10	花藥	_____
3	子葉	_____	11	散布;展開	sp_____
4	單子葉植物	_____	12	傳播;散發	d_____
5	雙子葉植物	_____	13	散播	sc_____
6	子房	_____	14	生殖器官	_____
7	雌蕊	_____	15	銀杏	_____
8	雄蕊	_____	16	花絲	_____

B

Complete the Sentences | 請在空格中填入最適當的答案,並視情況做適當的變化。

gymnosperm	angiosperm	ovary	monocot	pistil
cotyledon	stigma	stamen	anther	dicot

1 A _____ is a seed plant whose seeds are not in an enclosed ovary.
裸子植物是指種子不為子房所包覆的種子植物。

2 An _____ is a seed plant that produces flowers. 被子植物會開花的種子植物。

3 The first leaves of the embryo of a vascular plant are the _____.
子葉是指維管束植物中,最初由胚芽生出的葉子。

4 A _____ is a plant with seeds that has one cotyledon.
單子葉植物是指種子只有一片子葉的植物。

5 The female reproductive part of a flower is the _____.
花朵的雌性生殖器官為雌蕊。

6 The _____ is the top part of the pistil and receives the pollen.
柱頭位於雌蕊頂端,負責接收花粉。

7 The part of the flower which produces pollen is the _____.
花朵產生花粉的構造是雄蕊。

8 The _____ is the part of the stamen that bears pollen.
花藥是雄蕊負責產生花粉的部位。

C

Read and Choose | 閱讀下列句子,並且選出最適當的答案。

1 Trees (carry | spread) their seeds in order to increase their numbers.

2 Gymnosperms can (disperse | reproduce) their seeds by insects or the wind.

3 Pistils are the flower's (male | female) reproductive organs.

4 Stamens are the flower's (male | female) reproductive organs.

Look, Read, and Write ∣ 看圖並且依照提示，在空格中填入正確答案。

1  ▸ a seed plant whose seeds are not in an enclosed ovary

_____

3  ▸ the part of the stamen that bears pollen

_____

2  ▸ a seed plant that produces flowers

_____

4  ▸ the first leaf developed by the embryo of a seed plant

_____

E

Read and Answer ∣ 閱讀並且回答下列問題。　● 056

Pollination and Fertilization

Plants that reproduce sexually have both male and female parts. A plant must be pollinated in order to reproduce. Pollen from the stamen — the male part — must reach the pistil — the female part. There are two major ways this happens. The first is the wind. Sometimes, the wind carries pollen from one plant to another. However, this is not a very effective method.

Fortunately, many animals help pollinate plants. Usually, the animals are insects, such as bees and butterflies. Plants' flowers often produce nectar, which insects like. As the insects collect a plant's nectar, they pick up pollen. As the insects go from plant to plant, the pollen on them rubs off on the pistils of other plants. This pollinates the plants.

Now that the pollen has been transferred, the plant must be fertilized. The stigma of a plant has a pollen tube. At least one grain of pollen must go down that tube. This is not easy because the tube is so small, so plants often need many grains of pollen to ensure that one will go down the tube. Once that happens, then the male and female cells can unite. This results in the fertilization of the plant. And it can now reproduce.

Answer the questions.

1　What is the male part of the plant?　_____

2　What is the female part of the plant?　_____

3　What are insects looking for when they pick up pollen?　_____

4　Where in the stigma must the pollen go?　_____

Key Words
🔊 057

01 stimulus
[ˈstɪmjələs]

(n.) 刺激 *pl. stimuli* *a stimulus for 對某事物的激勵
*economic stimulus plan 經濟刺激方案

Anything that affects an organism and prompts a reaction is a **stimulus**.
影響有機體並使之產生反應的一切事物稱為刺激。

02 response
[rɪˈspɑns]

(n.) 反應；回覆 *in response to 作為對……的答覆
*make/give no response 不做回應

Responses and adaptations to a stimulus help an organism survive.
對刺激的反應及適應能幫助有機體生存。

03 tropism
[ˈtropɪzəm]

(n.) 向性；趨性 *phototropism 趨光性；向光性 *hydrotropism 向水性

Tropism is the response of a plant toward or away from a stimulus.
向性是指植物趨近或遠離某個刺激的反應。

04 carnivorous
[karˈnɪvərəs]

(a.) 肉食性的 *carnivore 食肉動物；食蟲植物

Carnivorous plants are plants that derive some nutrients by consuming insects. 肉食性植物是吃蟲來攝取營養的植物。

05 auxin
[ˈɔksɪn]

(n.) 茁長素（幫助植物生長的一種賀爾蒙）

Auxin can help to regulate or change the growth of plants.
茁長素有助於控制或改變植物的生長。

06 protective coloration
[prəˈtɛktɪv ˌkʌləˈreʃən]

(n.) 保護色 *coloration 染色；著色 *coloration of a flower 花卉的色彩

Due to their **protective coloration**, some animals can look the same as the background. 因為有保護色，有些動物看起來和背景一樣。

07 hybrid
[ˈhaɪbrɪd]

(n.) 雜種 *(a.)* 雜種的；混合而成的 *hybrid rose 雜交玫瑰
*hybrid car 油電混合車

A **hybrid** is the result of mating between two different species.
雜種是兩個不同物種交配的結果。

08 crossbreeding
[ˈkrɔsˌbridɪŋ]

(n.) 雜交育種（= interbreeding）

The process of creating hybrids is **crossbreeding**.
創造雜種的過程稱為雜交育種。

09 crossbreed
[ˈkrɔsˌbrid]

(n.) 雜交品種 *(v.)* 雜交繁育（= interbreed） *crossbred sheep/dog 混種羊／犬

If you **crossbreed** a horse and a donkey, the offspring will be a mule.
將馬和驢雜交所產生的下一代為騾。

10 evolution
[ˌɛvəˈluʃən]

(n.) 進化；進化論 *theory of evolution 進化論 *evolutionist 進化論者

Evolution is the process by which organisms physically change to adapt to their environment. 有機體改變身體結構來適應環境的過程，稱為進化。

carnivorous plants

protective coloration

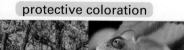

🔊 058

stimulate
[ˈstɪmjəˌlet]
刺激
Light, heat, and gravity can **stimulate** plants a lot. 光、熱和重力對植物有很大的刺激。

respond
[rɪˈspɑnd]
回應；回覆
Plants tend to **respond** to a stimulus more slowly than animals.
植物對刺激的反應往往比動物來得緩慢。

avoid
[əˈvɔɪd]
避開；避免
Prey animals try to **avoid** predators. 獵物試圖避開掠食性動物。

escape
[əˈskep]
逃離；逃跑
Prey animals try to **escape** from predators. 獵物試圖逃離掠食性動物。

evolve
[ɪˈvɑlv]
進化形成
Over time, animals **evolve** and develop new characteristics.
隨著時間的推移，動物進化並發展出新的特徵。

camouflage
[ˈkæməˌflɑʒ]
偽裝；掩飾
Some animals can **camouflage** themselves from predators.
有些動物利用偽裝來躲避掠食性動物。

mimic
[ˈmɪmɪk]
模仿；擬態
Some harmless snakes **mimic** more poisonous ones so that predators will leave them alone. 有些無毒的蛇會模仿較毒的蛇，讓掠食動物遠離牠們。

🔊 059

breed
[brid]
品種
The golden retriever is a **breed** of dog. 黃金獵犬是狗的一個品種。

species
[ˈspiʃiz]
物種
Dogs are a **species** of animal. 狗是動物的一個物種。

mimicry
[ˈmɪmɪkrɪ]
模仿；擬態
When animals imitate others in appearance, it is called **mimicry**.
動物模仿其他的外貌，稱為擬態。

camouflage
[ˈkæməˌflɑʒ]
偽裝；掩飾
Some animals use **camouflage** to blend in with their surroundings to hide from others. 有些動物利用偽裝的方式融入環境來躲藏敵人。

threatened species
受到威脅的物種
Threatened species are animals whose numbers are low.
受到威脅的物種是指數量很少的動物。

endangered species
瀕臨絕種的物種
Endangered species are animals whose numbers are very low.
瀕臨絕種的物種是指數量非常少的動物。

extinct species
絕種物種
Extinct species are animals that no longer exist on the planet.
絕種物種是指已從地球上消失的動物。

Checkup

A

Write | 請依提示寫出正確的英文單字或片語。

1	刺激 (n.)	_____	9	雜交繁育 (v.)	_____
2	反應;回覆 (n.)	_____	10	進化;進化論	_____
3	向性;趨性	_____	11	刺激 (v.)	_____
4	肉食性的	_____	12	回應;回覆 (v.)	_____
5	茁長素	_____	13	避開;避免	_____
6	保護色	_____	14	逃離;逃跑	_____
7	雜種	_____	15	進化形成	_____
8	雜交育種 (n.)	_____	16	模仿;擬態	_____

B

Complete the Sentences | 請在空格中填入最適當的答案,並視情況做適當的變化。

crossbreed	response	hybrid	protective coloration	evolution
carnivorous	auxin	tropism	crossbreeding	stimulus

1 Anything that affects an organism and prompts a reaction is a _____.
影響有機體並使之產生反應的一切事物稱為刺激

2 _____ and adaptations to a stimulus help an organism survive.
對刺激的反應及適應能幫助有機體生存。

3 _____ is the response of a plant toward or away from a stimulus.
向性是指植物趨近或遠離某種刺激的反應。

4 _____ plants are plants that derive some nutrients by consuming insects.
肉食性植物是吃蟲來攝取營養的植物。

5 _____ can help to regulate or change the growth of plants.
茁長素有助於控制或改變植物的生長。

6 A _____ is the result of mating between two different species.
雜種是兩個不同物種交配的結果。

7 If you _____ a horse and a donkey, the offspring will be a mule.
將馬和驢雜交所產生的下一代為騾。

8 _____ is the process by which organisms physically change to adapt to their environment. 有機體改變身體結構來適應環境的過程,稱為進化。

C

Read and Choose | 閱讀下列句子,並且選出最適當的答案。

1 Light, heat, and gravity can (stimulate | respond) plants a lot.

2 Plants tend to (stimulate | respond) to a stimulus more slowly than animals.

3 Prey animals try to (trap | avoid) predators.

4 Some animals can (camouflage | evolve) themselves from predators.

Look, Read, and Write I 看圖並且依照提示，在空格中填入正確答案。

 1
▸ the response of a plant toward or away from a stimulus

_____

 3
▸ a group of animals that have distinguishable characteristics from others of the same species

_____

 2
▸ plants that derive some nutrients by consuming insects

_____

 4
▸ an animal that is a mixture of two different breeds

_____

E

Read and Answer I 閱讀並且回答下列問題。　🔊 060

Tropisms

People know that animals often adapt to their environment. This is called evolution. It can take place over a very long time. And it can change animals very much. Plants can also adapt. Their adaptations are called tropisms.

Tropisms are the reactions of plants to external stimuli. These stimuli can be light, moisture, or gravity. Tropisms are involuntary, but they help plants survive.

Plants need light in order to live. Without light, they cannot undergo photosynthesis. So plants will always grow toward light. If they are in shadows or dark places, they will bend toward the light that they need to survive.

The same is true of moisture. Without water, plants will die. Plants' roots will grow toward the parts of the ground that have moisture. Plants' leaves will adapt so that they can trap as much moisture as possible.

Gravity is another force which causes tropisms. Stems will always move against gravity. This means that they will move in an upward direction. However, roots move with gravity. This means that they move downward.

What is NOT true?

1 Evolution is a change in plants.

2 Plants may react to light or gravity.

3 Plants will try to bend toward light.

4 Plants need water in order to live.

A

Write | 請依提示寫出正確的英文單字或片語。

1	界	_____	11	分類；分等級 _____
2	【動物】門	_____	12	貢獻；捐獻 _____
3	木質部	_____	13	蒸散 (v.) _____
4	形成層	_____	14	呼吸 (v.) _____
5	孢子	_____	15	使受精；使受粉 _____
6	假根	_____	16	授粉；傳粉 _____
7	被子植物	_____	17	柱頭 _____
8	裸子植物	_____	18	花藥 _____
9	刺激 (n.)	_____	19	雜交品種 _____
10	向性；趨性	_____	20	進化；進化論 _____

B

Choose the Correct Word | 請選出與鋪底字意思相近的答案。

1 Scientists categorize all life into five separate kingdoms.

   a. transport   b. classify   c. crossbreed

2 All stems hold the transportation system for plants.

   a. support   b. divide   c. carry

3 Trees spread their seeds in order to increase their numbers.

   a. pollinate   b. evolve   c. disperse

4 Prey animals try to escape from predators.

   a. trap   b. avoid   c. scatter

C

Complete the Sentences | 請在空格中填入最適當的答案，並視情況做適當的變化。

asexually	species	cambium	monocot

1 There are more than 1.5 million different _____ on Earth.
地球上有超過一百五十萬種不同的物種

2 The _____ is the layer of cells that separates the xylem and phloem.
形成層是分隔木質部和韌皮部的一層細胞。

3 Some plants reproduce _____.
有些植物為無性生殖。

4 A _____ is a plant with seeds that has one cotyledon.
單子葉植物是指種子只有一片子葉的植物。

CHAPTER 4

Science ②

The Human Body 人體

Key Words
🔘 061

01	**puberty**	*(n.)* 青春期　　*reach/enter puberty 到了青春期
	[ˈpjubɚtɪ]	Male and female humans are able to produce children when they reach **puberty**. 男性和女性到了青春期就能生育。

02	**adolescence**	*(n.)* 青春期；青少年時期　　*in one's adolescence 某人正值青少年時期 *in early/late adolescence 處於青春期初期／後期
	[ædlˈɛsn̩s]	Many changes in a person's body occur during **adolescence**. 人體在青春期會發生許多變化。

03	**reproductive system**	*(n.)* 生殖系統　　*reproductive organs 生殖器官　　*reproductive capacity 繁殖能力
	[ˌriprəˈdʌktɪv ˈsɪstəm]	The **reproductive system** is the parts of the body that enable humans to reproduce. 生殖系統是指能使人類進行繁殖的身體構造。

04	**menstruation**	*(n.)* 月經　　*(menstrual) period 生理期　　*menstrual pain 生理痛
	[ˌmɛnstrʊˈeʃən]	The monthly process of shedding the egg and the lining of the uterus is called **menstruation**. 每個月卵子及子宮內膜排出體外的過程，稱為月經。

05	**womb**	*(n.)* 子宮（= uterus）
	[wum]	A fetus grows in the mother's **womb** until it is ready to be born. 胎兒在母親的子宮內成長，直到可以出生為止。

06	**fetus**	*(n.)* 胎兒
	[ˈfitəs]	When a **fetus** grows enough to live in the outside world, the mother's uterus pushes the **fetus** out of her body. 當胎兒成長到足以在外面的世界生存，母親的子宮會將他推出體外。

07	**endocrine system**	*(n.)* 內分泌系統　　*endocrine disorder 內分泌失調　　*endocrinology 內分泌學
	[ˈɛndoˌkraɪn ˈsɪstəm]	The **endocrine system** is a system of glands that involve the release of hormones. 內分泌系統是一個分泌荷爾蒙的腺體系統。

08	**gland**	*(n.)* 腺體　　*sweat gland 汗腺　　*endocrine/exocrine gland 內／外分泌腺
	[glænd]	Humans have two kinds of **glands**: duct **glands** and ductless **glands**. 人的腺體有兩種：導管腺體（外分泌腺）與無導管腺體（內分泌腺）。

09	**metabolism**	*(n.)* 新陳代謝　　*increase one's metabolism 增加新陳代謝 *basal metabolic rate 基礎代謝率
	[mɛˈtæbl̩ˌɪzəm]	**Metabolism** is a set of chemical reactions that occur in living organisms to maintain life. 新陳代謝是發生於生物體內，用來維持生命的一系列化學反應。

10	**hormone**	*(n.)* 荷爾蒙；激素　　*growth hormone 生長激素 *female/male hormone 雌性／雄性激素
	[ˈhɔrmon]	The changes in a person's body during adolescence are due to the **hormones** released from glands. 人體在青春期的變化是由腺體分泌的荷爾蒙所致。

reproductive system

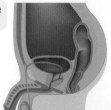

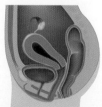

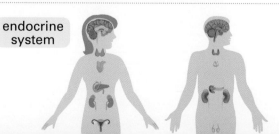
endocrine system

menstruate 月經來潮
[ˈmɛnstrʊˌet]
Women menstruate approximately once a month.
女人的月經大約一個月來一次。

implant 植入
[ɪmˈplænt]
If the egg is fertilized, it implants itself in the wall of the uterus.
卵子一旦受精，就會植入子宮壁。

become pregnant 懷孕 (= be pregnant)
[bɪˈkʌm ˈprɛgnənt]
Once the fertilized egg implants itself in the wall of the uterus, the woman becomes pregnant. 一旦受精卵植入子宮壁，就表示女人懷孕了。

deliver 接生；助產；生產
[dɪˈlɪvɚ]
Sometimes a baby is delivered by cesarean section.
有時嬰兒會以剖腹產的方式生產。

secrete 分泌
[sɪˈkrit]
Endocrine glands secrete hormones inside the body.
內分泌腺在人的體內分泌荷爾蒙。

release 排放
[rɪˈlis]
An egg cell is released every month from one of two ovaries.
每個月兩個卵巢會有其中一個排出卵細胞。

Word Families ● 063

Human Growth Stages 人類成長階段	embryo（受孕後八週內）胚胎　　fetus（受孕後八週以上）胎兒　infant 嬰兒；幼兒 (baby)　　toddler 學步兒童　　child 小孩　teen 青少年　adult 成年　middle age 中年　old age 老年

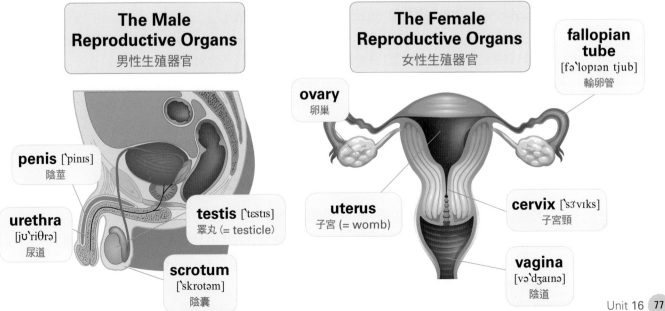

The Male Reproductive Organs 男性生殖器官

penis [ˈpinɪs] 陰莖

urethra [jʊˈriθrə] 尿道

testis [ˈtɛstɪs] 睪丸 (= testicle)

scrotum [ˈskrotəm] 陰囊

The Female Reproductive Organs 女性生殖器官

fallopian tube [fəˈlopɪən tjub] 輸卵管

ovary 卵巢

uterus 子宮 (= womb)

cervix [ˈsɝvɪks] 子宮頸

vagina [vəˈdʒaɪnə] 陰道

Checkup

A

Write | 請依提示寫出正確的英文單字或片語。

1	青春期	_____	9	內分泌系統 _____
2	青春期；青少年時期 _____	10	腺體 _____
3	生殖系統 _____	11	月經來潮 _____
4	月經 _____	12	植入 _____
5	子宮 _____	13	懷孕 _____
6	胎兒 _____	14	接生；助產 _____
7	新陳代謝 _____	15	分泌 s_____
8	荷爾蒙；激素 _____	16	排放 r_____

B

Complete the Sentences | 請在空格中填入最適當的答案，並視情況做適當的變化。

reproductive system	puberty	adolescence	fetus	hormone
endocrine system	metabolism	menstruation	womb	gland

1 Male and female humans are able to produce children when they reach _____. 男性和女性到了青春期就能生育。

2 Many changes in a person's body occur during _____.
人體在青春期會發生許多變化。

3 The monthly process of shedding the egg and the lining of the uterus is called _____. 每個月卵子及子宮內膜排出體外的過程，稱為月經。

4 When a _____ grows enough to live in the outside world, the mother's uterus pushes the fetus out of her body.
當胎兒成長到足以在外面的世界生存，母親的子宮會將他推出體外。

5 The _____ is a system of glands that involve the release of hormones. 內分泌系統是一個分泌荷爾蒙的腺體系統。

6 Humans have two kinds of _____: duct glands and ductless glands.
人的腺體有兩種：導管腺體（外分泌腺）與無導管腺體（內分泌腺）。

7 _____ is a set of chemical reactions that occur in living organisms to maintain life. 新陳代謝是發生於生物體內，用來維持生命的一系列化學反應。

8 The changes in a person's body during adolescence are due to the _____ released from glands. 人體在青春期的變化是由腺體分泌的荷爾蒙所致。

C

Read and Choose | 閱讀下列句子，並且選出最適當的答案。

1 Women (reproduce | menstruate) approximately once a month.

2 If the egg is fertilized, it (release | implants) itself in the wall of the uterus.

3 Once the fertilized egg implants itself in the wall of the uterus, the woman becomes (pregnant | delivered).

4 Endocrine glands (secrete | occur) hormones inside the body.

D

Look, Read, and Write | 看圖並且依照提示，在空格中填入正確答案。

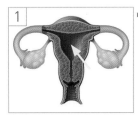
1 ▸ the organ in a female where babies develop
_____

3 ▸ the period during which a person develops from a child into an adult
_____

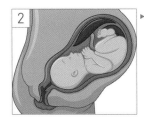
2 ▸ a baby inside the mother before it is born
_____

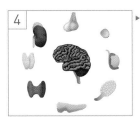
4 ▸ a system of glands that involves the release of hormones
_____

E

Read and Answer | 閱讀並且回答下列問題。 🔊 064

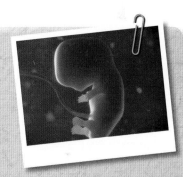

The Development of a Baby

When a woman becomes pregnant, a baby starts to grow in her body. For the next nine months, she will have another life inside her. Until the baby is born, the baby is called a fetus. The fetus goes through several stages of development over nine months.

At first, the new life is just an embryo. It starts growing cells and becoming larger. After three weeks, the body's organs begin to develop, and it takes a human shape. After two months, most of the organs are completely developed. Only the brain and spinal cord are not.

In the ninth week, the embryo is now said to be a fetus. The fetus starts to develop more quickly now. By week fourteen, doctors can determine if it is a male or a female. And after about four or five months of pregnancy, the mother can feel her baby moving around inside her. By the sixth month, the fetus is able to survive outside the womb. The fetus still needs about three more months to develop inside the mother. Finally, during the ninth month, most babies are born.

Fill in the blanks.

1 An unborn baby inside the mother is called a _____.

2 The fetus's organs are completely developed in two _____.

3 Doctors can tell if the baby will be a male or female by week _____.

4 A fetus can survive outside the _____ by the sixth month.

Key Words
🔊 065

01	**biotic factor** [baɪˋɑtɪk ˋfæktɚ]	*(n.)* 生物因子 Living things, such as animals, plants, and fungi, make up the biotic factors in an ecosystem. 像動物、植物以及真菌這樣的生物，組成了生態系統中的生物因子。
02	**abiotic factor** [ˌebaɪˋɑtɪk ˋfæktɚ]	*(n.)* 非生物因子 Nonliving things, such as water, minerals, and sunlight, make up the abiotic factors in an ecosystem. 像水、礦物以及陽光這樣的非生物，組成了生態系統中的非生物因子。
03	**niche** [nɪtʃ]	*(n.)* 生態棲位；小生境 The role or place of an organism in a community is its niche. 有機體在群落中佔有的角色或位置稱為生態棲位。
04	**symbiosis** [ˌsɪmbaɪˋosɪs]	*(n.)* 共生 *pl. symbioses* *endosymbiosis 內共生 *ectosymbiosis 外共生 Symbiosis occurs when two different kinds of organisms form close and long-term relationships. 兩種不同的有機體形成長期的密切關係，即為共生。
05	**mutualism** [ˋmjutʃʊəlɪzəm]	*(n.)* 互利共生 *mutualistic symbioses 互利共生 Mutualism is a type of symbiosis where both organisms benefit from the relationship. 互利共生屬於共生的一種，兩個有機體皆從中得利。
06	**parasitism** [ˋpærəsaɪˌtɪzm̩]	*(n.)* 寄生 *endoparasite 體內寄生蟲 *ectoparasite 體外寄生蟲 Parasitism is a type of symbiosis where one organism benefits at the expense of the host. 寄生屬於共生的一種，其中一方有機體受惠於消耗宿主。
07	**invasive species** [ɪnˋvesɪv ˋspiʃiz]	*(n.)* 入侵物種 *introduced/alien species 外來種 *non-native species 非本土物種 Species that move to a new ecosystem and cause problems there are called invasive species. 遷入新環境並造成當地問題的物種，稱為入侵物種。
08	**biome** [ˋbaɪˌom]	*(n.)* 生物群系（通常以各環境的優勢植被和氣候特徵來分類） There are six major kinds of ecosystems, called biomes, on Earth. 地球上有六大生態系統，稱為生物群系。
09	**ecological succession** [ˌɛkəˋlɑdʒɪkəl səkˋsɛʃən]	*(n.)* 生物演替 The gradual replacement of an ecological community by another is called ecological succession. 一個生態群落被另一個生態群落逐步取代的過程，稱為生物演替。
10	**carrying capacity** [ˋkærɪɪŋ kəˋpæsətɪ]	*(n.)* 環境負載力 Carrying capacity means the maximum population size that the resources in an area can support. 一地資源可養活的最大族群數量，稱為環境負載力。

Symbiosis

mutualism

parasitism

thrive
[θraɪv]

茁壯成長；繁榮興旺
Some species **thrive** when they move to a new environment.
有些物種遷移到新環境，會生長旺盛。

invade
[ɪnˋved]

侵入；侵略
Some species **invade** ecosystems from outside. 有些外來物種會侵入生態系統。

decompose
[ˌdikəmˋpoz]

分解
Dead animals quickly begin **decomposing**. 動物屍體很快就會開始分解。

rot
[rɑt]

腐爛
Dead animals quickly begin **rotting**. 動物屍體很快就會腐爛。

alter
[ˋɔltɚ]

改變
Invasive species can **alter** an ecosystem. 入侵物種會改變生態系統。

change

改變
Invasive species can **change** an ecosystem. 入侵物種會改變生態系統。

Ecological Succession　生態演替

pioneer species　先驅物種

Pioneer species are the first species living in a lifeless area and usually lead to ecological succession.
先驅物種是第一批進入無生命地區生活的物種，常會導致生態演替。

pioneer community　先驅群落

A pioneer community is formed by the appearance of pioneer species in an area.
一個區域出現的先驅物種構成先驅群落。

climax community　終極群落

A climax community is the final stage of succession.
終極群落是演替的最後一個階段。

grassland
草原

taiga [ˋtaɪgə]
北方針葉林

tundra
凍原

desert
沙漠

deciduous forest
落葉林

tropical rainforest
熱帶雨林

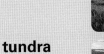

Biomes
生物群系

Checkup

Write | 請依提示寫出正確的英文單字或片語。

1	生物因子	_____	9	生物演替	_____
2	非生物因子	_____	10	環境負載力	_____
3	生態棲位	_____	11	茁壯成長	_____
4	共生	_____	12	侵入；侵略	_____
5	互利共生	_____	13	分解	_____
6	寄生	_____	14	腐爛	_____
7	入侵物種	_____	15	改變	_____
8	生物群系	_____	16	先驅物種	_____

B

Complete the Sentences | 請在空格中填入最適當的答案，並視情況做適當的變化。

symbiosis	niche	carrying capacity	biotic factor	parasitism
mutualism	biome	ecological succession	abiotic factor	invasive species

1 Living things, such as animals, plants, and fungi, make up the _____ in an ecosystem. 像動物、植物以及真菌這樣的生物，組成了生態系統中的生物因子。

2 Nonliving things, such as water, minerals, and sunlight, make up the _____ in an ecosytem.
像水、礦物以及陽光這樣的非生物，組成了生態系統中的非生物因子。

3 _____ occurs when two different kinds of organisms form close and long-term relationships. 兩種不同的有機體形成長期的密切關係，即為共生。

4 _____ is a type of symbiosis where both organisms benefit from the relationship. 互利共生屬於共生的一種，兩個有機體皆從中得利。

5 _____ is a type of symbiosis where one organism benefits at the expense of the host. 寄生屬於共生的一種，其中一方有機體受惠於消耗宿主。

6 There are six major kinds of ecosystems, called _____, on Earth. 地球上有六大生態系統，稱為生物群系。

7 The gradual replacement of an ecological community by another is called _____. 一個生態群落被另一個生態群落逐步取代的過程，稱為生物演替。

8 _____ means the maximum population size that the resources in an area can support. 一地資源可養活的最大族群數量，稱為環境負載力。

C

Read and Choose | 閱讀下列句子，並且選出最適當的答案。

1 Some species (thrive | decompose) when they move to a new environment.

2 Some species (invade | benefit) ecosystems from outside.

3 Invasive species can (alter | rot) an ecosystem.

4 A (pioneer | climax) community is the final stage of succession.

D

Look, Read, and Write | 看圖並且依照提示，在空格中填入正確答案。

1

▸ a type of symbiosis where one organism benefits at the expense of the host
_____

3

▸ the maximum population that the resources in an area can support
_____

2

▸ the first species living in a lifeless area and usually lead to ecological succession
_____

4

▸ a species that moves to a new ecosystem and causes problems there
_____

E

Read and Answer | 閱讀並且回答下列問題。 ◉ 068

How Ecosystems Change

Many ecosystems are thriving communities that are full of life. However, many of them were once empty and were barren lands. But they changed to become places with many kinds of organisms.

The first step is called primary succession. This happens in a place that has never had life on it. Soil must be made first. Then pioneer species come to the land. These are low-level organisms like lichens and mosses. Over time, the soil starts to be able to support more complicated organisms. These are various grasses. Once there is some minor vegetation, animals like insects and birds move in. Eventually, bushes and trees start to grow. Finally, even larger animals move in to the land.

Eventually, the ecosystem will grow enough that a climax community will be formed. This means that the ecosystem is fairly stable. The ecosystem will not change anymore unless something from outside affects it. It could be an invasive species. Or it could be a natural disaster. But unless something affects the ecosystem, it will never change.

What is NOT true?

1   Primary succession is the first step in the changing of an ecosystem.

2   Lichens are some of the first plants to live in a barren area.

3   Climax communities form quickly on barren lands.

4   Natural disasters can change some ecosystems.

Key Words 🔊 069

01	**geologist** [dʒɪˋɑlədʒɪst]	*(n.)* 地質學家　*geology 地質學 A **geologist** is a scientist who studies the earth. 研究地球的科學家稱為地質學家。
02	**seismograph** [ˋsaɪzməˏgræf]	*(n.)* 地震儀　*seismography 測震學　*seismographer 測震專家 A **seismograph** is an instrument that detects the strength of earthquakes. 地震儀是用來偵測地震強度的儀器。
03	**fault** [fɔlt]	*(n.)* 斷層　*fault zone 斷層帶　*active fault 活斷層 A **fault** is a break in the earth's crust and is related to earthquakes. 斷層是指地殼的斷裂處，與地震息息相關。
04	**watershed** [ˋwɑtəˏʃɛd]	*(n.)* 流域；分水嶺　*watershed 轉折點（= turning point） The area of land from which the water drains into a river or stream is a **watershed**. 水注入河流或溪流所涵蓋的區域稱為流域。
05	**floodplain** [ˋflʌdˏplen]	*(n.)* 沖積平原；氾濫平原　*floodway 分洪道；洩洪道　*flood fringe 洪水邊緣地 The flat land around a river that often floods is called the **floodplain**. 河流周圍經常氾濫的平坦陸地稱為沖積平原。
06	**deposition** [ˏdɛpəˋzɪʃən]	*(n.)* 堆積作用；沉機作用 **Deposition** is the settling of eroded material. 堆積作用是指被侵蝕物質的沉澱過程。
07	**lithosphere** [ˋlɪθəˏsfɪr]	*(n.)* 岩石圈　*asthenosphere（地球內部的）軟流圈 The crust and the upper mantle form the **lithosphere**. 地殼和上地函形成岩石圈。
08	**hydrosphere** [ˋhaɪdrəsfɪr]	*(n.)* 水圈 All of the water that is found on the earth's surface is the **hydrosphere**. 分布於地球表面的所有水稱為水圈。
09	**ore** [or]	*(n.)* 礦石　*iron ore 鐵礦 Any rock that has minerals or metals in it is **ore**. 內含礦物或金屬的岩石稱為礦石。
10	**gem** [dʒɛm]	*(n.)* 寶石 A **gem** is a precious stone like a diamond, ruby, or emerald. 寶石是指鑽石、紅寶石以及祖母綠這類的珍貴石頭。

atmosphere
crust
lithosphere
asthenosphere
mantle
hydrosphere
outer core
inner core

fault

floodplain

watershed

deposit
[dɪˈpɑzɪt]

使沉澱；使沉積

Rivers often **deposit** great amounts of silt at their deltas.
河流經常沉澱大量的泥沙於三角洲。

Nile Delta

transform
[trænsˈfɔrm]

使轉變；使改變

Great pressure can **transform** coal into a diamond.
巨大的壓力會使煤轉變為鑽石。

compress
[kəmˈprɛs]

擠壓；壓縮

Pressure inside the earth can **compress** rocks. 地球內部的壓力會擠壓岩石。

weather
[ˈwɛðə˞]

風化

The forces of erosion often **weather** rocks and make them smaller.
侵蝕力常會風化岩石，使其變小。

meander
[mɪˈændə˞]

緩慢而曲折地前進

Rivers **meander** in different directions as they flow to the ocean.
河流沿著不同的方向蜿蜒流入大海。

Forces in the Crust 地殼的作用力

tension

張力

Tension pulls apart the crust. 張力會將地殼拉斷。

compression

壓縮力

Compression pushes the crust together. 壓縮力會將地殼推擠在一起。

shear
[ʃɪr]

剪力

Shear tears or pushes one part of the crust past another.
剪力會將地殼的某部分撕扯或推擠過另一部分。

sediment
[ˈsɛdəmənt]

沉積物 (= deposit)

Sediment can be gravel, sand, silt, and dissolved materials.
沉積物可以是沙礫、沙子、泥沙或是溶解物質。

silt
[sɪlt]

泥沙；淤泥

Silt is sand or dirt that settles in bodies of water.
泥沙是指沉積在水域裡的沙子或泥土。

gem

luster
[ˈlʌstə˞]

光澤

A gemstone's **luster** is how much it shines.
光澤是指寶石的閃亮程度。

hardness

硬度

The **hardness** of gemstones varies, but diamonds are the hardest of all.
每種寶石的硬度相異，而鑽石是最硬的一種。

Checkup

A

Write I 請依提示寫出正確的英文單字或片語。

1	地質學家	_____	9 礦石	_____
2	地震儀	_____	10 寶石	_____
3	斷層	_____	11 使沉澱；使沉積	_____
4	流域；分水嶺	_____	12 使轉變；使改變	_____
5	沖積平原	_____	13 擠壓；壓縮	_____
6	堆積作用	_____	14 風化	_____
7	岩石圈	_____	15 緩慢而曲折地前進	_____
8	水圈	_____	16 張力	_____

B

Complete the Sentences I 請在空格中填入最適當的答案，並視情況做適當的變化。

geologist	fault	hydrosphere	watershed	flood plain
deposition	gem	lithosphere	seismograph	ore

1 A _____ is a scientist who studies the earth.
研究地球的科學家稱為地質學家。

2 A _____ is an instrument that detects the strength of earthquakes.
地震儀是用來偵測地震強度的儀器。

3 The area of land from which the water drains into a river or stream is a _____.
水注入河流或溪流所涵蓋的區域稱為流域。

4 _____ is the settling of eroded material. 堆積作用是指被侵蝕物質的沉澱過程。

5 A _____ is a break in the earth's crust and is related to earthquakes.
斷層是指地殼的斷裂處，與地震息息相關。

6 The crust and the upper mantle form the _____.
地殼和上地函形成岩石圈。

7 All of the water that is found on the earth's surface is the _____.
分布於地球表面的所有水稱為水圈。

8 Any rock that has minerals or metals in it is _____.
內含礦物或金屬的岩石稱為礦石。

C

Read and Choose I 閱讀下列句子，並且選出最適當的答案。

1 Rivers often (weather | deposit) great amounts of silt at their deltas.

2 Great pressure can (transport | transform) coal into a diamond.

3 Pressure inside the earth can (compress | detect) rocks.

4 Rivers (carry | meander) in different directions as they flow to the ocean.

Look, Read, and Write | 看圖並且依照提示，在空格中填入正確答案。

 1 ▸ a break in the earth's crust

_____

 3 ▸ to follow a path with a lot of turns and curves

_____

 2 ▸ the flat land around a river that often floods

_____

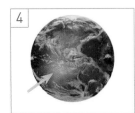 4 ▸ It refers to all of the water that is found on the earth's surface.

_____

E

Read and Answer | 閱讀並且回答下列問題。　◉ 072

Earthquakes

Sometimes, the ground suddenly begins to shake. Buildings and bridges move back and forth. They might even fall down. Places in the ground begin to crack. This is an earthquake. Earthquakes happen all the time all around the earth. Most of the time, they are so small that we cannot even feel them. But sometimes there are very large earthquakes. These can cause great damage, kill many people, and even change the way the earth looks.

The earth's crust is its top part. The crust is formed of many plates. These are called tectonic plates. There are seven large plates and around twelve smaller ones. These plates are enormous. But they also move really slowly. Sometimes they move back and forth against each other. This causes earthquakes.

The Richter scale measures the power of earthquakes. A level 2 quake is ten times as powerful as a level 1 quake. For each whole number increase, the power of the earthquake increases by ten. Levels 1 to 4 are weak earthquakes. Level 5 earthquakes can cause some damage. Levels 6 and 7 can be dangerous. Levels 8 and 9 can cause huge amounts of death and destruction.

Answer the questions.

1   What is the top part of the earth?　_____

2   How many large tectonic plates are there on the earth?　_____

3   What measures an earthquake's power?　_____

4   What do weak earthquakes measure?　_____

Matter 物質

01	**atom** [ˈætəm]	(n.) 原子 *carbon/hydrogen atom 碳／氫原子 *atomic number 原子序數（原子中的質子數量） Atoms are made of protons, neutrons, and electrons. 原子由質子、中子和電子組成。
02	**proton** [ˈprotɑn]	(n.) 質子 *protonation 質子化 *protonated atom 質子化原子 A **proton** is a particle in the nucleus of an atom that has a positive electric charge. 質子是原子核中帶正電的粒子。
03	**neutron** [ˈnjutrɑn]	(n.) 中子 *neutron bomb 中子彈 *neutron star 中子星 A **neutron** is a particle in the nucleus of an atom that has no electric charge. 中子是原子核中不帶電的粒子。
04	**electron** [ɪˈlɛktrɑn]	(n.) 電子 *electron microscope 電子顯微鏡 *negative electron 負電子 An **electron** has a negative electric charge and orbits an atom's nucleus. 電子帶負電，環繞原子核運動。
05	**nucleus** [ˈnjuklɪəs]	(n.) 原子核 The **nucleus** is the central part of an atom. 原子核是原子的中心。
06	**compound** [ˈkɑmpaʊnd]	(n.) 化合物；混合物 *chemical compound 化合物 *a compound of . . . and . . . 某兩物的混合物 A **compound** is formed by two or more elements. 化合物由兩種或兩種以上的元素組成。
07	**solution** [səˈluʃən]	(n.) 溶液 *a solution of sth. 某物的溶液 *saturated solution 飽和溶液 All **solutions** consist of at least one solute and one solvent. 所有的溶液都由至少一種溶質和一種溶劑組成。
08	**solute** [sɑˈljut]	(n.) 溶質；溶解物 A **solute** is a substance that dissolves in a solution. 溶質是溶液中的溶解物質。
09	**solvent** [ˈsɑlvənt]	(n.) 溶劑 A **solvent** is a substance that can dissolve another. 溶劑是可溶解其他物質之物。
10	**chemical formula** [ˈkɛmɪkḷ ˈfɔrmjələ]	(n.) 化學式 *molecular formula 分子式 *structural formula 結構式 A compound's **chemical formula** shows the symbols and subscripts for the elements that make it up. 化合物的化學式顯示了組成元素的符號和下標符號。

Atom

electron

neutron

nucleus

proton

chemical formula

$$CH_4$$

solute

unite 混合
[ju`naɪt]
Two or more elements can **unite** to create a compound.
兩種或兩種以上的元素可以混合，創造出化合物。

solvent

bond 結合
[bɑnd]
Two or more elements can **bond** to create a compound.
兩種或兩種以上的元素可以結合，創造出化合物。

dissolve 溶解
[dɪ`zɑlv]
Sugar and salt both **dissolve** in water. 糖和鹽都溶於水。

expand 膨脹
[ɪk`spænd]
Objects that **expand** become larger. 物體膨脹會變大。

contract 收縮
[kən`trækt]
Objects that **contract** become smaller. 物體收縮會變小。

solution

revolve 環繞……運動
[rɪ`vɑlv]
Electrons **revolve** around the nucleus. 電子環繞原子核運動。

orbit 環繞……運動
[`ɔrbɪt]
Electrons **orbit** the nucleus. 電子環繞原子核運動。

Word Families 🔊 075

acid 酸
Acids, like vinegar and lemon juice, taste sour.
像醋和檸檬汁這樣的酸類，味道是酸的。

base 鹼
Bases, like ammonia and baking soda, taste bitter.
像氨水和小蘇打這樣的鹼類，味道是苦的。

neutral 中性的
[`njutrəl]
Water is a **neutral** substance. 水是中性物質。

melting point 熔點
The melting point of water is 0 degrees Celsius. 水的熔點是攝氏 0 度。

boiling point 沸點
The boiling point of water is 100 degrees Celsius. 水的沸點是攝氏 100 度。

freezing point 冰點
The freezing point of water is 0 degrees Celsius. 水的冰點是攝氏 0 度。

Chemical Formulas for Common Compounds
常見化合物的化學式

water – H_2O 水
carbon dioxide – CO_2 二氧化碳
methane – CH_4 甲烷
[`mɛθen]
sugar – $C_{12}H_{22}O_{11}$ 糖

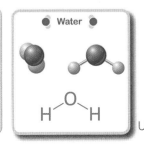
Water

Checkup

A

Write | 請依提示寫出正確的英文單字或片語。

1	原子	_____	9	溶液	_____
2	質子	_____	10	化學式	_____
3	中子	_____	11	混合	u_____
4	電子	_____	12	結合	b_____
5	原子核	_____	13	溶解	_____
6	化合物	_____	14	收縮	_____
7	溶質	_____	15	酸	_____
8	溶劑	_____	16	鹼	_____

B

Complete the Sentences | 請在空格中填入最適當的答案，並視情況做適當的變化。

electron	atom	proton	neutron	compound
solution	solute	solvent	nucleus	chemical formula

1 _____ are made of protons, neutrons, and electrons.
原子由質子、中子和電子組成。

2 A _____ is a particle in the nucleus of an atom that has a positive electric charge. 質子是原子核中帶正電的粒子。

3 An _____ has a negative electric charge and orbits an atom's nucleus.
電子帶負電，環繞原子核運動。

4 A _____ is formed by two or more elements.
化合物由兩種或兩種以上的元素組成。

5 The _____ is the central part of an atom. 原子核是原子的中心。

6 All _____ consist of at least one solute and one solvent.
所有的溶液都由至少一種溶質和一種溶劑組成。

7 A _____ is a substance that can dissolve another.
溶劑是可以溶解其他物質之物。

8 A _____ is a substance that dissolves in a solution.
溶質是溶液中的溶解物質。

C

Read and Choose | 閱讀下列句子，並且選出最適當的答案。

1 Two or more elements can (move | unite) to create a compound.

2 Objects that (expand | contract) become larger.

3 Objects that (expand | contract) become smaller.

4 Electrons (orbit | revolve) around the nucleus.

D

Look, Read, and Write | 看圖並且依照提示，在空格中填入正確答案。

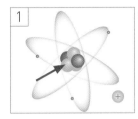
1
▸ a particle in the nucleus of an atom that has a positive electric charge

_____

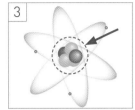
3
▸ the central part of an atom

_____

2
▸ a substance that dissolves in a solution

_____

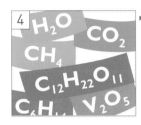
4
▸ a formula that shows the symbols and subscripts for the elements

_____

E

Read and Answer | 閱讀並且回答下列問題。 ⊙ 076

Elements

The entire universe is made of matter. And matter is made of either individual elements or compounds. Compounds are combinations of two or more elements. What is an element? It is matter made of only one type of atom. There are 117 elements. Most are natural. So they appear in nature. But scientists have made a few elements. They only appear in labs.

All elements have a similar structure. They have a nucleus. This is the element's core. Inside the nucleus are protons and neutrons. Elements have different numbers of them. For example, hydrogen has 1 proton and 0 neutrons. Helium has 2 protons and 2 neutrons. Oxygen has 8 protons and 8 neutrons. Gold has 79 protons and 118 neutrons.

Outside the nucleus are electrons. They orbit the nucleus. Electrons have negative charges. But protons have positive charges. Also, an element usually has the same number of protons and electrons. But they can sometimes be different.

What is true? Write T (true) or F (false).

1   There are 117 elements.   _____

2   Most elements are manmade.   _____

3   Protons and neutrons are in the nucleus.   _____

4   Electrons have positive charges.   _____

Key Words 🔊 077

01	**celestial** [sɪˈlɛstʃəl]	*(a.)* 天的;天空的 　*celestial globe 天球儀 　*celestial being 天神 There are many **celestial** bodies in outer space. 外太空有許多天體。
02	**rotation** [roˈteʃən]	*(n.)* 自轉;旋轉 　*the rotation of the earth 地球自轉 　*in rotation 輪流地 It takes 24 hours for Earth to make one complete **rotation**. 地球自轉一周耗時 24 小時。
03	**revolution** [ˌrɛvəˈluʃən]	*(n.)* 公轉;運行 　*revolution around sth. 圍繞某物運行 Earth's **revolution** around the sun causes the seasons. 地球繞太陽公轉形成了四季。
04	**lunar eclipse** [ˈlunɚ ɪˈklɪps]	*(n.)* 月蝕 　*in eclipse 處於蝕象 　*go into eclipse 進入蝕象 A **lunar eclipse** occurs when the earth moves between the sun and the moon. 月蝕發生於地球運行到太陽與月亮之間。
05	**solar eclipse** [ˈsolɚ ɪˈklɪps]	*(n.)* 日蝕 　*partial/total/annular eclipse 偏蝕/全蝕/環蝕 A **solar eclipse** occurs when the moon moves between the earth and the sun. 日蝕發生於月亮運行到地球與太陽之間。
06	**meteorite** [ˈmitɪərˌaɪt]	*(n.)* 隕石 　*meteor 流星 　*meteorite fall/find 墜落隕石/發現隕石 A **meteorite** is a piece of rock from space that strikes the surface of the earth or the moon. 隕石是來自太空的一塊岩石,撞擊於地球或月球表面。
07	**crater** [ˈkretɚ]	*(n.)* 隕石坑;環形山 　*impact crater 撞擊坑 　*Tycho crater 第谷坑(月球一隕石坑) The **craters** of the moon's surface resulted from meteorite collisions. 月球表面的隕石坑是隕石撞擊的結果。
08	**black hole** [blæk hol]	*(n.)* 黑洞 　*white hole 白洞 　*wormhole 蟲洞 When a high-mass star collapses, it can form a **black hole**. 當一個大質量的星體崩解時,會形成黑洞。
09	**supernova** [ˌsupɚˈnovə]	*(n.)* 超新星 　*pl. supernovas/supernovae* 　*nova 新星 　　　　　　　　　　　　　　　　　　　　　*supernova remnant 超新星殘骸 A **supernova** results when a high-mass star explodes and releases a huge amount of energy. 一個大質量的星體爆炸並釋放巨大能量時,會形成超新星。
10	**extraterrestrial** [ˌɛkstrətəˈrɛstrɪəl]	*(n.)* 外星生物 　*(a.)* 地球外的 　*extraterrestrial life 外星生命 　　　　　　　　　　　　　　　　　　　　*extraterrestrial being (= extraterrestrial) 外星人 An **extraterrestrial** is an alien. 外星生物就是外星人。

lunar eclipse

solar eclipse

crater

rotate
['rotet]

旋轉；轉動

Earth rotates on its axis every twenty-four hours.
地球每 24 小時繞地軸旋轉。

revolve
[rɪ'vɑlv]

公轉

It takes one year for Earth to revolve around the sun.
地球繞太陽公轉需耗時一年。

rotation

explode
[ɪk'splod]

爆炸；爆破

A supernova is formed when a high-mass star explodes with a huge amount of power. 當一個大質量的星體挾帶巨大能量爆炸時，便形成超新星。

release
[rɪ'lis]

釋放

The energy released by a supernova is more than all the energy the sun will create in its lifetime.
超新星所釋放的能量，比太陽一生中所產生的能量還大。

contain
[kən'ten]

包含

The Oort Cloud contains large numbers of comets and asteroids.
歐特雲內含大量的慧星和小行星。

surpass
[sɚ'pæs]

超越；大於

Scientists believe we cannot surpass the speed of light.
科學家認為人類無法超越光速。

exceed
[ɪk'sid]

超過；超出

Scientists believe we cannot exceed the speed of light.
科學家認為人類無法超過光速。

meteor
['mitɪɚ]

流星 (= shooting star)

A meteor is a piece of rock from space that burns up as it enters Earth's atmosphere. 流星是來自太空的一塊岩石，進入地球的大氣層時會燃燒。

comet
['kɑmɪt]

彗星

A comet is a ball of ice, dust, and frozen gases that orbits the sun.
慧星是繞著太陽運行的一團冰塊、塵埃以及冰凍氣體。

alien

外星人

Aliens are creatures that are not from the earth. 外星人是指地球以外的生物。

ET

外星生物

ET is short for extraterrestrial, and it means an alien.
ET 是 extraterrestrial 的簡稱，就是指外星人。

Types of Eclipses
月蝕與日蝕的種類

total lunar eclipse 月全蝕

partial lunar eclipse 月偏蝕

total solar eclipse 日全蝕

partial solar eclipse 日偏蝕

Checkup

A

Write | 請依提示寫出正確的英文單字或片語。

1	天的；天空的	_____
2	自轉；旋轉 (n.)	_____
3	公轉；運行 (n.)	_____
4	月蝕	_____
5	日蝕	_____
6	隕石	_____
7	黑洞	_____
8	超新星	_____
9	隕石坑；環形山	_____
10	外星生物	_____
11	旋轉；轉動 (v.)	_____
12	公轉 (v.)	_____
13	爆炸；爆破	_____
14	勝過；大於	s_____
15	超過；超出	e_____
16	流星	_____

B

Complete the Sentences | 請在空格中填入最適當的答案，並視情況做適當的變化。

solar eclipse	celestial	crater	black hole	extraterrestrial
lunar eclipse	meteorite	rotation	supernova	revolution

1 There are many _____ bodies in outer space. 外太空有許多天體。

2 Earth's _____ around the sun causes the seasons.
地球繞太陽公轉形成了四季。

3 It takes 24 hours for Earth to make one complete _____.
地球自轉一周耗時 24 小時。

4 A _____ is a piece of rock from space that strikes the surface of the earth or the moon. 流星是來自太空的一塊岩石，撞擊於地球或月球表面。

5 A _____ occurs when the moon moves between the earth and the sun. 日蝕發生於月亮運行到地球與太陽之間。

6 When a high-mass star collapses, it can form a _____.
當一個大質量的星體崩解時，會形成黑洞。

7 A _____ results when a high-mass star explodes and releases a huge amount of energy. 一個大質量的星體爆炸並釋放巨大能量時，會形成超新星。

8 An _____ is an alien. 外星生物就是外星人。

C

Read and Choose | 閱讀下列句子，並且選出最適當的答案。

1 It takes one year for Earth to (rotate | revolve) around the sun.

2 A supernova is formed when a high-mass star (explodes | releases) with a huge amount of power.

3 The Oort Cloud (exceeds | contains) large numbers of comets and asteroids.

4 Scientists believe we cannot (pass | surpass) the speed of light.

D

Look, Read, and Write **I 看圖並且依照提示，在空格中填入正確答案。**

1  ▸ It occurs when the earth moves between the sun and the moon.

_____

3  ▸ a large round hole in the ground caused by the impact of a meteorite

_____

2 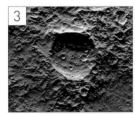 ▸ an exploding star that releases a huge amount of energy

_____

4  ▸ a piece of rock from space that strikes the surface of the earth or the moon

_____

E

Read and Answer **I 閱讀並且回答下列問題。** 🔊 080

Are We Alone?

For thousands of years, men have looked at the stars and asked, "Are we alone?" Men are fascinated by the stars and the possibility of there being life on other planets. Myths in many cultures tell stories about aliens coming to Earth. But no one knows if there really are aliens or not.

Nowadays, scientists are searching for life on other planets. Some believe there could be life on Mars. Others think the moons Europa or Io could have life. And others are looking at other star systems. They are trying to find Earth-like planets.

What does life need to survive on other planets? Life on Earth is all carbon based. That kind of life needs a star to provide heat and light. It needs an atmosphere with oxygen. It needs water.

Of course, other forms of life could be based on different elements. We don't know what they would need to survive. But we do know one thing: Men will continue looking for extraterrestrial life until we find it.

Fill in the blanks.

1   There are many _____ about aliens coming to Earth.

2   Some scientists are searching for _____ on other planets.

3   Some people believe the planet _____ could have aliens on it.

4   Life on Earth is _____ based.

A

Write | 請依提示寫出正確的英文單字或片語。

1	青春期	p_____	11	內分泌系統
2	新陳代謝	_____	12	腺體
3	共生	_____	13	生物演替
4	互利共生	_____	14	茁壯成長；繁榮
5	岩石圈	_____	15	使沈澱；使沈積
6	水圈	_____	16	使轉變；使改變
7	質子	_____	17	溶解
8	中子	_____	18	收縮
9	日蝕	_____	19	隕石坑；環形山
10	隕石	_____	20	外星生物

B

Choose the Correct Word | 請選出與鋪底字意思相近的答案。

1 Scientists believe we cannot exceed the speed of light.

   a. explode   b. surpass   c. transform

2 Two or more elements can unite to create a compound.

   a. compress   b. bond   c. expand

3 Electrons revolve around the nucleus.

   a. rotate   b. create   c. orbit

4 Dead animals quickly begin decomposing.

   a. rotting   b. depositing   c. contracting

C

Complete the Sentences | 請在空格中填入最適當的答案，並視情況做適當的變化。

adolescence	atom	parasitism	seismograph

1 Many changes in a person's body occur during _____.
人體在青春期會發生許多變化

2 _____ is a type of symbiosis where one organism benefits at the expense of the host.
寄生屬於共生的一種，其中一方有機體受惠於消耗宿主。

3 A _____ is an instrument that detects the strength of earthquakes.
地震儀是用來偵測地震強度的儀器。

4 _____ are made of protons, neutrons, and electrons.
原子由質子、中子和電子組成。

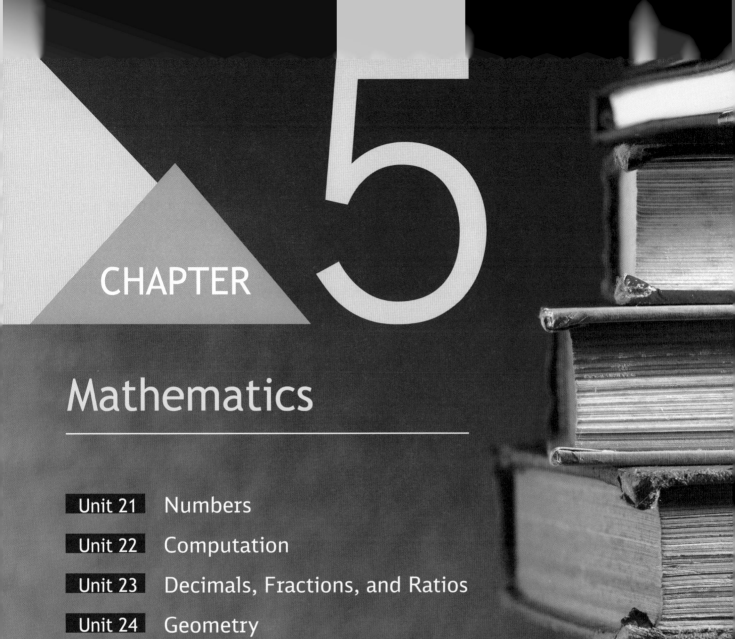

CHAPTER 5

Mathematics

Key Words 🔊 081

01	**Arabic numeral** [ˈærəbɪk ˈnjumərəl]	*(n.)* 阿拉伯數字 The Arabic numerals are the ten digits 0, 1, 2, 3, 4, 5, 6, 7, 8, and 9. 阿拉伯數字是指 0, 1, 2, 3, 4, 5, 6, 7, 8, 9 這 10 個數字。
02	**Roman numeral** [ˈromən ˈnjumərəl]	*(n.)* 羅馬數字 Roman numerals are letters that stand for numbers and were used by the Romans. 羅馬數字用字母代表數字，為羅馬人所使用。
03	**integer** [ˈɪntədʒɚ]	*(n.)* 整數　　*positive/negative integer 正／負整數 An integer is any positive or negative whole number. 整數是任何正整數或負整數。
04	**divisor** [dəˈvaɪzɚ]	*(n.)* 因數；除數 (= factor)　　*dividend 被除數　　*divisible 可除盡的 1, 3, and 7 are divisors of 21. 1、3、7 是 21 的因數。
05	**common divisor** [ˈkɑmən dəˈvaɪzɚ]	*(n.)* 公因數　　*greatest common divisor 最大公因數 1, 2, 3, and 6 are common divisors of 12 and 18. 1、2、3、6 是 12 和 18 的公因數。
06	**multiple** [ˈmʌltəpl̩]	*(n.)* 倍數　　*multiply 乘　　*multiplier 乘數 14, 21, 28, and 49 are multiples of 7. 14、21、28、49 是 7 的倍數。
07	**common multiple** [ˈkɑmən ˈmʌltəpl̩]	*(n.)* 公倍數　　*least/lowest common multiple 最小公倍數 12, 24, and 36 are common multiples of 4 and 6. 12、24、36 是 4 和 6 的公倍數。
08	**exponent** [ɪkˈsponənt]	*(n.)* 指數　　*exponentiation 指數運算　　*exponential function 指數函數 In 5^3, 5 is the base, and 3 is the exponent. 在 5^3 中，5 是底數，3 是指數。
09	**prime number** [praɪm ˈnʌmbɚ]	*(n.)* 質數 A number that can only be divided by itself or 1, like 7, is a prime number. 只能被自身和 1 整除的數稱為質數，例如 7 就是質數。
10	**prime factor** [praɪm ˈfæktɚ]	*(n.)* 質因數 3 and 2 are the prime factors of 12. 3 和 2 是 12 的質因數。

divisor

12　1, 2, 3, 4, 6, 12
18　1, 2, 3, 6, 9, 18

common divisor

multiple

4　4, 8, 12, 16, 20, 24...
6　6, 12, 18, 24, 30...

common multiple

Power Verbs 🔊 082

square
[skwɛr]

使成平方

When you **square** three, the result is nine.　3 的平方是 9。

break down into

分解成

6 can be **broken down into** the factors 3 and 2.　6 可分解為因數 3 和 2。

be expressed as

表示為

8=2×2×2 can **be expressed as** an exponent: 8=2³.
8=2×2×2 可用指數表示為：8=2³。

Word Families 🔊 083

million	百萬 One million is the number 1,000,000.　一百萬是數字 1,000,000。
billion	十億 One billion is one thousand million (1,000,000,000). 十億是一千個一百萬 (1,000,000,000)。
even number	偶數 An even number is any whole number ending with a 0, 2, 4, 6, or 8. 尾數為 0、2、4、6 或 8 的整數稱為偶數。
odd number	奇數 An odd number is any whole number ending with a 1, 3, 5, 7, or 9. 尾數為 1、3、5、7 或 9 的整數稱為奇數。
positive integer	正整數 A positive integer is any whole number 1 or above. 正整數是等於或大於 1 的整數。
negative integer	負整數 A negative integer is any whole number -1 or below. 負整數是等於或小於 -1 的整數。

-5　-4　-3　-2　-1　0　1　2　3　4　5
negative integer　　　　　　positive integer

Roman Numerals 羅馬數字

I = 1	**II** = 2	**III** = 3	**IV** = 4
V = 5	**VI** = 6	**VII** = 7	**VIII** = 8
IX = 9	**X** = 10	**L** = 50	**C** = 100
D = 500	**M** = 1,000		

Checkup

Write | 請依提示寫出正確的英文單字或片語。

1	阿拉伯數字	_____	9	質數	_____
2	羅馬數字	_____	10	質因數	_____
3	整數	_____	11	使成平方	_____
4	因數;除數	_____	12	分解成	_____
5	公因數	_____	13	表示為	_____
6	倍數	_____	14	十億	_____
7	公倍數	_____	15	偶數	_____
8	指數	_____	16	奇數	_____

B

Complete the Sentences | 請在空格中填入最適當的答案,並視情況做適當的變化。

Arabic numeral	common multiple	prime number	multiple	integer
Roman numeral	common divisor	prime factor	exponent	divisor

1 The _____ are the ten digits 0, 1, 2, 3, 4, 5, 6, 7, 8, and 9.
阿拉伯數字是指 0, 1, 2, 3, 4, 5, 6, 7, 8, 9 這 10 個數字。

2 An _____ is any positive or negative whole number.
整數是任何正整數或負整數。

3 1, 3, and 7 are _____ of 21.
1、3、7 是 21 的因數。

4 1, 2, 3, and 6 are _____ of 12 and 18.
1、2、3、6 是 12 和 18 的公因數。

5 14, 21, 28, and 49 are _____ of 7.
14、21、28、49 是 7 的倍數。

6 12, 24, and 36 are _____ of 4 and 6.
12、24、36 是 4 和 6 的公倍數。

7 In 5^3, 5 is the base, and 3 is the _____. 在 5^3 中,5 是基數,3 是指數。

8 3 and 2 are the _____ of 12.
3 和 2 是 12 的質因數。

C

Read and Choose | 閱讀下列句子,並且選出最適當的答案。

1 When you (multiply | square) three, the result is nine.

2 6 can be (broken | divided) down into the factors 3 and 2.

3 An (even | odd) number is any whole number ending with a 1, 3, 5, 7, or 9.

4 A (positive | negative) integer is any whole number -1 or below.

D

Look, Read, and Write I 看圖並且依照提示，在空格中填入正確答案。

1
I II III
IV V VI
VII VIII IX

▸ letters that stand for numbers and were used by the Romans

_____

3
2, 3, 5, 7, 11, 13, 17,...

▸ a number that can only be divided by itself or 1

_____

2

▸ a small number written above and to the right of another number to show how many times that number is to be multiplied by itself

_____

4
1, 2, 3,...
-1, -2, -3,...

▸ any positive or negative whole number

_____

E

Read and Answer I 閱讀並且回答下列問題。　 084

Roman Numerals

We count with numbers today. The decimal system we use is very easy. But not every culture has counted the same way. Many systems are different. In ancient Rome, the Romans used Roman numerals. But these were not actually numerals. Instead, they were letters.

The Romans used the letters I, V, X, L, C, D, and M to stand for certain quantities. For example, I was 1, V was 5, X was 10, L was 50, C was 100, D was 500, and M was 1,000. To make larger numbers, they just added more letters. So 2 was II, and 3 was III. 6 was VI, and 7 was VII. However, the number 4 was not IIII. Instead, it was IV. Why did they do that? When a letter was going to change to one with a greater value, the Romans put the smaller letter in front of the bigger letter. That meant they should subtract that amount, not add to it. So 9 was IX. 40 was XL. 90 was XC. And 900 was CM.

Doing that was not difficult. But Romans could not count very high since it was hard to write large numbers. For example, what was 3,867? In Roman numerals, it was MMMDCCCLXVII. How about doing addition, subtraction, multiplication, or division? Can you imagine dividing MMCCXII by CCLXIV?

What is true? Write T(true) or F(false).

1　The Romans used letters for numbers.　_____

2　V meant 10 to the Romans.　_____

3　XL was 90 to the Romans.　_____

4　The Romans could not count very high numbers.　_____

Key Words
🔊 085

01 expression
[ɪkˈsprɛʃən]

(n.) 式　　*exponential expression 指數式

An **expression** is a part of a number sentence that has numbers and operation signs but does not have an equal sign.
式是算式的一部分，有數字和運算符號，但是沒有等號。

02 equation
[ɪˈkweʃən]

(n.) 等式；方程式　　*quadratic equation 二次方程式
*solve an equation 解方程式

An **equation** is a number sentence which shows that two quantities are equal. (5+x=12)　等式是一個算式，用來表示兩個量相等。(5+x=12)

03 variable
[ˈvɛrɪəbḷ]

(a.) 變數；未知數　　*dependent variable 應變數；依變數
*independent variable 自變數

A **variable** is a letter or symbol that represents an unknown number. (3+y=7)
未知數是一個字母或符號，用來表示未知的數字。(3+y=7)

04 inverse operation
[ɪnˈvɝs ˌɑpəˈreʃən]

(n.) 逆運算

Addition and subtraction are **inverse operations**.
加法和減法互為逆運算。

05 divisible
[dəˈvɪzəbḷ]

(a.) 可除盡的　　*be divisible by 可被某數除盡

10 is **divisible** by 2 because 10÷2=5, and there is no remainder.
10 可被 2 除盡，因為 10÷2=5，而且沒有餘數。

06 long division
[lɔŋ dəˈvɪʒən]

(n.) 長除法　　*long division symbol 長除法符號

Writing down every step in the process of a division problem is called **long division**.　寫下除法運算過程中的每個步驟，稱為長除法。

07 short division
[ʃɔrt dəˈvɪʒən]

(n.) 短除法

Not writing down the steps in the process of a division problem is called **short division**.　不寫下除法運算過程中的步驟，稱為短除法。

08 computation
[ˌkɑmpjuˈteʃən]

(n.) 計算

Computation is any type of mathematical calculation.
計算是指任何類型的數學推算。

09 order of operations
[ˈɔrdɚ ɑv ˌɑpəˈreʃənz]

(n.) 運算次序

The **order of operations** gives the order in which calculations are done first in an expression.　運算次序用來指定一個式子裡，哪些運算要先算。

10 mental math
[ˈmɛntḷ mæθ]

(n.) 心算（ = mental arithmetic ）

Mental math is solving a math problem in one's head.
心算是在心裡解數學題。

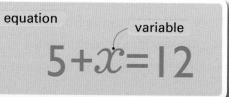

expression
$(20+3)-7$

equation
variable
$5+x=12$

bring down　拿下來

When doing long division, you must often bring down certain numbers.
做長除法時，經常必須把某些數字拿下來。

carry　拿；帶

When doing long division, you must often carry certain numbers.
做長除法時，經常必須拿一些數字。

vary　變化

In an equation, a variable can vary. 在方程式中，變數會變化。

change　改變

In an equation, a variable can change. 在方程式中，變數會改變。

rewrite　改寫
[ri`raɪt]

To solve the equation x-6=15, rewrite it as an addition problem.
解方程式 x-6=15 的時候，要將算式改寫為加法題。

estimate　估算；估計
[`ɛstə,met]

Estimate the sums and differences. 估算出和以及差。

property　性質

There are certain properties in addition. 加法有某些性質。

rule　規則

There are certain rules in addition. 加法有某些規則。

commutative property of addition　加法交換律

Numbers can be added in any order, and the sum will be the same.
數字相加的順序可以交換，其和不變。
ex. 2+3=3+2

associative property of addition　加法結合律

Numbers can be grouped in any way, and the sum will be the same.
數字可以任意結合，其和不變。
ex. 2+(3+5)=(2+3)+5

identity property of addition　加法單位元

When you add zero to any number, the sum is that number.
任何數加上 0 得其本身。
ex. 25+0=25

$$2+6=8 \quad 3\times4=12$$
$$2=8-6 \quad 3=12\div4$$
$$10\div2=5$$
divisible

inverse operation

Checkup

A

Write I 請依提示寫出正確的英文單字或片語。

1	式 _____	9	運算次序 _____
2	方程式 _____	10	心算 _____
3	變數；未知數 _____	11	拿下來 b_____
4	逆運算 _____	12	變化 v_____
5	可除盡的 _____	13	改寫 _____
6	短除法 _____	14	估算；估計 _____
7	長除法 _____	15	性質 _____
8	計算 _____	16	規則 _____

B

Complete the Sentences I 請在空格中填入最適當的答案，並視情況做適當的變化。

variable	long division	expression	inverse operation	divisible
equation	short division	computation	order of operations	mental math

1 An _____ is a part of a number sentence that has numbers and operation signs but does not have an equal sign.
式是算式的一部分，有數字和運算符號，但是沒有等號。

2 An _____ is a number sentence which shows that two quantities are equal. 等式是一個算式，用來表示兩個量相等。

3 10 is _____ by 2 because 10÷2=5, and there is no remainder.
10 可被 2 除盡，因為 10÷2=5，而且沒有餘數。

4 Not writing down the steps in the process of a division problem is called _____. 不寫下除法運算過程中的步驟，稱為短除法。

5 Writing down every step in the process of a division problem is called _____. 寫下除法運算過程中的每個步驟，稱為長除法。

6 _____ is any type of mathematical calculation. 計算是指任何類型的數學推算。

7 A _____ is a letter or symbol that represents an unknown number.
未知數是一個字母或符號，用來表示未知的數字。

8 The _____ gives the order in which calculations are done first in an expression. 運算次序用來指定一個式子裡，哪些運算要先算。

C

Read and Choose I 閱讀下列句子，並且選出最適當的答案。

1 When doing long division, you must often (come | bring) down certain numbers.

2 In an equation, a variable can (vary | represent).

3 To solve the equation x-6=15, (estimate | rewrite) it as an addition problem.

4 There are certain (variables | properties) in addition.

Look, Read, and Write | 看圖並且依照提示，在空格中填入正確答案。

1
$$20 \div 5 + 8$$
▸ a part of a number sentence that does not have an equal sign

_____

3
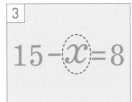
▸ a letter or symbol that represents an unknown number

_____

2
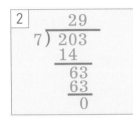
▸ the operation of division in which the sequence of steps are written down

_____

4

▸ solving a math problem in one's head

_____

E

Read and Answer | 閱讀並且回答下列問題。 ⊙ 088

The Order of Operations

In math, some problems are easy to solve. For example, this problem: 2+3=5. That is a simple problem. But sometimes there are more complicated problems. For example, how about this problem: 2+3×4? How do you solve this? Do you do the addition or the multiplication first? Is the answer 14 or 20?

In math, there is something called the order of operations. These tell the order in which you should solve a math problem. There are three simple rules: 1) Do the calculations inside parentheses first. 2) Moving from left to right, solve all multiplication and division problems first. 3) Moving from left to right, solve all addition and subtraction problems next.

Let's look at the problem above one more time: 2+3×4. How do we solve it? First, we must multiply 3×4. That's 12. Then we add 2+12. That's 14. So the correct answer is 14.

How about a more complicated problem? Look at this problem: 3×(3+4)−1. First, we must solve the problem in parentheses. So 3+4 is 7. Next, we do the multiplication problem. So 3×7 is 21. Last, we do the subtraction problem. So 21−1 is 20. The answer is 20.

Fill in the blanks.

1 Solve complicated problems in math by using the _____ of operations.

2 You should solve problems in _____ first.

3 Solve multiplication and _____ problems before you solve addition and subtraction problems.

4 You should always move from _____ to right when solving a math problem.

Unit 23 Decimals, Fractions, and Ratios

Key Words 🔊 089

01 equivalent decimal
[ɪˈkwɪvələnt ˈdɛsɪml̩]

(n.) 等值小數　　*infinite decimal 無窮小數　　*recurring decimal 循環小數

0.3 and 0.30 are equivalent decimals. (0.3=0.30)
0.3 與 0.30 為等值小數。(0.3=0.30)

02 like fractions
[laɪk ˈfrækʃənz]

(n.) 同分母分數

$\frac{1}{5}$ and $\frac{3}{5}$ are like fractions. $\frac{1}{5}$ 和 $\frac{3}{5}$ 為同分母分數。

03 unlike fractions
[ʌnˈlaɪk ˈfrækʃənz]

(n.) 異分母分數

$\frac{2}{3}$ and $\frac{2}{5}$ are unlike fractions. $\frac{2}{3}$ 和 $\frac{2}{5}$ 為異分母分數。

04 least common denominator
[list ˈkɑmən dɪˈnɑməˌnetɚ]

(n.) 最小公分母（LCD = least/lowest common denominator）

When you find a common denominator of fractions, you have to find their LCD. 要找出分數的公分母，就必須找到它們的最小公分母。

05 fraction bar
[ˈfrækʃən bɑr]

(n.) 分數線

A fraction bar is the same as the division sign. ($\frac{1}{6}$ =1÷6)
分數線等同於除號。($\frac{1}{6}$ =1÷6)

06 ratio
[ˈreʃo]

(n.) 比；比例　　*length-to-width ratio 長寬比
*a ratio of 3:2 / three to two 三比二的比例

A ratio is a comparison of the size of two numbers or two amounts.
「比」是兩個數或量的大小比較。

07 proportion
[prəˈporʃən]

(n.) 比例式　　*in direct/inverse proportion 成正／反比
*continued proportion 連比例式（三個以上的比相等）

A proportion is an equation that shows two ratios are equal.
比例式是一個等式，用來表示兩個比相等。

08 scale
[skel]

(n.) 尺度

A scale is a series of numbers placed at fixed distances on a graph.
尺度是圖上以固定間距所標示的一系列數字。

09 percent
[pɚˈsɛnt]

(n.) 百分比

A percent is the ratio of a number to 100.
百分比是某數比一百的比例。

10 probability
[ˌprɑbəˈbɪlətɪ]

(n.) 機率；或然率　　*the theory of probability = probability theory 機率論
*conditional probability 條件機率

The probability of something is the chance that it will occur.
某件事的機率是指其發生的機會。

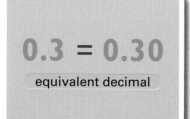

0.3 = 0.30
equivalent decimal

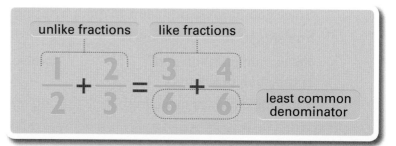

unlike fractions　　like fractions

$$\frac{1}{2} + \frac{2}{3} = \frac{3}{6} + \frac{4}{6}$$

least common denominator

compare [kəm`pɛr]	相比 A ratio compares the size of two numbers. 比是用來比較兩個數的大小。
be represented by	表示為 A ratio can be represented by a fraction. (3:5 = $\frac{3}{5}$) 比可以分數表示。
be written as	寫成 A ratio can be written as a fraction. (3:5 = $\frac{3}{5}$) 比可寫為分數。
be expressed as	表示為 Probability can be expressed as a fraction. (25%= $\frac{1}{4}$) 機率可以分數表示。
be likely to	很可能 A high probability means something is likely to happen. 高機率表示某件事很可能發生。

Word Families 🔊 091

denominator [dɪ`nɑmə,netɚ]	分母 The denominator of the fraction $\frac{3}{4}$ is 4. 分數 $\frac{3}{4}$ 的分母為 4。	3 — numerator — fraction bar 4 — denominator
numerator [`njumə,retɚ]	分子 The numerator of the fraction $\frac{3}{4}$ is 3. 分數 $\frac{3}{4}$ 的分子為 3。	
decimal sum	小數的和 A decimal sum is the result of adding two decimals. 小數的和是兩個小數相加的結果。	
decimal difference	小數的差 A decimal difference is the result of subtracting two decimals. 小數的差是兩個小數相減的結果。	
decimal product	小數的積 A decimal product is the result of multiplying two decimals. 小數的積是兩個小數相乘的結果。	
decimal quotient	小數的商 A decimal quotient is the result of dividing two decimals. 小數的商是兩個小數相除的結果。	

2 to 5
2 : 5
$\frac{2}{5}$ — ratio

$\frac{1}{3} = \frac{2}{6}$
1 : 3 = 2 : 6 — proportion

$\frac{1}{4} = \frac{25}{100} =$ 25% — percent

Checkup

A

Write | 請依提示寫出正確的英文單字或片語。

1	等值小數	_____	9	最小公分母 _____
2	同分母分數	_____	10	分數線 _____
3	異分母分數	_____	11	相比 _____
4	比	_____	12	表示為 _____
5	比例式	_____	13	寫為 _____
6	尺度	_____	14	很可能 _____
7	百分比	_____	15	分母 _____
8	機率；或然率	_____	16	分子 _____

B

Complete the Sentences | 請在空格中填入最適當的答案，並視情況做適當的變化。

proportion	percent	ratio	like fractions	common denominator
equivalent	probability	scale	unlike fractions	fraction bar

1 0.3 and 0.30 are _____ decimals.
0.3 與 0.30 為等值小數。

2 $\frac{2}{3}$ and $\frac{2}{5}$ are _____. $\frac{2}{3}$ 和 $\frac{2}{5}$ 為異分母分數。

3 When you find a _____ of fractions, you have to find their LCD.
要找出分數的公分母，就必須找到它們的最小公分母。

4 A _____ is an equation that shows two ratios are equal.
比例式是一個等式，用來表示兩個比相等。

5 A _____ is a series of numbers placed at fixed distances on a graph.
尺度是圖上以固定間距所標示的一系列數字。

6 The _____ of something is the chance that it will occur.
某件事的機率是指其發生的機會。

7 A _____ is the same as the division sign.
分數線等同於除號。

8 A _____ is a comparison of the size of two numbers or two amounts.
比是用來比較兩個數的大小。

C

Read and Choose | 閱讀下列句子，並且選出最適當的答案。

1 A ratio (compares | confirm) the size of two numbers.

2 A ratio can be (rounded | represented) by a fraction.

3 Probability can be (expressed | fixed) as a fraction.

4 A high probability means something is (unlikely | likely) to happen.

D

Look, Read, and Write I 看圖並且依照提示，在空格中填入正確答案。

1

$$\frac{2}{7}, \frac{2}{5}$$

▸ fractions with different denominator

_____

3

▸ the ratio of a number to 100

_____

2

a : b = c : d

▸ an equation that shows two ratios are equal

_____

4

▸ the chance that something will occur

_____

E

Read and Answer I 閱讀並且回答下列問題。　092

Percentages, Ratios, and Probabilities

The weatherman may say, "There is a 70% chance of rain." He is telling you the probability of rain. At 70%, this means that, in the current weather conditions, it will rain 70 times out of 100.

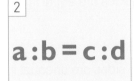

Weather forecasts often use percentages. So do sports. An announcer may say, "The basketball player shoots 52%." This means that for every 100 shots he takes, he makes 52.

Ratios are a way to compare two things to one another. For example, a classroom has 20 children. There are 12 boys and 8 girls. You can say, "The ratio of boys to girls is 12 to 8." Or you can write the ratio as 12:8 or $\frac{12}{8}$. Perhaps there are 5 cats and 8 dogs. You can say the ratio of cats to dogs is 5 to 8, 5:8, or $\frac{5}{8}$. All three ways express ratios.

Probability expresses the odds, or chances, of something happening. If you flip a coin, there is a 1 in 2 chance of a certain side showing because a coin has two sides. If you roll a die, there is a 1 in 6 chance of the number 4 appearing. Perhaps there are 10 cookies. Three are oatmeal cookies. If you grab one cookie at random, there is a 3 in 10 chance you will get an oatmeal cookie.

What is NOT true?

1　Weather forecasts often use ratios.

2　A ratio can compare two things to each other.

3　Probability is the chance that something will happen.

4　There is a 1 in 6 chance of the number 4 appearing when you roll a die.

Key Words 🔊 093

01	**quadrilateral** [ˌkwɑdrɪˈlætərəl]	*(n.)* 四邊形　*(a.)* 四邊形的 Four-sided polygons are called quadrilaterals. 四個邊的多邊形稱為四邊形。
02	**isosceles** [aɪˈsɑslˌiz]	*(a.)* 二等邊的；等腰的 An isosceles triangle is one in which two sides are equal in length. 等腰三角形是有兩個邊等長的三角形。
03	**scalene** [ˈskelin]	*(a.)* 不等邊的　*(n.)* 不等邊三角形 A scalene triangle is one in which all three sides are unequal in length. 不等邊三角形是三個邊皆不等長的三角形。
04	**surface area** [ˈsɝfɪs ˈɛrɪə]	*(n.)* 表面積 The surface area is the amount of space a two-dimensional figure occupies.　平面圖形所佔的大小稱為表面積。
05	**circumference** [səˈkʌmfərəns]	*(n.)* 周長；圓周　*diameter 直徑　*radius 半徑 *be . . . in circumference = have a circumference of . . . 周長為…… The circumference of a circle is the distance around the circle. 圓周長是指圓的外圍長度。
06	**prism** [ˈprɪzm̩]	*(n.)* 角柱；稜柱　*triangular prism 三稜柱 Prisms have two congruent and parallel bases. 角柱有兩個全等且平行的底面。
07	**line symmetry** [laɪn ˈsɪmɪtrɪ]	*(n.)* 線對稱 Figures that have line symmetry can be folded in half along a line. 線對稱的圖形可以沿著一條線對折。
08	**rotational symmetry** [roˈteʃənl̩ ˈsɪmɪtrɪ]	*(n.)* 軸對稱 A pinwheel has rotational symmetry. 紙風車屬於軸對稱。
09	**clockwise** [ˈklɑkˌwaɪz]	*(a.)* 順時針方向的　*in a clockwise direction 依順時針方向 Clockwise is moving in the same direction as the hands of a clock. 順時針方向是和時鐘指針移動的方向相同。
10	**counterclockwise** [ˌkaʊntəˈklɑkˌwaɪz]	*(a.)* 逆時針方向的　*in a counterclockwise direction 依逆時針方向 Counterclockwise is moving in the opposite direction of the hands of a clock.　逆時針方向是和時鐘指針移動的方向相反。

prism
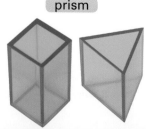

line symmetry

rotational symmetry

clockwise　counterclockwise

Power Verbs

🔊 094

convert
[kən'vɝt]

換算；轉換
Convert inches to centimeters. 將英寸換算為公分。

circumference

turn

使轉動；使旋轉
Turn the compass clockwise to form a 90° angle.
將圓規順時針轉動，畫出一個 90 度角。

diameter

radius

calculate
['kælkjə,let]

計算；估計
People calculate the size of an angle with a protractor. 人們利用量角器來計算角度大小。

measure
['mɛʒɚ]

測量；估量
People measure the size of an angle with a protractor. 人們利用量角器來測量角度大小。

construct
[kən'strʌkt]

作（圖）(= draw)
Construct a prism that has a total of eight sides. 作出一個合計有 8 個邊的角柱圖。

Word Families

🔊 095

trapezoid
['træpə,zɔɪd]

梯形
A trapezoid is a quadrilateral that has two parallel and two nonparallel sides.
梯形是有兩邊平行而兩邊不平行的四邊形。

rhombus
['rɑmbəs]

菱形
A rhombus is a parallelogram with angles that are not 90 degrees.
菱形是一種平行四邊形，內角皆不為 90 度。

Types of Triangles
三角形的種類

acute triangle
銳角三角形

right triangle
直角三角形

obtuse triangle
鈍角三角形

equilateral triangle
(=regular triangle)
等邊三角形

isosceles triangle
等腰三角形

scalene triangle
不等邊三角形

protractor

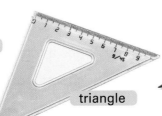
triangle

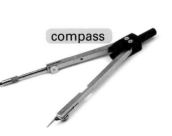
compass

Checkup

A

Write | 請依提示寫出正確的英文單字或片語。

1	四邊形 _____	9	順時針方向的 _____
2	二等邊的;等腰的 _____	10	逆時針方向的 _____
3	不等邊的 _____	11	換算;轉換 _____
4	表面積 _____	12	轉動;轉向 _____
5	周長;圓周 _____	13	計算;估計 _____
6	角柱;稜柱 _____	14	作(圖) _____
7	線對稱 _____	15	梯形 _____
8	軸對稱 _____	16	菱形 _____

B

Complete the Sentences | 請在空格中填入最適當的答案,並視情況做適當的變化。

surface area	isosceles	counterclockwise	scalene	prism
quadrilateral	rotational	circumference	clockwise	line

1   An _____ triangle is one in which two sides are equal in length.
等腰三角形是有兩個邊等長的三角形。

2   Four-sided polygons are called _____. 四個邊的多邊形稱為四邊形。

3   A _____ triangle is one in which all three sides are unequal in length.
不等邊三角形是三個邊皆不等長的三角形。

4   The _____ is the amount of space a two-dimensional figure occupies. 平面圖形所佔的大小稱為表面積。

5   _____ have two congruent and parallel bases.
角柱有兩個全等且平行的底面。

6   The _____ of a circle is the distance around the circle.
圓周長是指圓的外圍長度。

7   A pinwheel has _____ symmetry. 紙風車屬於軸對稱。

8   Figures that have _____ symmetry can be folded in half along a line.
線對稱的圖形可以沿著一條線對折。

C

Read and Choose | 閱讀下列句子,並且選出最適當的答案。

1   (Convert | Calculate) inches to centimeters.

2   (Draw | Turn) the compass clockwise to form a 90° angle.

3   (Measure | Construct) a prism that has a total of eight sides.

4   A (trapezoid | rhombus) is a quadrilateral that has two parallel and two nonparallel sides.

D

Look, Read, and Write | 看圖並且依照提示，在空格中填入正確答案。

1 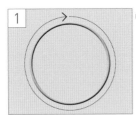 ▸ the distance around the outside of a circle

_____

3  ▸ a triangle that has two sides of equal length

_____

2 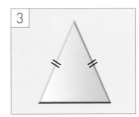 ▸ a solid figure that has two congruent and parallel bases

_____

4  ▸ a quadrilateral that has two parallel and two nonparallel sides

_____

E

Read and Answer | 閱讀並且回答下列問題。　⊙ 096

Solid Figures in Real Life

Solid figures include cubes, prisms, pyramids, cylinders, cones, and spheres. Everywhere you look, you can see solid figures. Many buildings are rectangular prisms. A door is one, too. So are the bulletin board in your classroom and this book you are reading right now.

Pyramids are not very common. But some of them are really famous. Think about Egypt for a minute. What comes to mind? The pyramids, right? There are huge pyramids all over Egypt.

Cones are among people's favorite solid figures. Why is that? The reason is that ice cream cones are solid figures. There are often many cones in areas where there is road construction, too. Construction workers put traffic cones on the street to show people where they can and cannot drive.

Of course, spheres are everywhere. People would not be able to play most sports without them. They need soccer balls, baseballs, basketballs, tennis balls, and many other spheres. Oranges, grapefruit, peaches, plums, and cherries are fruits that are shaped like spheres, too.

Answer the questions.

1 What kind of solid figures are doors? _____

2 What kind of solid figures are the famous buildings in Egypt? _____

3 What kind of solid figures are traffic cones? _____

4 What kind of solid figures are tennis balls? _____

A

Write | 請依提示寫出正確的英文單字或片語。

1	阿拉伯數字	_____	11	質數	_____
2	羅馬數字	_____	12	質因數	_____
3	整數	_____	13	心算	_____
4	方程式；等式	_____	14	使成平方	_____
5	變數；未知數	_____	15	變化	v _____
6	比；比例	_____	16	最小公分母	_____
7	比例式	_____	17	分數線	_____
8	機率；或然率	_____	18	表面積	_____
9	二等邊的	_____	19	周長；圓周	_____
10	不等邊的	_____	20	梯形	_____

B

Choose the Correct Word | 請選出與鋪底字意思相近的答案。

1 When doing long division, you must often bring down certain numbers.

   a. calculate   b. come   c. carry

2 In an equation, a variable can vary.

   a. convert   b. fix   c. change

3 Probability can be expressed as a fraction.

   a. changed   b. written   c. measured

4 Construct a prism that has a total of eight sides.

   a. Draw   b. Represent   c. Line

C

Complete the Sentences | 請在空格中填入最適當的答案，並視情況做適當的變化。

line symmetry	computation	exponent	unlike fractions

1 In 5^3, 5 is the base, and 3 is the _____.
在 5^3 中，5 是基數，3 是指數。

2 _____ is any type of mathematical calculation.
計算是指任何類型的數學推算。

3 $\frac{2}{3}$ and $\frac{2}{5}$ are _____.
$\frac{2}{3}$ 和 $\frac{2}{5}$ 為異分母分數。

4 Figures that have _____ can be folded in half along a line.
線對稱的圖形可以沿著一條線對折。

CHAPTER 6

Language • Visual Arts • Music

Key Words 🔊 097

01	**legend** [ˈlɛdʒənd]	(n.) 傳說；傳奇故事　*a living legend 活著的傳奇人物 *legend has it that . . . 傳說…… A legend is a well-known story passed down from the past and which is often about brave people or adventures. 傳說是從古代流傳下來的著名故事，通常和勇士及冒險有關。
02	**adventure** [ədˈvɛntʃɚ]	(n.) 冒險　*adventure novel 冒險小說　*have a spirit of adventure 具有冒險精神 *The Adventures of Tom Sawyer* is a popular American novel by Mark Twain. 《湯姆歷險記》是由馬克・吐溫所著的美國小說，廣受歡迎。
03	**epic** [ˈɛpɪk]	(n.) 史詩　(a.) 史詩般的；堅苦卓絕的 *an epic poem/film 史詩／史詩式電影　*an epic achievement 壯舉 An epic is a long poem that tells the story of great heroes. 史詩是講述著偉大英雄事蹟的長篇詩。
04	**Homer** [ˈhomɚ]	(n.) 荷馬 Homer was a blind poet in ancient Greece who told two great epics, the *Iliad* and the *Odyssey*. 荷馬是古希臘的盲眼詩人，他講述了兩部偉大的史詩：《伊里亞德》與《奧德賽》。
05	**Iliad** [ˈɪlɪəd]	(n.) 伊里亞德 The *Iliad* tells the story of the Trojan War. 《伊里亞德》講述特洛伊戰爭的故事。
06	**Odyssey** [ˈɑdəsɪ]	(n.) 奧德賽 The *Odyssey* tells the story of how Odysseus returned home after the Trojan War. 《奧德賽》講述了特洛伊戰爭後，奧德修斯如何返鄉的故事。
07	**Achilles** [əˈkɪliz]	(n.) 阿基里斯　*Achilles' heel 阿基里斯的腳踝（喻致命的弱點、缺陷） *Achilles tendon 阿基里斯腱 Achilles was the greatest of all of the Greek warriors. 阿基里斯是希臘最偉大的戰士。
08	**Hector** [ˈhɛktɚ]	(n.) 赫克特 Hector was the greatest of all of the Trojan warriors. 赫克特是特洛伊最偉大的戰士。
09	**Odysseus** [oˈdɪsjus]	(n.) 奧德修斯（= Ulysses 尤里西斯） Odysseus was the king of Ithaca and the main character of the *Odyssey*. 奧德修斯是伊薩卡的國王，也是《奧德賽》中的主角。
10	**Cyclops** [ˈsaɪklɑps]	(n.) 獨眼巨人 The Cyclops was a huge giant that only had one eye in the middle of his forehead. 獨眼巨人是高大的巨人，其獨眼長在額頭中間。

Achilles

The Triumph of Achilles

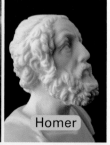
Homer

carry off　強行帶走；抓走
Paris **carried off** Helen and took her to Troy. 帕里斯擄走海倫，把她帶到特洛伊。

abduct　誘拐；綁架
[əbˋdʌkt]
Paris **abducted** Helen and took her to Troy. 帕里斯誘拐海倫，把她帶去特洛伊。

kidnap　誘拐；綁架
[ˋkɪdnæp]
Paris **kidnapped** Helen and took her to Troy. 帕里斯綁架海倫，把她帶去特洛伊。

assault　攻擊；襲擊
[əˋsɔlt]
The Greeks **assaulted** Troy to get Helen back.
為了救回海倫，希臘攻擊特洛伊。

lay siege to　包圍
[le sidʒ tu]
The Greeks **laid siege to** Troy to get Helen back.
為了救回海倫，希臘包圍特洛伊。

The Abduction of Helen

challenge　挑戰；質疑
[ˋtʃælɪndʒ]
Achilles **challenged** Hector to a one-on-one battle.
阿基里斯單挑赫克特。

blind　弄瞎
[blaɪnd]
Odysseus **blinded** the Cyclops in its own cave.
奧德修斯在獨眼巨人的洞穴中將他弄瞎。

Trojan Horse

Paris　帕里斯
Paris was a prince of Troy and was the one who abducted Helen from Greece.
帕里斯是特洛伊的王子，也是將海倫從希臘拐走的人。

Helen　海倫
Helen of Troy was said to be the most beautiful woman in the world.
特洛伊的海倫是傳說中世界上最漂亮的女人。

golden apple　金蘋果
Paris awarded the **golden apple** to Aphrodite, who gave him Helen of Troy as his reward. 帕里斯將金蘋果給了阿芙蘿黛蒂，她則贈之以特洛伊的海倫當作獎賞。

Trojan War　特洛伊戰爭
[ˋtrodʒən wɔr]
The **Trojan War** was between the Greeks and the Trojans and lasted for ten years. 特洛伊戰爭是發生於希臘與特洛伊之間的十年之戰。

Trojan Horse　特洛伊木馬
Many Greek warriors hid in the **Trojan Horse**, so they were able to defeat the Trojans. 許多希臘戰士躲在特洛伊木馬裡，如此他們才能擊敗特洛伊人。

Achilles' heel　阿基里斯的腳踝
An **Achilles' heel** was the only weak place on Achilles, so he was vulnerable there. 阿基里斯的腳踝是他唯一的弱點，所以那裡是他最脆弱的地方。

Checkup

A

Write | 請依提示寫出正確的英文單字或片語。

1 傳說；傳奇故事 _____
2 冒險 _____
3 史詩 _____
4 荷馬 _____
5 伊里亞德 _____
6 奧德賽 _____
7 阿基里斯 _____
8 赫克特 _____
9 奧德修斯 _____
10 獨眼巨人 _____
11 強行帶走；抓走 _____
12 誘拐；綁架 _____
13 攻擊；襲擊 _____
14 特洛伊戰爭 _____
15 特洛伊木馬 _____
16 阿基里斯的腳踝 _____

B

Complete the Sentences | 請在空格中填入最適當的答案，並視情況做適當的變化。

Achilles	adventure	Homer	*Odyssey*	epic
Hector	Odysseus	legend	Cyclops	*Iliad*

1 A _____ is a well-known story passed down from the past and which is often about brave people or adventures.
傳說是從古代流傳下來的著名故事，通常和勇士及冒險有關。

2 The _____ of Tom Sawyer is a popular American novel by Mark Twain.
《湯姆歷險記》是由馬克・吐溫所著的美國小說，廣受歡迎。

3 An _____ is a long poem that tells the story of great heroes.
史詩是講述著偉大英雄事蹟的長篇詩。

4 The _____ tells the story of the Trojan War. 《伊里亞德》講述有關特洛伊戰爭的故事。

5 The _____ tells the story of how Odysseus returned home after the Trojan War. 《奧德賽》講述了特洛伊戰爭後，奧德修斯如何返鄉的故事。

6 _____ was the greatest of all of the Greek warriors.
阿基里斯是希臘最偉大的戰士。

7 _____ was the greatest of all of the Trojan warriors.
赫克特是特洛伊最偉大的戰士。

8 _____ was the king of Ithaca and the main character of the *Odyssey*.
奧德修斯是伊薩卡的國王，也是《奧德賽》中的主角。

C

Read and Choose | 閱讀下列句子，並且選出最適當的答案。

1 Paris (abducted | carried) off Helen and took her to Troy.

2 The Greeks (assaulted | returned) Troy to get Helen back.

3 Achilles (kidnapped | challenged) Hector to a one-on-one battle.

4 Odysseus (blinded | blind) the Cyclops in its own cave.

D

Look, Read, and Write I 看圖並且依照提示，在空格中填入正確答案。

1  ▸ a blind poet in ancient Greece who told the *Iliad* and the *Odyssey*

_____

3  ▸ the only weak place on Achilles; a small but mortal weakness

_____

2  ▸ to surround a city or building with soldiers

_____

4  ▸ a huge giant that only had one eye in the middle of his forehead

_____

E

Read and Answer I 閱讀並且回答下列問題。　🔘 100

The *Iliad* and the *Odyssey*

Two of the greatest works of literature are also very old. They are the epic poems the *Iliad* and the *Odyssey*. Both were told by Homer and tell stories about the ancient Greeks.

The *Iliad* is about the Trojan War. Paris abducted Helen and took her to Troy. Helen was the most beautiful woman in the world. So all of the Greeks joined together to fight the Trojans. There were many great Greek warriors. There were Agamemnon, Menelaus, Odysseus, and Ajax. But Achilles was the greatest warrior of all. The war lasted for ten years. Many people died. Finally, thanks to Odysseus, the Greeks used the Trojan Horse to win. The Greeks pretended to leave. They left behind a giant horse. The Trojans took the horse into their city. But many Greek warriors were hiding inside it. At night, the Greeks came out of the horse. Inside the city, they managed to capture and defeat Troy.

The *Odyssey* tells the tale of Odysseus's return home after the war. It took him ten years to get home. He had many strange adventures. He had to fight a fearsome Cyclops. He met magical women like Circe and Calypso. And all of his men died. Finally, though, with help from the gods, Odysseus arrived home.

What is true? Write T(true) or F(false).

1 The *Iliad* was about the adventures of Odysseus.   _____

2 The greatest Greek warrior was Achilles.   _____

3 The Trojans hid in the Trojan Horse.   _____

4 Odysseus and all of his men arrived home after ten years.   _____

Key Words
🔊 101

01	**literal** [ˈlɪtərəl]	*(a.)* 照字面的；逐字的　　*(adv.)* literally 逐字地 *literal translation 直譯；逐字翻譯　　*literal meaning 原義；字面意義 When you want to say exactly what you mean, you use **literal** language: I'm tired. 當你想完全依照你的意思說出來，可以直接照字面說：「我累了」。
02	**figurative** [ˈfɪgjərətɪv]	*(a.)* 比喻的；象徵的　　*in a/the figurative sense 在比喻的意義上 When you are very tired, you might say "I'm dead," which is **figurative** language. 當你非常的累，你可以說「我累斃了」，這是比喻性語言。
03	**figure of speech** [ˈfɪgjə ɑv spitʃ]	*(n.)* 修辭 A **figure of speech**, like "time flies," is an expression that is not meant to be taken literally. 修辭這種詞語不能從字面上來解釋，例如「時光飛逝」。
04	**imagery** [ˈɪmɪdʒərɪ]	*(n.)* 意象；比喻　　*visual imagery 視覺意象 Writers use **imagery** to give their works more creativity and imagination. 作家運用意象為作品增添創造力和想像力。
05	**simile** [ˈsɪmə,lɪ]	*(n.)* 明喻；直喻 A **simile** is a comparison that uses as or like as in "busy as a bee." 明喻是使用了「如」或「像」的比較手法，例如：「如蜜蜂般忙碌」。
06	**metaphor** [ˈmɛtəfə]	*(n.)* 隱喻；暗喻　　*a metaphor for sth. 某事物的象徵　　*mixed metaphor 混合隱喻 A **metaphor** is often hidden in the words, such as in "She is an angel." 隱喻通常隱含在文字中，例如：「她是個天使」。
07	**symbol** [ˈsɪmbl]	*(n.)* 象徵；符號　　*a symbol of sth. 某事物的象徵 　　　　　　　　　　　*the symbol for sth. 代表某事物的符號 The cross is a **symbol** of Christianity. 十字架是基督教的象徵。
08	**personification** [pə,sɑnəfəˈkeʃən]	*(n.)* 擬人法；化身　　*the personification of sth./sb. 某事物／某人的化身 When writers use **personification**, they give a thing or an animal certain human qualities. 作家使用擬人法時，會賦予事物或動物某些人類特質。
09	**hyperbole** [haɪˈpɝbəlɪ]	*(n.)* 誇飾法；誇張的句子　　*be filled with hyperboles 充斥著誇張的言辭 **Hyperbole** is the use of exaggeration. 誇飾法運用了誇大的手法。
10	**onomatopoeia** [,ɑnə,mætəˈpiə]	*(n.)* 擬聲法　　*onomatopoetic words 象聲詞 Words like "buzz," "hiss," and "moo" are examples of **onomatopoeia**. 像「嗡嗡」、「嘶嘶」和「哞」這些字都是擬聲法的例子。

Figure of Speech

simile
 busy as a bee

metaphor
 She is an angel.

personification
 My dog is speaking to me.

hyperbole
 I worked all day and all night.

stand for
象徵；代表
Sometimes a heart **stands for** love. 有時候愛心代表愛情。

symbolize
[ˈsɪmbl̩ˌaɪz]
象徵；標誌
Sometimes a heart **symbolizes** love. 有時候愛心象徵愛情。

represent
[ˌrɛprɪˈzɛnt]
代表；呈現
What do you think the skull **represents**? 你認為骷髏頭代表什麼？

amuse
[əˈmjuz]
娛樂；消遣
People perform comedies to **amuse** others. 人們演出喜劇來娛樂他人。

entertain
[ˌɛntəˈten]
娛樂；款待
People perform comedies to **entertain** others. 人們演出喜劇來娛樂他人。

personify
[pəˈsɑnəˌfaɪ]
擬人化
Aesop **personified** many animals in his fables by giving them certain human qualities. 伊索藉由賦予動物某些人的特質，來使寓言故事中的動物擬人化。

exaggerate
[ɪgˈzædʒəˌret]
誇大
People often **exaggerate** when they speak or write.
人們在說話或是寫作時，常會誇大。

Word Families 🔊 103

tragedy
悲劇
A **tragedy** is a play in which something bad or tragic happens to the characters.
悲劇是主角遭遇不幸或發生悲劇的戲劇。

comedy
喜劇
A **comedy** is a play that is based on humor. 喜劇是以幽默為基礎的戲劇。

drama
戲劇
A **drama** is a story with dialog that can be performed as a play.
戲劇是有對話的故事，能以劇本的形式演出。

dramatist
劇作家
A **dramatist** is a person who writes dramas. 編寫戲劇的人稱為劇作家。

pen name
筆名
Some writers use a **pen name**, which is not their real name.
有時作家會使用非真實姓名的筆名。

pseudonym
[ˈsudn̩ˌɪm]
化名
Mark Twain was the **pseudonym** of Samuel Clemens.
塞繆爾・克萊門斯化名為馬克・吐溫。

anonymous
[əˈnɑnəməs]
匿名
When no one knows the author of a work, it is **anonymous**.
無法得知作品的作者時，就稱之為匿名作品。

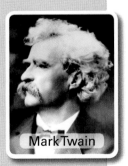
Mark Twain

Checkup

A

Write | 請依提示寫出正確的英文單字或片語。

1	照字面的;逐字的 _____	9	修辭 _____
2	比喻的;象徵的 _____	10	擬聲法 _____
3	意象;比喻 _____	11	象徵;代表 st_____
4	明喻;直喻 _____	12	象徵;標誌 sy_____
5	隱喻;暗喻 _____	13	娛樂;消遣 a_____
6	象徵;符號 _____	14	使娛樂;款待 e_____
7	擬人法 _____	15	擬人化 _____
8	誇飾法 _____	16	誇大 _____

B

Complete the Sentences | 請在空格中填入最適當的答案,並視情況做適當的變化。

metaphor	figurative	figure of speech	simile	literal
imagery	personification	onomatopoeia	hyperbole	symbol

1 When you want to say exactly what you mean, you use _____ language: I'm tired. 當你想完全依照你的意思說出來,可以直接照字面說:「我累了」。

2 When you are very tired, you might say "I'm dead," which is _____ language. 當你非常的累,你可以說「我累斃了」,這是比喻性語言。

3 A _____, like "time flies," is an expression that is not meant to be taken literally. 修辭這種詞語不能從字面上來解釋,例如「時光飛逝」。

4 A _____ is often hidden in the words, such as in "She is an angel." 隱喻通常隱含在文字中,例如:「她是個天使」。

5 Writers use _____ to give their works more creativity and imagination. 作家運用「意象」為作品增添創造力和想像力。

6 The cross is a _____ of Christianity. 十字架是基督教的象徵。

7 When writers use _____, they give a thing or an animal certain human qualities. 作家使用擬人法時,會賦予事物或動物某些人類特質。

8 Words like "buzz," "hiss," and "moo" are examples of _____. 像「嗡嗡」、「嘶嘶」和「哞」這些字,是擬聲法的例子。

C

Read and Choose | 閱讀下列句子,並且選出最適當的答案。

1 Sometimes a heart (symbolizes | stands) for love.

2 People perform comedies to (represent | amuse) others.

3 Aesop (exaggerated | personified) many animals in his fables by giving them certain human qualities.

4 Mark Twain was the (pseudonym | anonymous) of Samuel Clemens.

Look, Read, and Write ▎看圖並且依照提示，在空格中填入正確答案。

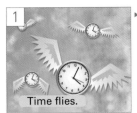
Time flies.

▸ an expression that is not meant to be taken literally

_____

She is an angel.

▸ a word or phrase for one thing that is used to refer to another thing

_____

I worked all day and all night.

▸ the use of exaggeration

_____

▸ to give a thing or an animal certain human qualities

_____

E

Read and Answer ▎閱讀並且回答下列問題。　🔊 104

Figures of Speech

a sea of sand

Writers can be creative. To do this, they can use figures of speech. There are many of these. Four are similes, metaphors, hyperbole, and personification.

Similes and metaphors are both comparisons. But they are not the same. Similes use "as" or "like" to compare two things. For example, "strong as an ox" and "dark like night" are similes. Metaphors are comparisons between two unlike things that seem to have nothing in common. "The stars are diamonds in the sky" and "There is a sea of sand" are metaphors.

There were a million people.

Hyperbole is also a figure of speech. It is a form of exaggeration. People often exaggerate when they speak or write. For instance, "There were a million people in the store" is hyperbole. "I worked all day and all night" is, too.

Finally, people often give objects and animals human characteristics. This is personification. "The wind is whispering" is one example. So is "My dog is speaking to me." The wind and a dog are not humans. But in both cases, they have human characteristics. So they are examples of personification.

Fill in the blanks.

1　Similes and metaphors are two kinds of _____ of speech.

2　A _____ is a comparison that uses *like* or *as*.

3　_____ is a form of exaggeration.

4　_____ gives animals or objects human characteristics.

Key Words ● 105

01	**sentence fragment** [ˈsɛntəns ˈfrægmənt]	*(n.)* 句子片段 *fragment 碎片；片段（fragments of conversation 談話的片段、隻言片語） A **sentence fragment** is part of a sentence or an incomplete sentence. 句子片段是指句子的一部分或是不完整的句子。
02	**comma splice** [ˈkɑmə splaɪs]	*(n.)* 逗點謬誤（= comma fault） Improperly using a comma to join two clauses is a **comma splice**. 逗點謬誤是指不當使用逗號來連接兩個子句。
03	**direct object** [dəˈrɛkt ˈɑbdʒɪkt]	*(a.)* 直接受詞 A **direct object** is a noun or pronoun that receives the action of the verb. 直接受詞是接受動詞行為的名詞或代名詞。
04	**indirect object** [ˌɪndəˈrɛkt ˈɑbdʒɪkt]	*(v.)* 間接受詞 An **indirect object** is the person or thing that receives the direct object from the subject. 間接受詞是從主詞接受直接受詞的人或物。
05	**interjection** [ˌɪntəˈdʒɛkʃən]	*(n.)* 感嘆詞（如：oh 噢、alas 哎呀） People use **interjections** to show strong emotions. 人們用感嘆詞來表示強烈的情感。
06	**pronoun** [ˈpronaʊn]	*(n.)* 代名詞 *personal pronoun 人稱代名詞 *indefinite pronoun 不定代名詞 People use **pronouns** as substitutions for nouns. 人們用代名詞來代替名詞。
07	**nominative case** [ˈnɑmənətɪv kes]	*(n.)* 主格（= subjective case） *in the nominative (case) 用主格 The **nominative case** refers to the subject of a sentence: I, we, you, he, she, and they. 主格是句子的主詞，例如：I、we、you、he、she、they。
08	**objective case** [əbˈdʒɛktɪv kes]	*(n.)* 受格（= accusative case） *objective pronoun 受格代名詞 *in the objective (case) 用受格 The **objective case** refers to the object of a sentence: me, us, you, him, her, and them. 受格是句子的受詞，例如：me、us、you、him、her、them。
09	**possessive case** [pəˈzɛsɪv kes]	*(n.)* 所有格 *possessive pronoun 所有格代名詞 *possessive adjective 所有格形容詞 The **possessive case** shows ownership by someone or something: John's house, the ship's captain. 所有格顯示某人或某物的所有權，例如：「約翰的房子」、「船的船長」。
10	**coordinating conjunction** [koˈɔrdn̩etɪŋ kənˈdʒʌŋkʃən]	*(n.)* 對等連接詞 *subordinating conjunction 從屬連接詞 *correlative conjunction 關係連接詞 **Coordinating conjunctions** include and, but, or, nor, and so, and they connect two words, phrases, or clauses. 對等連接詞包含 and、but、or、nor、so，用來連接兩個單字、片語或是子句。

I love him.

direct object

I gave him a book.

indirect object direct object

modify
[ˈmɑdəˌfaɪ]

修飾
Adjectives modify nouns, so they provide more information about them.
形容詞用來修飾名詞，提供更多名詞的相關訊息。

qualify
[ˈkwɑləˌfaɪ]

修飾
Adjectives qualify nouns, so they provide more information about them.
形容詞用來修飾名詞，提供更多名詞的相關訊息。

replace
[rɪˈples]

取代
Pronouns replace nouns. 代名詞取代名詞。

take the place of

代替
Pronouns take the place of nouns. 代名詞代替名詞。

complete
[kəmˈplit]

使完整
Use a subject and a verb to complete a sentence.
用主詞和動詞使句子完整。

agree with

和……一致
The subject of a sentence must agree with the verb.
句子的主詞要和動詞一致。

Word Families ● 107

personal pronoun	人稱代名詞 *I*, *you*, *he*, *she*, *it*, *we*, and *they* are personal pronouns. I、you、he、she、it、we 以及 they 是人稱代名詞。
reflexive pronoun	反身代名詞 *Myself*, *yourself*, *himself*, *herself*, *itself*, *ourselves*, and *themselves* are reflexive pronouns. myself、yourself、himself、herself、itself、ourselves 以及 themselves 是反身代名詞。
possessive adjective	所有格形容詞 *My*, *your*, *his*, *her*, *its*, and *our* are possessive adjectives. my、your、his、her、its 以及 our 是所有格形容詞。
gender [ˈdʒɛndɚ]	性 A word's gender indicates if it is masculine or feminine. 單字的性顯示它為陽性或是陰性。
number	數 A word's number indicates if it is singular or plural. 單字的數顯示它為單數或複數。

Checkup

A

Write | 請依提示寫出正確的英文單字或片語。

1	句子片段	_____	9	所有格	_____
2	逗點謬誤	_____	10	對等連接詞	_____
3	直接受詞	_____	11	修飾	m_____
4	間接受詞	_____	12	修飾	q_____
5	感嘆詞	_____	13	取代	r_____
6	代名詞	_____	14	使完整	_____
7	主格	_____	15	所有格形容詞	_____
8	受格	_____	16	（單字的）性	_____

B

Complete the Sentences | 請在空格中填入最適當的答案，並視情況做適當的變化。

possessive case	objective case	fragment	interjection	indirect
nominative case	comma splice	pronoun	coordinating	direct

1 A sentence _____ is part of a sentence or an incomplete sentence.
句子片段是指句子的一部分或是不完整的句子。

2 An _____ object is the person or thing that receives the direct object from the subject.
間接受詞是從主詞接受直接受詞的人或物。

3 A _____ object is a noun or pronoun that receives the action of the verb.
直接受詞是接受動詞行為的名詞或代名詞。

4 People use _____ to show strong emotions. 人們用感嘆詞來表示強烈的情感。

5 People use _____ as substitutions for nouns. 人們用代名詞來代替名詞。

6 The _____ refers to the object of a sentence.
受格是句子的受詞。

7 The _____ shows ownership by someone or something.
所有格顯示某人或某物的所有權。

8 _____ conjunctions include and, but, or, nor, and so.
對等連接詞包含 and、but、or、nor 以及 so。

C

Read and Choose | 閱讀下列句子，並且選出最適當的答案。

1 Pronouns (replace | take) the place of nouns.

2 Adjectives (indicate | modify) nouns, so they provide more information about them.

3 Myself, yourself, himself, and themselves are (personal | reflexive) pronouns.

4 A word's (number | gender) indicates if it is singular or plural.

Look, Read, and Write | 看圖並且依照提示，在空格中填入正確答案。

1

He handsome

▸ a part of a sentence or an incomplete sentence

_____

3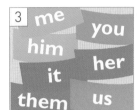

▸ It refers to the object of a sentence, like _me_, _us_, or _you_.

_____

2

It's okay, it was not your fault.

▸ improperly using a comma to join two clauses

_____

4 Wendy **and** Joe

▸ a word (like "and" or "but") that connects two words, phrases, or clauses

_____

E

Read and Answer | 閱讀並且回答下列問題。 ⊙ 108

Common Mistakes in English

Writing in English is not easy. There are many grammar rules. So you have to be very careful. Two common mistakes are sentence fragments and comma splices.

A sentence fragment is an incomplete sentence. A sentence must always have a subject and a verb. Look at the following sentence fragments:

attends the school   **My father, who is a doctor**

Neither of these is complete. The first fragment needs a subject. The second fragment needs a verb. Make them complete sentences like this: "Jane attends the school." "My father, who is a doctor, is home now."

Comma splices are also common mistakes. These are sentences that use a comma to connect two independent clauses. Look at the following comma splices:

My brother studies hard, he's a good student.   I'm sorry, it was an accident.

Neither of these is correct. The first sentence either needs a period or the word _because_: "My brother studies hard because he's a good student." The second sentence needs a period, not a comma: "I'm sorry. It was an accident."

What is true? Write T(true) or F(false).

1   There are no grammar rules in English.   _____

2   A sentence fragment is a complete sentence.   _____

3   A comma splice is good grammar.   _____

4   A comma splice often needs a period instead of a comma.   _____

Renaissance Art 文藝復興藝術

01	**Renaissance** [rə`nesṇs]	*(n.)* 文藝復興 *Renaissance painter 文藝復興時代畫家 *Renaissance art 文藝復興時代藝術 The **Renaissance** was the most glorious period in the history of European art. 文藝復興是歐洲藝術史上最輝煌的時期。
02	**rebirth** [ri`bɝθ]	*(n.)* 再生；重生 *the rebirth of sth. 某事物的復興 *spiritual rebirth 精神的重生 The Renaissance was the time of the **rebirth** of the arts. 文藝復興是藝術重生的時代。
03	**Humanism** [`hjumən͵ɪzəm]	*(n.)*（文藝復興時期的）人文主義 *humanism（小寫）人道主義；人文主義 *secular humanism 世俗人文主義 **Humanism** stressed the importance of man and his role in the world. 人文主義強調人和人在世界的角色之重要性。
04	**harmony** [`hɑrmənɪ]	*(n.)* 和諧 *in harmony 和諧地 *in harmony with sth. 與某事物協調一致 Renaissance artists were interested in the **harmony** of the human body. 文藝復興的藝術家關注人體的和諧度。
05	**perspective** [pɚ`spɛktɪv]	*(n.)* 透視法 *in / out of perspective 用／不用透視法 *perspective drawing 透視圖畫 Renaissance artists used **perspective** to make their paintings look more real. 文藝復興的藝術家運用透視法使畫作更寫實。
06	**realistic** [͵rɪə`lɪstɪk]	*(a.)* 寫實主義的；寫實的 *realism 寫實主義 *realistic painting 寫實繪畫 Paintings in the Renaissance were **realistic**, so the subjects looked like they did in real life. 文藝復興的畫作為寫實主義，主題會以真實生活中的面貌呈現。
07	**enrich** [ɪn`rɪtʃ]	*(v.)* 使富裕；使豐富 *enrich A with B 用 B 使 A 豐富 *a life-enriching experience 充實人生的經驗 **Enriched** by trade, Europeans prospered during the Renaissance. 透過貿易致富的歐洲人在文藝復興時期昌隆興盛。
08	**mural** [`mjʊrəl]	*(n.)* 壁畫 *(a.)* 牆壁的；掛或畫在牆壁上的 *mural decoration 壁飾 *mural painting 壁畫 A **mural** is a painting that is made on a wall. 壁畫是創作於牆壁上的畫。
09	**fresco** [`frɛsko]	*(n.)* 濕壁畫；濕壁畫法 *fresco secco 乾壁畫；乾壁畫法 *in fresco 用濕壁畫法 Michelangelo decorated the ceiling of the Sistine Chapel with some beautiful **frescoes**. 米開朗基羅在西斯汀教堂的天花板上裝飾了一些美麗的濕壁畫。
10	**plaster** [`plæstɚ]	*(n.)* 灰泥 *wet plaster 濕灰泥 A fresco is a painting that is made on **plaster** attached to a wall or ceiling. 濕壁畫是在牆面或天花板所鋪的灰泥上繪畫的畫作。

mural

the fresco of the Sistine Chapel

last 　持續
The Renaissance, which began in Italy, lasted from about 1400 to 1600.
文藝復興興起於義大利，由 1400 年持續到 1600 年。

prosper 　繁榮；昌盛
[ˋprɑspɚ]
Many Italian cities like Florence and Rome prospered during the Renaissance.
許多義大利城市如佛羅倫斯和羅馬，在文藝復興期間社會非常繁榮。

flourish 　繁榮；昌盛
[ˋflɝɪʃ]
Painting, sculpture, and architecture flourished during the Renaissance.
繪畫、雕刻以及建築在文藝復興期間非常興盛。

admire 　欽佩；欣賞
[ədˋmaɪr]
Renaissance artists admired Greek and Roman art.
文藝復興的藝術家崇尚希臘及羅馬藝術。

fascinate 　強烈吸引；迷住
[ˋfæsṇ͵et]
Renaissance artists were fascinated by how the Greeks and Romans had depicted the human body.
文藝復興的藝術家為希臘人及羅馬人描繪人體的方式而著迷。

depict 　描繪；描述
[dɪˋpɪkt]
Renaissance artists depicted people in a more realistic manner.
文藝復興的藝術家以更寫實的手法來描繪人物。

portray 　描繪；描寫
[porˋtre]
Renaissance artists portrayed people in a more realistic manner.
文藝復興的藝術家以更寫實的手法來描繪人物。

Word Families 🔊 111

Famous Renaissance Works
著名文藝復興作品

Mona Lisa 蒙娜麗莎

The Last Supper 最後的晚餐

Pietà 聖殤

David 大衛像

The Birth of Venus 維納斯的誕生

Famous Renaissance Artists
著名文藝復興藝術家

Leonardo da Vinci 李奧納多・達文西

Michelangelo 米開朗基羅

Raphael 拉斐爾

Giotto 喬托

Donatello 多那太羅

Botticelli 波提切利

Mona Lisa　　Pietà

David

Checkup

A

Write | 請依提示寫出正確的英文單字或片語。

1	文藝復興	_____	9	濕壁畫	_____
2	再生；重生	_____	10	灰泥	_____
3	人文主義	_____	11	持續	_____
4	和諧	_____	12	繁榮；昌盛	p _____
5	透視法	_____	13	繁榮；昌盛	f _____
6	寫實主義的；寫實的	_____	14	欽佩；欣賞	_____
7	使富裕；使豐富	_____	15	強烈吸引；迷住	_____
8	壁畫	_____	16	描畫；描述	d _____

B

Complete the Sentences | 請在空格中填入最適當的答案，並視情況做適當的變化。

plaster	harmony	realistic	mural	Renaissance
rebirth	perspective	enrich	fresco	Humanism

1 The _____ was the most glorious period in the history of European art.
文藝復興是歐洲藝術史上最輝煌的時期。

2 The Renaissance was the time of the _____ of the arts.
文藝復興是藝術重生的時代。

3 _____ stressed the importance of man and his role in the world.
人文主義強調人和人在世界的角色之重要性。

4 Renaissance artists were interested in the _____ of the human body.
文藝復興的藝術家關注人體的和諧度。

5 Renaissance artists used _____ to make their paintings look more real.
文藝復興的藝術家運用透視法使畫作更寫實。

6 _____ by trade, Europeans prospered during the Renaissance.
透過貿易致富的歐洲人在文藝復興時期昌隆興盛。

7 Michelangelo decorated the ceiling of the Sistine Chapel with some beautiful
_____. 米開朗基羅在西斯汀教堂的天花板上裝飾了一些美麗的濕壁畫。

8 A fresco is a painting that is made on _____ attached to a wall or ceiling.
濕壁畫是在牆面或天花板所鋪的灰泥上繪畫的畫作。

C

Read and Choose | 閱讀下列句子，並且選出最適當的答案。

1 The Renaissance (lasted | fascinated) from about 1400 to 1600.

2 Many Italian cities like Florence and Rome (prospered | portrayed) during the Renaissance.

3 Renaissance artists (depicted | admired) Greek and Roman art.

4 Renaissance artists (portrayed | attached) people in a more realistic manner.

D Look, Read, and Write | 看圖並且依照提示，在空格中填入正確答案。

 ▸ the time of the rebirth of the arts in European history

_____

 ▸ a painting that is made on a wall

_____

 ▸ a painting that is made on plaster attached to a wall or ceiling

_____

 ▸ a method of showing distance in a picture by making far away objects smaller

_____

E Read and Answer | 閱讀並且回答下列問題。　⊙ 112

Renaissance Artists

During the Renaissance, there were many brilliant artists. These included Raphael, Botticelli, Giotto, and Donatello. But two are considered greater than the others. One is Leonardo da Vinci. The other is Michelangelo Buonarroti.

Leonardo

Leonardo da Vinci was a true Renaissance man. He could do many things well. He was an engineer and scientist. He was an inventor, architect, and artist. He was one of the greatest men in history. As an artist, he painted one of the world's most famous pictures: the *Mona Lisa*. Another famous painting is *The Last Supper*. It shows Jesus and his apostles together. Leonardo made many other famous works. But those two are the most well known.

Michelangelo

Michelangelo was an incredible sculptor. He created two of the most famous statues of all time. The first was *David*. The second was *Pietà*. *Pietà* is a sculpture of Mary holding the body of Jesus after he died. Michelangelo was also a great painter. He painted the frescoes on the ceiling of the Sistine Chapel. The most famous of these frescoes is the *Creation of Adam*. It shows God and Adam reaching out to one another.

Answer the questions.

1 When did Raphael and Botticelli paint? _____

2 What kind of a person was Leonardo da Vinci? _____

3 What were two of Leonardo da Vinci's most famous works? _____

4 What were two of Michelangelo's most famous statues? _____

Key Words 🔊 113

01	**genre painting** [ˈʒɑnrə ˈpentɪŋ]	*(n.)* 風俗畫 Genre painting flourished in the 19th century in the United States. 風俗畫盛行於 19 世紀的美國。
02	**Hudson River School** [ˈhʌdsn̩ ˈrɪvɚ skul]	*(n.)* 哈德遜河畫派 The Hudson River School was one group of landscape painters in the 19th century in America. 哈德遜河畫派是美國 19 世紀的一群風景畫家。
03	**luminism** [ˈlumənɪzəm]	*(n.)* 透光主義 Luminism was an American landscape painting style from the 1850s to the 1870s and was characterized by the effects of light on landscapes. 透光主義是美國 1850 年代到 1870 年代的風景畫風格，強調光在風景中的效果。
04	**silversmith** [ˈsɪlvɚˌsmɪθ]	*(n.)* 銀匠　*blacksmith 鐵匠　*silverware 銀器 Paul Revere was a famous silversmith who created beautiful works of silver. 保羅・瑞維爾是一位知名的銀匠，他創作過許多美麗的銀器。
05	**patronage** [ˈpætrənɪdʒ]	*(n.)* 資助　*under the patronage of sb. 在某人的贊助下 Many artists required the patronage of a sponsor for them to be able to afford to paint. 許多藝術家需要贊助者的資助才得以創作。
06	**self-portrait** [ˈsɛlfˈportret]	*(n.)* 自畫像 A self-portrait is a picture the artist makes of himself or herself. 自畫像是藝術家描繪自己的畫像。
07	**watercolor** [ˈwɑtɚˌkʌlɚ]	*(n.)* 水彩；水彩畫　*in watercolor 用水彩　*watercolorist 水彩畫家 Artists like Winslow Homer used watercolors to make beautiful paintings. 溫斯洛・霍默等藝術家運用水彩來創作美麗的畫作。
08	**photography** [fəˈtɑgrəfɪ]	*(n.)* 攝影　*landscape photography 風景攝影 *photography exhibit 攝影展 Photography is the art of taking pictures with a camera. 攝影是利用相機拍照的藝術。
09	**expressionism** [ɪkˈsprɛʃənˌɪzəm]	*(n.)* 表現主義　*expressionist 表現主義藝術家　*abstract expressionism 抽象畫派 Expressionism uses symbols and exaggeration to represent emotions. 表現主義用象徵和誇大的手法來呈現情感。
10	**pop art** [pɑp ɑrt]	*(n.)* 普普藝術；流行藝術　*pop 通俗藝術；通俗文化　*pop artist 普普藝術家 Pop art is a visual art movement which began in the 1950s and is characterized by themes and techniques drawn from popular mass culture. 普普藝術是興起於 1950 年代的視覺藝術運動，特色是從通俗大眾文化中找尋主題和技法。

a painting of the Hudson River School

self-portrait

watercolor

pop art

engrave
[ɪnˈgrev]
雕刻
Silversmiths engraved designs into various works of silver.
銀匠在各種銀器上雕刻圖案。

etch
[ɛtʃ]
蝕刻
Silversmiths etched designs into various works of silver.
銀匠在各種銀器上蝕刻圖案。

pose
擺姿勢
A person must pose while an artist paints his or her portrait.
藝術家在替人畫像時，被畫者要擺姿勢。

idealize
[aɪˈdɪəlˌaɪz]
將……理想化
Many artists idealize the subject they are painting.
許多藝術家會美化其所描繪的主題。

abound
[əˈbaʊnd]
充滿
New ideas and techniques in paintings abounded.
畫作裡充滿了新的構思和技法。

photograph
[ˈfotəˌgræf]
拍照
Ansel Adams often photographed beautiful scenes in nature.
安塞爾‧亞當斯經常拍攝大自然美景。

John James Audubon

Word Families 🔊 115

contemporary
[kənˈtɛmpəˌrɛrɪ]
當代的
Contemporary art is art that is currently being made.
當代藝術是指時下創作的藝術。

modern
現代的
Modern art refers to art made during modern times.
現代藝術是指現代創作的藝術。

Famous American Artists
著名美國藝術家

Thomas Moran

John James Audubon (J.J. Audubon), naturalist painter
約翰‧詹姆士‧奧杜邦，自然主義畫家

Thomas Moran, landscape painter 湯瑪斯‧莫蘭，風景畫家

Winslow Homer, landscape painter 溫斯洛‧霍默，風景畫家

James McNeill Whistler, portraitist, landscape painter 詹姆斯‧惠斯勒，肖像及風景畫家

Ansel Adams, photographer 安塞爾‧亞當斯，攝影師

Checkup

A

Write | 請依提示寫出正確的英文單字或片語。

1	風俗畫	_____	9	水彩；水彩畫 _____
2	透光主義	_____	10	哈德遜河畫派 _____
3	銀匠	_____	11	雕刻 en_____
4	資助	_____	12	蝕刻 et_____
5	攝影	_____	13	擺姿勢 _____
6	表現主義	_____	14	將……理想化 _____
7	普普藝術	_____	15	充滿 _____
8	自畫像	_____	16	拍照 _____

B

Complete the Sentences | 請在空格中填入最適當的答案，並視情況做適當的變化。

expressionism	patronage	luminism	silversmith	photography
genre painting	self-portrait	pop art	watercolor	Hudson River School

1 _____ flourished in the 19th century in the United States.
風俗畫盛行於 19 世紀的美國。

2 _____ was an American landscape painting style from the 1850s to the 1870s and was characterized by the effects of light on landscapes.
透光主義是美國 1850 年代到 1870 年代的風景畫風格，強調光在風景中的效果。

3 Paul Revere was a famous _____ who created beautiful works of silver.
保羅・瑞維爾是位出名的銀匠，他創作過許多美麗的銀器。

4 Many artists required the _____ of a sponsor for them to be able to afford to paint. 許多藝術家需要贊助者的資助才得以創作。

5 A _____ is a picture the artist makes of himself or herself.
自畫像是藝術家描繪自己的畫像。

6 Artists like Winslow Homer used _____ to make beautiful paintings.
溫斯洛・霍默等藝術家運用水彩來創作美麗的畫作。

7 _____ uses symbols and exaggeration to represent emotions.
表現主義用象徵和誇大的手法來呈現情感。

8 _____ is a visual art movement which began in the 1950s.
普普藝術是興起於 1950 年代的視覺藝術運動。

C

Read and Choose | 閱讀下列句子，並且選出最適當的答案。

1 Silversmiths (enlarged | engraved) designs into various works of silver.

2 A person must (etch | pose) while an artist paints his or her portrait.

3 Ansel Adams often (photographed | afforded) beautiful scenes in nature.

4 New ideas and techniques in paintings (depicted | abounded).

D

Look, Read, and Write I 看圖並且依照提示，在空格中填入正確答案。

1 ▸ a style of painting depicting scenes from ordinary life
_____

3 ▸ a picture the artist makes of himself or herself
_____

2 ▸ a group of American landscape painters who painted the landscapes along the Hudson River
_____

4 ▸ an American landscape painting style concerned with the depiction of effects of light
_____

E

Read and Answer I 閱讀並且回答下列問題。 ◉ 116

Nineteenth Century American Landscapes

Fallen Monarchs

In the nineteenth century, much of America was not settled. So there were few cities. Not many people lived in the countryside. So there were many beautiful places for artists to paint landscapes.

One group of landscape artists was called the Hudson River School. The Hudson River flows through New York. These artists painted the land in this area. Much of it was forest. But there were also farms, fields, and many mountains. Thomas Cole was the first Hudson River School artist. Frederic Edwin Church and Asher Durand were two others. The Hudson River School artists were Romantics. So they idealized the landscapes they painted. They painted the scenes the way they wanted the land to look, not the way that it actually looked.

Around the same time, there was another school of artists. They were called Naturalists, or Realists. They painted nature as it appeared. William Bliss Baker was one of these artists. He also painted in the Hudson River area. But his paintings look very different from the Hudson River School artists' paintings. Baker's works are realistic. His painting _Fallen Monarchs_ is one of the most beautiful of the Naturalist paintings.

What is true? Write T(true) or F(false).

1 There were few places in America to paint landscapes. _____

2 The Hudson River School artists painted in New York City. _____

3 Thomas Cole idealized his landscapes. _____

4 William Bliss Baker was a Naturalist. _____

A World of Music 音樂的世界

01	**repeat sign** [rɪˈpit saɪn]	*(n.)* 反覆記號 A **repeat sign** shows which section of the music needs to be repeated. 反覆記號顯示哪一節音樂要重複演奏。
02	**refrain** [rɪˈfren]	*(n.)* 副歌（= chorus） The **refrain** is the part of the song that is repeated. 副歌是指歌曲中重複的部分。
03	**rondo** [ˈrɑndo]	*(n.)* 迴旋曲 In the Classical Period, **rondo** was often used for the last movement of a sonata, concerto, or symphony. 在古典時期，迴旋曲常被使用於奏鳴曲、協奏曲和交響曲的最後樂章。
04	**chorus** [ˈkorəs]	*(n.)* 合唱曲　*Hallelujah Chorus 哈利路亞大合唱（韓德爾《彌賽亞》中的知名段落） A **chorus** is a piece of music written to be sung by a large group of people. 合唱曲是由一群人合唱的一段音樂。
05	**chord** [kɔrd]	*(n.)* 和弦　*strike/touch a chord (in/with sb.) 觸（某）人心弦；引起（某人）共鳴 A **chord** is made of two or more musical sounds played at the same time. 和弦是同時演奏兩個或多個樂音。
06	**monotone music** [ˈmɑnəˌton ˈmjuzɪk]	*(n.)* 單音音樂（= monophony = monophonic music）　*monotone 單音調 **Monotone music** is music that has a single tone. 單音音樂是只有單一曲調的音樂。
07	**polyphonic music** [pɑlɪˈfɑnɪk ˈmjuzɪk]	*(n.)* 複音音樂（= polyphony）　*homophony 主音音樂 Music with two or more different tones is **polyphonic music**. 複音音樂是指音樂中含有兩條或兩條以上的不同曲調。
08	**a cappella** [ˌɑkəˈpɛlə]	*(n.)* 阿卡貝拉；無伴奏合唱（純人聲合唱）　*(a.)* 沒有樂器伴奏的 **A cappella** music is vocal music without instrumental accompaniment. 阿卡貝拉音樂是一種無樂器伴奏、僅由人聲演唱的音樂。
09	**canon** [ˈkænən]	*(n.)* 卡農　*Pachelbel's Canon 帕海貝爾卡農 = Canon and Gigue in D　D 大調卡農與吉格 *Pachelbel's Canon* is the most famous piece of music by Johann Pachelbel. 《帕海貝爾卡農》是約翰‧帕海貝爾最著名的音樂作品。
10	**spiritual** [ˈspɪrɪtʃʊəl]	*(n.)* 聖歌；靈歌 A **spiritual** is a kind of music that is based on religion. 靈歌是一種以宗教為主的音樂。

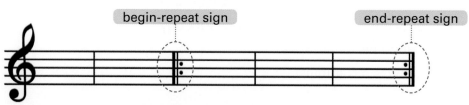

begin-repeat sign　　end-repeat sign

dotted note

repeat	重複;複誦
[rɪˋpit]	The refrain of a song repeats throughout it. 歌曲的副歌會在整首歌中反覆出現。

inspire	鼓舞;激勵
[ɪnˋspaɪr]	Spirituals often inspire the people who hear them. 靈歌常能鼓舞聆聽者。

motivate	激發;刺激
[ˋmotəˏvet]	Spirituals often motivate the people who hear them. 靈歌常能激發聆聽者。

comfort	安慰;使舒服
[ˋkʌmfət]	Music often comforts people. 音樂常能安慰人心。

console	撫慰;安慰
[kənˋsol]	Music often consoles people. 音樂常能撫慰人心。

Word Families ◉ 119

begin-repeat sign	開始反覆記號
	The begin-repeat sign shows where the music to be repeated begins. 開始反覆記號顯示音樂從何處開始重複。
end-repeat sign	結束反覆記號
	The end-repeat sign shows where the music to be repeated ends. 結束反覆記號顯示音樂在何處結束重複。
dotted note	附點音符
	A dotted note indicates the note should be played longer by half. 附點音符表示該音符演奏的音長要增加一半。
tied note	連結音符
	Tied notes combine two notes and indicate they are to be played as a single note. 連結音符是兩個音符的結合,表示它們要當成一個音演奏。

Musical Instructions
音樂指南

crescendo [krɪˋʃɛnˏdo]	<	漸強
decrescendo [ˏdikrəˋʃɛndo]	>	漸弱
accelerando [ækˏsɛləˋrændo]	accel	漸快
ritardando [ˏritɑrˋdændo]	rit / ritard	漸慢

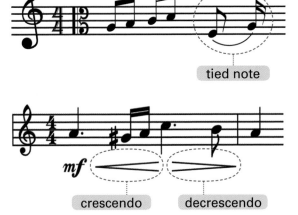

tied note

crescendo   decrescendo

Checkup

A

Write | 請依提示寫出正確的英文單字或片語。

1	反覆記號	_____	
2	副歌	_____	
3	迴旋曲	_____	
4	合唱曲	_____	
5	和弦	_____	
6	單音音樂	_____	
7	複音音樂	_____	
8	無伴奏合唱	_____	

9 卡農 _____
10 聖歌；靈歌 _____
11 重複；複誦 _____
12 鼓舞；激勵 _____
13 激發；刺激 _____
14 安慰 _____
15 附點音符 _____
16 漸弱 _____

B

Complete the Sentences | 請在空格中填入最適當的答案，並視情況做適當的變化。

polyphonic	chord	refrain	spiritual	repeat sign
monotone	canon	chorus	rondo	a cappella

1 A _____ shows which section of the music needs to be repeated.
反覆記號顯示哪一節音樂要重複演奏。

2 The _____ is the part of the song that is repeated. 副歌是指歌曲中重複的部分。

3 In the Classical Period, _____ was often used for the last movement of a sonata, concerto, or symphony.
在古典時期，迴旋曲常被使用於奏鳴曲、協奏曲和交響曲的最後樂章。

4 A _____ is made of two or more musical sounds played at the same time.
和弦是同時演奏兩個或多個樂音。

5 Music with two or more different tones is _____ music.
複音音樂是指音樂中含有兩條或兩條以上的不同曲調。

6 _____ music is music that has a single tone. 單音音樂是只有單一曲調的音樂。

7 Pachelbel's _____ is the most famous piece of music by Johann Pachelbel.
《帕海貝爾卡農》是約翰・帕海貝爾最著名的音樂作品。

8 A _____ is a kind of music that is based on religion.
靈歌是一種以宗教為主的音樂。

C

Read and Choose | 閱讀下列句子，並且選出最適當的答案。

1 The refrain of a song (repeats | shows) throughout it.

2 Spirituals often (inspire | sing) the people who hear them.

3 Music often (comforts | composes) people.

4 A (tied | dotted) note indicates the note should be played longer by half.

Look, Read, and Write I 看圖並且依照提示，在空格中填入正確答案。

1  ▸ the part of the song that is repeated

_____

3  ▸ vocal music without instrumental accompaniment

_____

2  ▸ a piece of music written to be sung by a large group of people

_____

4  ▸ a kind of music that is based on religion

_____

E

Read and Answer I 閱讀並且回答下列問題。 120

Spirituals

Music is often associated with religion. In Christianity, there are many kinds of songs people sing. There are hymns, carols, chants, and others. Another type of music is the spiritual.

Spirituals were first written in the eighteenth century in the United States. They were written because there was a revival of interest in religion in the U.S. then. Spirituals were often very inspiring songs. They were about stories and themes from the Bible. In style, they were a kind of folk music or folk hymn.

Spirituals were often sung by black Americans. Yet there were also many white spirituals, too. Many of the blacks who made these spirituals were slaves from Africa. So spirituals had a strong African influence. They later combined with European and American influences. The result was spirituals.

Nowadays, spiritual music is called gospel music. It is a form of music that is very religious. All kinds of people sing and listen to gospel music. It inspires people and gives them comfort as well.

Fill in the blanks.

1 Hymns, carols, and chants are kinds of music associated with _____.

2 The first spirituals appeared in the U.S. in the _____ century.

3 The stories told in spirituals came from the _____.

4 People call spirituals _____ music today.

A

Write I 請依提示寫出正確的英文單字或片語。

1	傳說;傳奇故事	_____	11 誘拐;綁架	a _____
2	史詩	_____	12 包圍	_____
3	照字面的;逐字的	_____	13 阿基里斯的腳踝	_____
4	比喻的;象徵的	_____	14 修辭	_____
5	句子片段	_____	15 擬聲法	_____
6	文藝復興	_____	16 修飾	_____
7	透視法	_____	17 合唱曲	_____
8	風俗畫	_____	18 繁榮;昌盛	p _____
9	表現主義	_____	19 當代的	_____
10	副歌	_____	20 聖歌;靈歌	_____

B

Choose the Correct Word I 請選出與鋪底字意思相近的答案。

1 Adjectives qualify nouns, so they provide more information about them.

a. represent   b. replace   c. modify

2 Renaissance artists portrayed people in a more realistic manner.

a. depicted   b. painted   c. fascinated

3 Painting, sculpture, and architecture flourished during the Renaissance.

a. etched   b. prospered   c. admired

4 Music often consoles people.

a. inspires   b. motivates   c. comforts

C

Complete the Sentences I 請在空格中填入最適當的答案,並視情況做適當的變化。

rebirth	*Iliad*	metaphor	chord

1 The _____ tells the story of the Trojan War.
《伊里亞德》講述有關特洛伊戰爭的故事。

2 A _____ is often hidden in the words, such as in "She is an angel."
隱喻通常隱含在文字中,例如:「她是個天使」。

3 The Renaissance was the time of the _____ of the arts.
文藝復興是藝術重生的時代。

4 A _____ is made of two or more musical sounds played at the same time.
和弦是同時演奏兩個或多個樂音。

Index

ANSWERS
AND
TRANSLATIONS

Unit 01 • A Nation of Diversity (p.12)

A
1 diversity　2 ethnic group　3 melting pot
4 national identity　5 authority
6 democratic republic　7 constitution
8 amendment　9 party　10 compromise
11 ratify　12 establish　13 amend　14 bear/carry
15 reach a compromise　16 Bill of Rights

B
1 diversity　2 ethnic group　3 National identity
4 democratic republic　5 Constitution　6 authority
7 amendment　8 parties

C
1 ratified　2 amend　3 bear　4 compromise

D
1 melting pot　2 diversity　3 amendment
4 freedom of speech

E 權利法案
　　1787 年，美國的領導者開始起草《美國憲法》，這是國家的最高法律。然而許多美國人民並不開心，因為他們擔心國家政府的力量，他們深知這樣的強權政府會奪走人民的權力。於是他們希望在《美國憲法》中增加修正案，賦予人民和政府特定的權力。他們立下十條憲法修正案，統稱為《權利法案》。《權利法案》於 1791 年生效，正式成為法律。

　　第一條修正案與自由相關，人民擁有言論、宗教與新聞的自由，以及和平集會的權利。第二條修正案允許人民持有武器。第三條修正案聲明政府不得於民房駐軍。第四條修正案保障人民不受無理搜查與拘捕。第五條修正案說明，任何人不得因同一罪行而受二次審判。第六條修正案規定人民有權要求迅速審判。第七條修正案賦予人民要求陪審團審判的權利。第八條修正案禁止過重保釋金。第九及第十條修正案保障人民及政府行使《美國憲法》中未規定事項的權利。

以下何者為「是」？請在空格中填入「T」或「F」。
1 美國人民想要一個強權政府。(F)
2 《權利法案》於 1787 年成為法律。(F)
3 《美國憲法》的前十條修正案為《權利法案》。(T)
4 第一條修正案賦予人民言論自由。(T)

Unit 02 • The American Electoral System (p.16)

A
1 primary　2 caucus　3 candidate　4 delegate
5 nominee　6 nomination　7 convention　8 ballot
9 voting/polling station　10 electoral college
11 nominate　12 vie　13 raise　14 donate
15 cast a ballot/vote　16 voting/polling booth

B
1 primary　2 candidate　3 delegate　4 caucus
5 nomination　6 conventions　7 electoral college
8 voting station

C
1 nominates　2 run　3 raise　4 cast

D
1 nominee　2 donate　3 poll　4 ballot

E 美國總統選舉制度
　　美國有許多政黨，其中勢力最大的兩黨是共和黨與民主黨。總統大選的前兩年左右，兩黨的黨員開始競選總統，他們想獲得黨的提名為總統候選人。這些人會進行募款，並到全國各地演講。

　　美國每四年選一次總統。在選舉年的時候，各州會舉行初選或是黨代表大會，這時他們也會選出黨代表，而候選人則希望盡力爭取黨代表的支持。新罕布夏州是全美國第一個進行初選的州，愛荷華州則是第一個召開黨代表大會的州。各州進行初選或黨代表大會期間，支持度低的從政者會退選。一旦某位候選人得到足夠的黨代表支持，就能獲得提名代表黨參選總統。到了七月或八月，兩黨召開大會，正式提名正副總統的候選人。接著，總統選戰正式展開。兩黨的參選人造訪各州、進行演講，努力贏得選民支持。十一月的第一個星期二，美國選民會決定誰將成為下一屆的總統。

填空
1 共和黨與民主黨是勢力最大的政黨。(Republican)
2 美國每四年選一次新總統。(four)
3 新罕布夏州是全美國第一個進行初選的州。(primary)
4 選舉日是十一月的第一個星期二。(Tuesday)

Unit 03 • History and Culture (p.20)

A
1 historian　2 archaeologist　3 timeline
4 interpretation　5 primary source
6 secondary source　7 artifact　8 chronology
9 historical figure　10 oral history　11 interpret
12 translate　13 utilize　14 B.C.　15 A.D.　16 historic

B
1 Archaeologists　2 Historians　3 interpretation
4 artifacts　5 primary source　6 chronology
7 historical figures　8 oral history

C
1 interpret　2 utilize　3 take　4 stands

D
1 timeline　2 artifact　3 decade　4 archaeologist

E 歷史學家做些什麼？
　　歷史學家研究過去，他們關切過去的事件以及生活在昔日的人們。歷史學家不只是單純得知人名、日期和地點，而是試著詮釋過去的事件，了解事情發生的原因以及人的行為動機。他們也想知道事件彼此之間的因果關係。

　　因此，歷史學家必須研究許多資料。首先，他們必須運用事件發生時所記錄下來的第一手資料，可能是期刊、書籍、報章或照片，現在也有可能是錄影記錄。歷史學家從原始資料中得知重要事件目擊者的觀點。此外，他們會採用非事件目擊者所記錄的第二手資料。優秀的歷史學家會在研究過程中同時採用這兩種資料。

　　歷史分為許多種類，有的歷史學家喜歡政治史，有的研究軍事史，有人著重於經濟史，也有人偏好社會史或文化史。這些歷史都很重要，它們能幫助我們更加了解過去。
* eyewitness 目擊者

下列何者為「非」？(3)
1 歷史學家想要了解過去。
2 歷史學家常會運用第一手資料。
3 優秀的歷史學家只使用第一手資料。
4 有些人研究經濟史或軍事史。

Unit 04 • The Native People of North America (p.24)

A

1 ancestral　2 hunter-gatherer　3 mound
4 totem pole　5 potlatch　6 craft　7 dwelling
8 remains　9 wampum　10 clan　11 impact
12 affect　13 be urged to　14 be forced to
15 set aside　16 teepee

B

1 ancestral　2 hunter-gatherers　3 crafts
4 mound builders　5 dwellings　6 Wampum
7 clan　8 remains

C

1 (a)　2 (b)　3 (c)

D

1 remains　2 igloo　3 hogan　4 wampum

E 阿納薩齊印地安人

　　現今北美洲有許多印地安部落，過去定居於此的部落更多，然而其中像是馬雅和阿茲提克都已不復存在。這樣的情況在數個世紀以前，也曾發生在另一個印地安部落身上，他們是阿納薩齊人。

　　一千多年前，阿納薩齊人居住於現今的美國西南部地區。他們有個令人印象深刻的文化：獨特的手工陶器。部分族人甚至住在嵌入懸崖的房子裡。然而，在 1200 年左右，阿納薩齊人突然消失了，沒有人確定發生了什麼事。有人相信另一個部落在戰爭中擊敗了阿納薩齊人，也有人認為他們是感染疾病而滅亡，多數考古學家則認為是旱災所致。當時阿納薩齊人居住的西南部地區缺雨，然而部落的人口眾多，只要一陣子不下雨，很快就會缺水，也許是某次旱災使他們遷移到別處。至今僅存工藝品和阿納薩齊建築遺跡，至於他們到哪裡去了卻不得而知。

回答下列問題。
1 有些印地安部落發生了什麼事？(They disappeared.)
2 阿納薩齊人過去住在哪裡？(in the Southwest)
3 阿納薩齊人何時消失？(around 1200)
4 阿納薩齊人為何消失？(No one is sure why.)

Unit 05 • The Age of Exploration (p.28)

A

1 trader　2 raider　3 pirate　4 merchant　5 barter
6 navigation　7 caravel　8 expedition
9 Age of Exploration　10 Cape of Good Hope
11 raid　12 invade　13 attack　14 navigate
15 barter　16 dominate

B

1 traders　2 raiders　3 Merchants　4 Navigation
5 caravel　6 expedition　7 Barter
8 Age of Exploration

C

1 raided　2 bartered　3 navigate　4 dominated

D

1 pirate　2 expedition　3 navigation　4 caravel

E 地理大發現

　　1453 年，鄂圖曼土耳其人擊敗拜占庭帝國，並攻佔了首都君士坦丁堡。突然間，歐洲通往亞洲的陸路變得更加

危險。當時，許多歐洲人會向中國和其他亞洲國家購買香料，此時他們無法透過陸路購買，於是開始嘗試走海路。

　　地理大發現於是展開，許多歐洲人開始向南繞行非洲。最初只有葡萄牙和西班牙向南航行，接著其他歐洲人也開始跟隨他們的腳步。

　　在 1488 年，巴爾托洛梅烏‧迪亞士成為第一個航行至非洲最南端好望角的歐洲人，他同時也發現了前往印度的水路。1498 年，瓦斯科‧達伽馬航越印度洋，在印度登陸，並於 1499 年返回葡萄牙。

　　此時，美洲已經被發現了。不過人們依舊不了解地球有多大。最後，在 1519 年，斐迪南‧麥哲倫自西班牙啟航，途經南美洲的南端並深入太平洋，而後他死於與菲律賓原住民的衝突中。然而在 1522 年，他的船員返回西班牙，完成了航行環繞世界的創舉！

下列何者為「非」？(1)
1 歐洲人於 1453 年擊敗拜占庭帝國。
2 地理大發現始於 15 世紀。
3 巴爾托洛梅烏‧迪亞士航行繞過非洲的南端。
4 麥哲倫的船員率先航行環繞世界。

Review Test 1

A

1 melting pot　2 national identity　3 primary
4 caucus　5 archaeologist　6 artifact　7 craft
8 dwelling　9 raider　10 expedition　11 ratify
12 amend　13 electoral college　14 nominate
15 B.C.　16 A.D.　17 clan　18 be forced to
19 barter　20 dominate

B

1 (b)　2 (c)　3 (a)　4 (b)

C

1 diversity　2 conventions　3 chronology
4 remains

Unit 06 • The Spanish Conquerors (p.34)

A

1 smallpox　2 downfall　3 Machu Picchu
4 quipus　5 missionary　6 mestizo　7 enslave
8 El Dorado　9 Spaniard　10 conquistador
11 demand　12 break out　13 drive away/out
14 retreat　15 infect　16 collapse

B

1 Spaniards　2 conquistadors　3 downfall
4 Machu Picchu　5 enslaved　6 quipus
7 Mestizos　8 missionaries

C

1 (a)　2 (b)　3 (c)

D

1 missionary　2 smallpox　3 conquistador
4 El Dorado

E 西班牙人征服新大陸

　　克里斯多福‧哥倫布於 1492 年發現美洲時，當地已有數百萬的居民。他們有的建立起偉大的帝國，其中兩個便是阿茲提克和印加。然而幾年之後，西班牙人卻把他們雙雙擊敗。

阿茲提克帝國位於現在的墨西哥地區，是一個非常好戰的民族，也曾征服許多鄰國，但是他們並沒有槍砲這類的現代武器。赫爾南多・科特斯於 1519 年侵略阿茲提克帝國，雖然只帶了五百名左右的士兵，卻獲得許多鄰近部落的支持，這些部落對阿茲提克恨之入骨。科特斯和他的士兵行軍前往阿茲提克首都特諾奇提特蘭的路上，爆發了多場戰役。他最終在 1521 年攻下這座城市，征服了阿茲提克帝國。

　　印加帝國位於南美洲的安地斯山脈。 1531 年，法蘭西斯克・皮澤洛帶著 182 名士兵抵達此地。當時的印加帝國已經非常衰弱，他們才剛經歷了一場內戰。就在 1532 年，皮澤洛和他的士兵俘虜了印加帝國的帝王。隔年，他們將自己的帝王拱上寶座，成功地擊敗印加帝國。

* the Americas (North America and South America)
美洲（北美與南美） capture 俘虜；佔領　throne 王座

填空
1　美洲的兩個偉大帝國是阿茲提克和印加帝國。(Aztec)
2　阿茲提克沒有像大砲這樣的現代武器。(weapons)
3　阿茲提克的首都是特諾奇提特蘭。(Tenochtitlan)
4　法蘭西斯克・皮澤洛征服了印加帝國。(Pizarro)

Unit 07 ● Colonial America (p.38)

A
1 fur trade　2 trapper　3 ally　4 charter
5 cash crop　6 apprentice　7 Mayflower Compact
8 triangular trade　9 indentured servant
10 House of Burgesses　11 ally　12 tolerate
13 issue　14 be engaged in　15 grant　16 bestow
B
1 fur trade　2 allies　3 charter　4 cash crop
5 indentured servants　6 triangular trade
7 Mayflower Compact　8 House of Burgesses
C
1 allied　2 tolerated　3 granted　4 issued
D
1 trapper　2 cash crop　3 apprentice
4 House of Burgesses
E　五月花號

　　英國有一群稱為清教徒的人，他們與大部分的英國人不同。這些人擁有某種宗教信仰不被認同，因此他們想離開英國，前往新大陸。清教徒租了一艘名為「五月花號」的船，帶他們前往美洲。

　　清教徒於 1620 年離開，在海上航行兩個月後抵達美洲。他們原本的目的地是哈德遜河一帶，卻在普利茅斯岩登陸，位置在現今科德角的麻薩諸塞州。儘管如此，清教徒仍決定定居於此。

　　第一個冬天相當煎熬，許多清教徒因此喪生。不過當地的印地安人和他們和平相處，印地安首領薩莫塞特帶著史廣多與清教徒一起生活。史廣多和其他印地安人教導清教徒如何種田。那一年，清教徒的作物豐收，和印地安人舉辦了一場為期三天的盛大宴會，也就是感恩節的由來。

　　每一年，清教徒殖民地越來越壯大，更多的殖民從英國前來，此處成為非常成功的殖民地。

以下何者為非？(3)
1　清教徒搭乘五月花號來到美洲。
2　清教徒在普利茅斯岩登陸。

3　史廣多是清教徒的領袖。
4　第一個感恩節在 1621 年舉辦。

Unit 08 ● The Declaration of Independence (p.42)

A
1 territory　2 intolerable　3 militia　4 troop
5 patriot　6 mercenary　7 profiteering
8 turning point　9 Loyalist　10 minuteman
11 enact　12 repeal　13 repay　14 enlist
15 desert　16 conflict
B
1 territories　2 intolerable　3 militias
4 minutemen　5 troops　6 Loyalist
7 profiteering　8 Boston Massacre
C
1 enacted　2 enlisted　3 deserted　4 disputes
D
1 profiteering　2 patriot　3 mercenary　4 conflict
E　法印戰爭導致美國革命

　　18 世紀歐洲各國之間經常發生戰爭，通常在歐洲本土打仗，然而有時候也會在其他地方發動戰爭，美洲就是其中之一。在 1750 至 1760 年代之間，英國與法國在北美爆發一場戰爭，有人稱之為「法印戰爭」，有些人則稱其為「七年戰爭」。基本上，英國和美國殖民地站在同一陣線；法國和印地安人在另一陣線。

　　英國獲得勝利，法國因此退出大部分的北美，並讓出許多殖民地給英國。然而對英國而言，戰爭付出的代價非常昂貴，因此，英國國王喬治三世想要提高殖民地的賦稅。他宣稱英國保護殖民地，所以殖民地居民要負擔更高的稅。

　　英國通過許多稅法，其中包含《印花稅法》和《茶稅法》，其他新增的稅法也不勝其數。美國人憎恨課稅，認為並不公平。他們將新增的稅法稱為「不可容忍法案」。最終，英國的種種行為導致了殖民地的戰爭。美國人起義，並脫離英國獲得自由。

回答下列問題。
1　「法印戰爭」另一個名稱為？ (the Seven Years' War)
2　誰贏了「法印戰爭」？ (the British)
3　「法印戰爭」期間，英國的國王為誰？ (King George III)
4　美國人稱《印花稅法》和《茶稅法》為何？
　(the Intolerable Acts)

Unit 09 ● Post-Civil War (p.46)

A
1 Jim Crow Laws　2 abolition　3 Reconstruction
4 industrialization　5 monopoly　6 regulation
7 isolationism　8 stock market　9 depression
10 unemployment　11 abolish　12 get rid of
13 reconstruct/rebuild　14 industrialize
15 regulate　16 Southerner
B
1 Jim Crow Laws　2 abolition　3 Industrialization
4 monopoly　5 regulation　6 Isolationism
7 Great Depression　8 unemployment

C

1 abolish   2 reconstruct   3 regulated
4 industrialized

D

1 Reconstruction   2 depression   3 unemployment
4 industrialization

E 咆哮的二〇年代與經濟大蕭條

　　1920 年代的美國經濟強盛、生活富足。由於第一次世界大戰才剛結束，人民嚮往和平不要戰爭。他們有工作，能賺大錢，也買得起許多新創的科技產品。人們搬到郊區，住進房子，有了閒暇能夠走出戶外享受愜意的生活。

　　然而 1929 年 10 月 24 日當天股市狂洩，數百萬人的生活瞬間變調。人們一下子就從股票中損失了數十億，企業紛紛破產。公司一倒閉，數百萬人民也頓失工作，失業率隨之攀升。當時的總統赫伯特・胡佛被指責為造成經濟問題的罪魁禍首。1932 年富蘭克林・羅斯福被選為新一屆的美國總統。

　　羅斯福提出一個終止經濟大蕭條的政策，稱為「新政」。他提高了政府在經濟中的影響力，並試圖由政府提供人們就業機會。在 1930 年代期間，美國的生活非常艱苦，這樣的日子直至 1941 年的第二次世界大戰才終止。不久，美國的經濟開始復甦。

以下何者為非？ (3)

1 1920 年代的美國經濟富裕。
2 股市於 1929 年狂洩。
3 富蘭克林・羅斯福是股市狂洩時的總統。
4 經濟大蕭條終止於第二次世界大戰。

Unit 10 ● The United States in the Modern Age (p.50)

A

1 surprise attack   2 atomic bomb
3 nuclear weapon   4 Cold War   5 desegregation
6 union   7 corrupt   8 demonstration   9 suffrage
10 superpower   11 declare   12 embark
13 disembark   14 encounter   15 strike   16 confront

B

1 surprise attack   2 Nuclear weapons   3 Cold War
4 desegregation   5 corrupt   6 unions   7 suffrage
8 superpower

C

1 declared   2 disembarked   3 embarked
4 protested

D

1 capitalist   2 corrupt   3 suffrage   4 Cold War

E 冷戰

　　第二次世界大戰由 1939 年持續到 1945 年，戰爭一結束，另一場戰爭旋即爆發，這是美國與蘇聯之間的另一種戰爭，稱為「冷戰」。美國擁護自由與民主，蘇聯卻支持暴政與共產主義，所以他們在世界各地不同的地方較量。

　　冷戰期間發生許多事件，多非真正的戰爭。發生於 1948 年和 1949 年的「柏林封鎖」是其中一個事件，1961 年柏林圍牆的建造也是其一。當然，期間也發生過一些戰爭，像韓戰與越戰也都屬於冷戰的一部分，因為美蘇兩方各支持一方。甚至連 1950 年代和 1960 年代的太空競賽也屬於冷戰之一，核子競賽亦是，美蘇雙方皆擁有大量核武，不過他們從未真正使用。

　　冷戰最終於 1980 年代結束，這要歸功於美國總統隆納・雷根，蘇聯開始瓦解。1989 年柏林圍牆倒塌，東歐國家開始走向自由。接著在 1991 年，蘇聯正式垮臺，冷戰也隨之告終。

* tyranny 暴政   communism 共產主義

填空

1 美國擁護自由與民主。(freedom)
2 「柏林封鎖」發生於 1948 年和 1949 年。(Berlin)
3 太空競賽也屬於冷戰之一。(Cold War)
4 美國總統隆納・雷根結束冷戰並擊敗蘇聯。
　 (Ronald Reagan)

Review Test 2

A

1 smallpox   2 downfall   3 fur trade   4 charter
5 territory   6 intolerable/unbearable   7 abolition
8 Reconstruction   9 surprise attack   10 atomic bomb
11 break out   12 drive away/out   13 issue   14 grant
15 enact   16 repeal   17 depression
18 unemployment   19 suffrage   20 superpower

B

1 (b)   2 (b)   3 (a)   4 (a)

C

1 conquistadors   2 indentured servants   3 militias
4 monopoly

Unit 11 ● Classifying Living Things (p.56)

A

1 classification   2 kingdom   3 phylum   4 division
5 class   6 genus   7 species   8 prokaryote
9 bacterium   10 biodiversity   11 categorize
12 classify   13 divide   14 contain   15 contribute
16 fungi kingdom

B

1 kingdoms   2 classification   3 phylum
4 Divisions   5 class   6 species   7 Prokaryotes
8 biodiversity

C

1 classify   2 contributes   3 contain   4 Vascular

D

1 kingdom   2 genus   3 biodiversity   4 prokaryotes

E 界

　　地球上有許多有機生物，有的彼此之間大不相同，也有許多擁有某些相似性。因此科學家將有機體分成五個獨立的界，分別為動物界、植物界、原生生物界、真菌界以及細菌界，每個界的生物都有一定的相似性。

　　最大的是動物界，包含了超過八十萬種物種，大多數可分為脊椎與無脊椎動物。動物包括哺乳動物、爬行動物、鳥類、兩棲動物以及昆蟲。

　　第二大的是植物界，有喬木、灌木、花卉、藤類以及青草。第三大的是單細胞的原生生物界，包含原生動物、水藻和矽藻。第四大的為真菌界，大部分的真菌是菇類，也有一些是黴菌、酵母菌和地衣。最後是細菌界，包含某些種類的細菌以及病毒等各種病原體。

* pathogen 病原體

以下何者為「是」？請在空格中填入「T」或「F」。
1 有機體可分為五個不同的界。(T)
2 最大的界是植物界。(F)
3 昆蟲和水藻屬於原生生物界。(F)
4 真菌是指菇類和酵母菌。(T)

Unit 12 • Plant Structure (p.60)

A
1 epidermis 2 root hair 3 taproot 4 xylem
5 phloem 6 cambium 7 transpiration
8 respiration 9 cortex 10 chloroplast
11 transpire 12 respire 13 function 14 operate
15 hold 16 simple leaf
B
1 Respiration 2 Transpiration 3 Root hairs
4 phloem 5 cambium 6 taproot 7 cortex
8 Chloroplasts
C
1 transpire 2 respire 3 function 4 compound
D
1 epidermis 2 xylem 3 simple leaf 4 chloroplast

E 根、莖、葉
　　植物有許多構造，其中最重要的三個是根、莖以及葉，他們都具備了各種功能。
　　根位於植物的底部，生長在地底，負責把植物固定於地面，防止植物被雨水沖走或是被風吹走。同時，植物也藉由根部來吸收地面的水和各種礦物質等養分。
　　莖部擔負幾個重責大任。首先，它們將水和養分從根部輸送到葉子。如果水分和養分過剩，莖也會將它們儲存起來。莖也負責將像汁液這樣的養分從葉子往下輸送到根部，最後還有支撐葉子的功能。
　　葉子也佔有非常重要的角色，其包含的葉綠體能夠行使光合作用，如此植物才能製造糖分作為食物。同時，葉子吸收二氧化碳，將其轉換成氧氣，讓地球上所有其他動物都能呼吸。

填空
1 植物最重要的三個構造是根、莖、葉。(stems)
2 根負責吸收地面的水和礦物質。(minerals)
3 植物的莖可以儲存養分和水。(stem)
4 葉綠體能夠行使光合作用。(Chloroplasts)

Unit 13 • Plants without Seeds (p.64)

A
1 seedless 2 spore 3 rhizoid 4 frond
5 fertilization 6 fertilized egg
7 asexual reproduction 8 sexual reproduction
9 asexually 10 gamete 11 fertilize 12 pollinate
13 reproduce 14 regenerate 15 branch out
16 rhizome
B
1 seedless 2 spore 3 rhizoids 4 Fertilization
5 fertilized egg 6 sexual reproduction
7 asexually 8 gamete
C
1 pollinate 2 fertilized 3 reproduce 4 branch

D
1 spore 2 rhizome 3 pollinate
4 asexual reproduction

E 有性生殖與無性生殖
　　所有的植物都需要繁殖來產生新的植物，它們繁殖的方式可分為有性生殖與無性生殖兩種。
　　有性生殖需要同種的雄株與雌株，以這種方式繁殖的植物會開花，花朵是它們保存生殖器官和種子的地方。雄性生殖器官為雄蕊，上面有需要傳到雌株的花粉。雌性生殖器官為雌蕊，一旦花粉傳送至此，植物就完成了受粉，花朵裡的種子開始成長。不久後種子會發芽，代表它們即將長成幼小植物。
　　第二種生殖方式為無性生殖，這種方式只需要一株親代便可完成。無性生殖可分為多種方式，例如，新生植物可以直接從原植物長出，也有植物靠鱗莖來繁殖，洋蔥和馬鈴薯就屬於鱗莖。這種植物的部分結構可直接生根，變成新植物。無性生殖不需要花粉，也沒有雄株與雌株之分，新植物直接從原植物中生長。

以下何者為「非」？(4)
1 植物有兩種生殖方式。
2 植物的生殖器官位於花朵。
3 種子發芽可以長成新植物。
4 無性生殖需要雄株與雌株。

Unit 14 • Flowers and Seeds (p.68)

A
1 angiosperm 2 gymnosperm 3 cotyledon
4 monocot 5 dicot 6 ovary 7 pistil 8 stamen
9 stigma 10 anther 11 spread 12 disperse
13 scatter 14 reproductive organ 15 ginkgo
16 filament
B
1 gymnosperm 2 angiosperm 3 cotyledons
4 monocot 5 pistil 6 stigma 7 stamen
8 anther
C
1 spread 2 disperse 3 female 4 male
D
1 gymnosperm 2 angiosperm 3 anther
4 cotyledon

E 授粉與受精
　　有性生殖的植物具有雄性和雌性的構造，一株植物必須受粉才能繁殖，來自雄蕊（雄性構造）的花粉必須要抵達雌蕊（雌性構造）。這個過程主要依靠兩個方式：一為風，有時候風會將花粉攜帶至另一株植物上，然而，這並不是非常有效率的方法。
　　所幸許多動物都能幫忙授粉，通常以昆蟲為主，如蜜蜂和蝴蝶。植物的花朵常常產生昆蟲喜愛的花蜜，昆蟲採集花蜜的同時也會沾上花粉，所以當昆蟲穿梭於植物之間，身上的花粉就會抹在其他植物的雌蕊上，完成了授粉。
　　既然花粉已經傳遞完成，植物必須準備受精。植物的柱頭有一根花粉管，至少要有一粒花粉順著管子滑下。然而這並不容易，因為花粉管很小，所以植物需要許多粒的花粉，才能確保有一個會滑下管中。一旦成功，雄細胞與雌細胞才能結合。結果導致受精作用，植物得以繁殖。

回答下列問題。
1 植物的雄性構造為何？(the stamen)
2 植物的雌性構造為何？(the pistil)
3 昆蟲採花粉時，要尋找哪裡？(nectar)
4 花粉要送到柱頭的哪裡？(in the pollen tube)

Unit 15 ● Adaptations (p.72)

A

1 stimulus 2 response 3 tropism 4 carnivorous
5 auxin 6 protective coloration 7 hybrid
8 crossbreeding 9 crossbreed 10 evolution
11 stimulate 12 respond 13 avoid 14 escape
15 evolve 16 mimic

B

1 stimulus 2 Responses 3 Tropism 4 Carnivorous
5 Auxin 6 hybrid 7 crossbreed 8 Evolution

C

1 stimulate 2 respond 3 avoid 4 camouflage

D

1 tropism 2 carnivorous plants 3 breed
4 crossbreed

E 植物的向性

　　我們知道動物會適應環境，稱為演化，演化的過程可能需要很長的時間，動物也會產生很大的改變。其實植物也會適應環境，稱為向性。

　　向性是指植物對外在刺激的反應，這些刺激可能是光、水分或是地心引力。向性是非自主的行為，卻有助於植物生存。

　　植物需要光來維生，沒有光就無法行使光合作用，因此植物會一直往光源的方向生長。假如它們被陰影遮蔽或處於暗處，就會向有光的地方彎曲，如此才能生存。

　　水分對植物也一樣，沒有水分，植物就會死亡。植物的根會朝著有水分的土壤生長，葉子也會適應環境，才能盡可能地鎖住水分。

　　另一種會造成向性的力量是地心引力，莖總是往地心引力的反方向生長，也就是向上生長。然而根卻是順著地心引力的方向生長，所以它們會往下紮根。

以下何者為非？(1)
1 演化是發生在植物身上的改變。
2 植物會對光或地心引力做出反應。
3 植物會試著向有光的地方彎曲。
4 植物需要水來維生。

Review Test 3

A

1 kingdom 2 phylum 3 xylem 4 cambium
5 spore 6 rhizoid 7 angiosperm 8 gymnosperm
9 stimulus 10 tropism 11 classify 12 contribute
13 transpire 14 respire 15 fertilize 16 pollinate
17 stigma 18 anther 19 crossbreed 20 evolution

B

1 (b) 2 (a) 3 (c) 4 (b)

C

1 species 2 cambium 3 asexually 4 monocot

Unit 16 ● The Human Body (p.78)

A

1 puberty 2 adolescence 3 reproductive system
4 menstruation 5 womb/uterus 6 fetus
7 metabolism 8 hormone 9 endocrine system
10 gland 11 menstruate 12 implant
13 become pregnant 14 deliver 15 secrete
16 release

B

1 puberty 2 adolescence 3 menstruation
4 fetus 5 endocrine system 6 glands
7 Metabolism 8 hormones

C

1 menstruate 2 implants 3 pregnant 4 secrete

D

1 womb/uterus 2 fetus 3 adolescence
4 endocrine system

E 嬰兒的發育

　　當一個女人懷孕，嬰兒就在她的體內開始成長。接下來的九個月裡，她的體內會孕育著另一個生命。小孩誕生前稱為胎兒，他在九個月裡經歷數個階段的發展。

　　剛開始這個新生命只是個胚胎，爾後開始生長細胞並且變大。三週後，身體的器官開始發展，逐漸成為人形。二個月後，大部分的器官皆已發育完整，只有大腦和脊髓尚未發展完成。

　　到了第九週時，胚胎就會被稱為胎兒，生長的速度也更加快速。到了第 14 週，醫生會檢查胎兒是男是女。懷孕的四到五個月後，母親可以感受到胎動。第六個月時，胎兒已經可以在子宮外存活，不過仍須在母體內生長三個月，最後在第九個月時，大部分的嬰兒就會出生。

填空
1 母體內尚未出生的嬰兒稱為胎兒。(fetus)
2 胚胎的器官在兩個月後發展完成。(months)
3 醫生在第 14 週時，可以判斷嬰兒是男是女。(fourteen)
4 胎兒到了第六個月時，可以在子宮外存活。(womb)

Unit 17 ● Ecosystems (p.82)

A

1 biotic factor 2 abiotic factor 3 niche
4 symbiosis 5 mutualism 6 parasitism
7 invasive species 8 biome
9 ecological succession 10 carrying capacity
11 thrive 12 invade 13 decompose 14 rot
15 alter/change 16 pioneer species

B

1 biotic factors 2 abiotic factors 3 Symbiosis
4 Mutualism 5 Parasitism 6 biomes
7 ecological succession 8 Carrying capacity

C

1 thrive 2 invade 3 alter 4 climax

D

1 parasitism 2 pioneer species
3 carrying capacity 4 invasive species

許多生態系統是充滿生命的繁榮群落，不過它們過去也一度是空無一物的貧瘠土地，最後卻變成了充滿許多有機體的地方。

第一個階段為初級演替，發生在一地尚未出現任何生命時。先要有土壤，接著先驅物種進入這片土地。先驅物種是像地衣和苔蘚這樣的低階有機體。隨著時間的過去，這裡的土壤開始可以維持更複雜的有機體，也就是各種的禾本科植物。一旦有了一些低階植被，昆蟲和鳥類等動物就會移入，灌木與喬木最終也會開始生長。最後，甚至連更大型的動物都會進駐此地。

這個生態系統最後會發展完整，形成一個終極群落，表示它已經相當安定。除非有外來的影響，這個生態系統才會改變。有可能是出現了入侵物種，或是發生天災。不過若是沒有外來影響，這個生態系統永遠不會改變。

* barren lands 貧瘠的土地

以下何者為「非」？(3)
1 初級演替是生態系統改變的第一階段。
2 地衣是首批進入貧瘠地區的植物。
3 終極群落很快就能在貧瘠之地形成。
4 天災可能會改變一些生態系統。

Unit 18 ● Earth and Resources (p.86)

A
1 geologist　2 seismograph　3 fault　4 watershed
5 floodplain　6 deposition　7 lithosphere
8 hydrosphere　9 ore　10 gem　11 deposit
12 transform　13 compress　14 weather
15 meander　16 tension

B
1 geologist　2 seismograph　3 watershed
4 Deposition　5 fault　6 lithosphere
7 hydrosphere　8 ore

C
1 deposit　2 transform　3 compress　4 meander

D
1 fault　2 floodplain　3 meander　4 hydrosphere

E 地震

有時候地面會突然開始震動，建築物與橋樑也隨之前後晃動，甚至倒塌，地面各處開始裂開，這就是地震。世界各地時時刻刻都在發生地震，通常很輕微，我們感覺不到。然而有的時候，也會發生非常大的地震，可能造成嚴重的損害，奪走無數性命，甚至改變地貌。

地殼是地球的最上層，由許多板塊組成，稱為構造板塊。地球一共有七大板塊與大約十二塊較小的板塊。這些板塊很龐大，不過移動速度很緩慢。有時候它們會彼此碰撞，於是產生地震。

芮氏地震規模用來測量地震的威力，規模二級是一級的十倍，每增加一個整數，威力也隨之增加十倍。規模一級到四級屬於輕微地震，五級會造成一些損害，六到七級非常危險，八到九級會造成嚴重的死亡和破壞。

回答下列問題。
1 地球的最上層為何？(the crust)
2 地球上有幾個大型的構造板塊？(seven)
3 什麼用來測量地震的威力？(the Richter scale)
4 輕微地震的規模為何？(one to four on the Richter scale)

Unit 19 ● Matter (p.90)

A
1 atom　2 proton　3 neutron　4 electron
5 nucleus　6 compound　7 solute　8 solvent
9 solution　10 chemical formula　11 unite　12 bond
13 dissolve　14 contract　15 acid　16 base

B
1 Atoms　2 proton　3 electron　4 compound
5 nucleus　6 solutions　7 solvent　8 solute

C
1 unite　2 expand　3 contract　4 revolve

D
1 proton　2 solute　3 nucleus　4 chemical formula

E 元素

整個宇宙是由物質組成的，而物質則由個別的元素或是化合物構成。化合物是指兩種或兩種以上元素的結合。那麼什麼是元素呢？元素是只含一種原子的物質，一共有117個，大部分是自然元素，存在於大自然中。但是科學家也會製造一些元素，就只在實驗室裡出現。

所有的元素都有一個類似結構，就是有原子核，這是元素的核心。原子核內部有質子和中子，每種元素的質子數與中子數並不相同。例如，氫有一個質子和零個中子，氦有兩個質子和兩個中子，氧有八個質子和八個中子，金則有79個質子和118個中子。

原子核的外圍有電子，繞行原子核運動，同時帶有負電。不過質子帶的是正電。此外，一個元素的質子與電子數量通常相同，偶爾也會相異。

以下何者為「是」？請在空格中填入「T」或「F」。
1 元素有117種。(T)
2 大部分的元素為人造的。(F)
3 質子與中子位於原子核內。(T)
4 電子帶正電。(F)

Unit 20 ● The Universe (p.94)

A
1 celestial　2 rotation　3 revolution
4 lunar eclipse　5 solar eclipse　6 meteorite
7 black hole　8 supernova　9 crater
10 extraterrestrial/alien　11 rotate　12 revolve
13 explode　14 surpass　15 exceed　16 meteor

B
1 celestial　2 revolution　3 rotation　4 meteorite
5 solar eclipse　6 black hole　7 supernova
8 extraterrestrial

C
1 revolve　2 explodes　3 contains　4 surpass

D
1 lunar eclipse　2 supernova　3 crater　4 meteorite

E 宇宙只有我們嗎？

數千年以來，人們仰望星空問：「宇宙只有我們嗎？」人們陶醉於漫天星斗，為其他星球可能存在生命所著迷。許多文化都有外星人降臨地球的神話故事，卻沒有人知道外星人是否真的存在。

而今科學家一直在尋找其他星球上的生命。有些人認為火星上可能存在生命，有些人則認為歐羅巴（木衛二）或埃歐（木衛一）可能存在生命，還有一些人試圖從其他星系尋找與地球類似的行星。

其他星球生命生存的條件是什麼呢？地球上的所有生命全是碳基生命，需要來自恆星提供的熱和光、充滿氧氣的大氣層，也需要水分。

當然，其他的生命形式可能以不同的元素為生命基礎，我們不知道他們需要的生存條件，但有一件事是確定的：在找到外星生物前，人們絕對會繼續探索下去。

填空
1 有很多關於外星人來到地球的神話。(myths)
2 有些科學家一直在尋找其他星球上的生命。(life)
3 有人認為火星上有外星人。(Mars)
4 地球上的所有生命全是碳基生命。(carbon)

Review Test 4

A
1 puberty　2 metabolism　3 symbiosis
4 mutualism　5 lithosphere　6 hydrosphere
7 proton　8 neutron　9 solar eclipse
10 meteorite　11 endocrine system　12 gland
13 ecological succession　14 thrive　15 deposit
16 transform　17 dissolve　18 contract　19 crater
20 extraterrestrial/alien

B
1 (b)　2 (b)　3 (c)　4 (a)

C
1 adolescence　2 Parasitism　3 seismograph
4 Atoms

Unit 21 ● Numbers (p.100)

A
1 Arabic numeral　2 Roman numeral　3 integer
4 divisor　5 common divisor　6 multiple
7 common multiple　8 exponent　9 prime number
10 prime factor　11 square　12 break down into
13 be expressed as　14 billion　15 even number
16 odd number

B
1 Arabic numerals　2 integer　3 divisors
4 common divisors　5 multiples
6 common multiples　7 exponent　8 prime factors

C
1 square　2 broken　3 odd　4 negative

D
1 Roman numerals　2 exponent　3 prime number
4 integer

E 羅馬數字

今日我們都用數字來計數，我們所用的十進位制很簡單，不過並非每個文化都使用相同的計數法，方法各異。古羅馬人使用羅馬數字，它們並非真正的數字，而是字母。

羅馬人使用字母 I、V、X、L、C、D、M 來代表某些數，例如 I 是 1，V 是 5，X 是 10，L 是 50，C 是 100，D 是 500，M 是 1,000。為了數出更大的數字，羅馬人會再增加字母，因此 2 是 II，3 是 III，6 是 VI，7 是 VII。

不過 4 並不是 IIII 而是 IV。羅馬人為什麼要這麼做？當一個數字要變成較大的數值時（如 III 變成 IV），羅馬人有時候是在大數字（V）前面放上小數字（I），表示要減去那個量，而不是加上（IV＝V－I）。所以說，9 是 IX，40 是 XL，90 是 XC，900 是 CM。

這樣的作法雖不困難，但是遇到特大的數字時，羅馬人就算不下去了，因為太難寫了。例如 3,867 要怎麼表示？用羅馬數字會變成 MMMDCCCLXVII。那麼又要怎麼作加減乘除？你可以想像用 MMCCXII 除以 CCLXIV 嗎？

以下何者為「是」？請在空格中填入「T」或「F」。
1 羅馬人使用字母當數字。(T)
2 對羅馬人來說，V 代表 10。(F)
3 對羅馬人來說，XL 代表 90。(F)
4 羅馬人無法計算很大的數字。(T)

Unit 22 ● Computation (p.104)

A
1 expression　2 equation　3 variable
4 inverse operation　5 divisible　6 short division
7 long division　8 computation
9 order of operations　10 mental math
11 bring down　12 vary　13 rewrite　14 estimate
15 property　16 rule

B
1 expression　2 equation　3 divisible
4 short division　5 long division　6 Computation
7 variable　8 order of operations

C
1 bring　2 vary　3 rewrite　4 properties

D
1 expression　2 long division　3 variable
4 mental math

E 運算順序

在數學中，有些題目很好解，例如 2+3=5 就是個簡單的題目。不過有時候會碰到較複雜的問題，例如 2+3×4 要怎麼計算？要先作加法還是先作乘法？答案是 14 還是 20？

數學裡有所謂的運算次序，用來說明解題的順序。有三個簡單的規則：第一，括號內先算；第二，由左向右先作乘除；第三，由左向右再作加減。

再看一次上面的題目：2+3×4，我們要怎麼解呢？先將 3×4 得 12，再將 2+12 得到 14，所以正確答案為 14。

更複雜的問題怎麼辦？看看這一題：3×(3+4)-1。首先要先算括號內的問題：3+4 是 7，接著作乘法：3×7 得 21，最後作減法：21-1 為 20，所以答案是 20。

填空
1 使用運算次序來解複雜的題目。(order)
2 先解括號內的問題。(parentheses)
3 先乘除，後加減。(division)
4 解數學題時，一定要由左而右運算。(left)

Unit 23 ● Decimals, Fractions, and Ratios (p.108)

A
1 equivalent decimal　2 like fractions
3 unlike fractions　4 ratio　5 proportion
6 scale　7 percent　8 probability

9 least/lowest common denominator　10 fraction bar
11 compare　12 be represented by / be expressed as
13 be written as　14 be likely to
15 denominator　16 numerator

B

1 equivalent　2 unlike fractions
3 common denominator　4 proportion　5 scale
6 probability　7 fraction bar　8 ratio

C

1 compares　2 represented　3 expressed　4 likely

D

1 unlike fractions　2 proportion　3 percent
4 probability

E 百分比、比與機率

　　氣象播報員可能會說：「降雨機率為 70%」，這是在說明下雨的機率。70% 表示以目前的天氣狀況來說，100 次的機會有 70 次會下雨。氣象預報經常使用百分比，運動比賽也是，播報員可能會說：「這名籃球選手的命中率為 52%」，表示每 100 次的投籃有 52 次會投中。

　　「比」是用來比較兩件事物的方法。例如，教室的 20 個孩童中，有 12 個男生、8 個女生，你可以說：「男女生的比為 12 比 8」，也可以寫成 12：8 或 $\frac{12}{8}$。假設有 5 隻貓和 8 隻狗，你可以說貓比狗是 5 比 8、5：8 或 $\frac{5}{8}$。這三種都是比的表示法。

　　機率表示事情發生的機會。如果你輕拋一個硬幣，顯示某一面的機會為二分之一，因為一個硬幣有兩面。如果你擲一顆骰子，出現 4 的機會為六分之一。又或者有十片餅乾，其中有三片為燕麥餅乾，你隨機取一塊，拿到燕麥餅乾的機會是十分之三。

以下何者為「非」？(1)
1 氣象預報常使用比。
2 比是用來比較兩件事物。
3 機率表示事情發生的機會。
4 擲一顆骰子，出現 4 的機會為六分之一。

Unit 24 • Geometry (p.112)

A

1 quadrilateral　2 isosceles　3 scalene
4 surface area　5 circumference　6 prism
7 line symmetry　8 rotational symmetry
9 clockwise　10 counterclockwise　11 convert
12 turn　13 calculate　14 construct　15 trapezoid
16 rhombus

B

1 isosceles　2 quadrilaterals　3 scalene
4 surface area　5 Prisms　6 circumference
7 rotational　8 line

C

1 Convert　2 Turn　3 Construct　4 trapezoid

D

1 circumference　2 prism　3 isosceles triangle
4 trapezoid

E 生活中的立體圖形

　　立體圖形包含立方體、角柱、角錐、圓柱、圓錐以及球體，放眼所見幾乎都有立體圖形。許多建築物是長方柱，門、教室的布告欄和你現在正在讀的書也都是。

　　角錐並不常見，不過有些卻赫赫有名。想一下埃及，什麼出現在你腦海中呢？金字塔，對吧？埃及四處可見高大的金字塔。

　　圓錐是人們最愛的立體圖形之一。為什麼呢？因為冰淇淋就是立體圖形。道路施工處也常有很多圓錐出現，施工工人會在道路上設置交通錐，告知駕駛此處是否可通行。

　　當然，球體也遍佈各地。如果沒有球體，大部分的運動都無法進行了。人們需要足球、棒球、籃球、網球以及其他球體。橘子、葡萄柚、桃子、梅子和櫻桃，也都屬於球狀的水果。

回答下列問題。
1 門屬於哪種立體圖形？(rectangular prisms)
2 埃及最出名的建築屬於哪種立體圖形？(pyramids)
3 交通錐屬於哪種立體圖形？(cones)
4 網球屬於哪種立體圖形？(spheres)

Review Test 5

A

1 Arabic numeral　2 Roman numeral
3 integer / whole number　4 equation　5 variable
6 ratio　7 proportion　8 probability　9 isosceles
10 scalene　11 prime number　12 prime factor
13 mental math　14 square　15 vary
16 least/lowest common denominator
17 fraction bar　18 surface area　19 circumference
20 trapezoid

B

1 (c)　2 (c)　3 (b)　4 (a)

C

1 exponent　2 Computation　3 unlike fractions
4 line symmetry

Unit 25 • Stories, Myths, and Legends (p.118)

A

1 legend　2 adventure　3 epic　4 Homer　5 Iliad
6 Odyssey　7 Achilles　8 Hector　9 Odysseus
10 Cyclops　11 carry off　12 abduct/kidnap
13 assault　14 Trojan War　15 Trojan Horse
16 Achilles' heel

B

1 legend　2 Adventures　3 epic　4 *Iliad*
5 *Odyssey*　6 Achilles　7 Hector　8 Odysseus

C

1 carried　2 assaulted　3 challenged　4 blinded

D

1 Homer　2 lay siege to　3 Achilles' heel　4 Cyclops

E 《伊里亞德》與《奧德賽》

　　兩部最偉大的文學作品都非常古老，它們是史詩《伊里亞德》與《奧德賽》，兩者皆為荷馬所著的古希臘故事。

　　《伊里亞德》是關於特洛伊戰爭的故事。帕里斯誘拐了世上最美麗的女人海倫，並把她帶到特洛伊，於是所有的希臘人團結起來，對特洛伊人開戰。希臘有許多偉大的戰士，像是阿伽門農、墨涅拉俄斯、奧德修斯和阿賈克斯，不過其中最偉大的戰士是阿基里斯。戰爭持續了十年之久，許多人也因此戰亡。最終，因為奧德修斯，希臘人利用特洛伊木馬贏了戰爭。希臘人假裝撤退，只留下一座巨大的木馬。特洛伊人將木馬帶進城內，卻不知裡頭藏匿了許多希臘戰士。趁著黑夜時，希臘人走出木馬，從城內攻佔並擊敗特洛伊。

《奧德賽》是關於奧德修斯戰後返鄉的故事。奧德修斯花了十年的時間才回到家鄉，途中歷經許多奇特的冒險。他必須打敗可怕的獨眼巨人，也遭遇女巫瑟茜和卡呂普索。奧德修斯的士兵全都陣亡。他最後得到諸神相助，才得以返家。

以下何者為「是」？請在空格中填入「T」或「F」。
1 《伊里亞德》是關於奧德修斯的冒險。(F)
2 最偉大的希臘戰士是阿基里斯。(T)
3 特洛伊人藏匿於特洛伊木馬。(F)
4 奧德修斯和他的所有士兵歷經十年才得以返家。(F)

Unit 26 ● Learning about Literature (p.122)

A
1 literal　2 figurative　3 imagery　4 simile
5 metaphor　6 symbol　7 personification
8 hyperbole　9 figure of speech　10 onomatopoeia
11 stand for　12 symbolize　13 amuse
14 entertain　15 personify　16 exaggerate

B
1 literal　2 figurative　3 figure of speech
4 metaphor　5 imagery　6 symbol
7 personification　8 onomatopoeia

C
1 stands　2 amuse　3 personified　4 pseudonym

D
1 figure of speech　2 hyperbole　3 metaphor
4 personification

E 修辭

作家也許要有想像力，因此他們會使用修辭法。修辭法有許多種，其中四種為明喻、隱喻、誇飾和擬人。

明喻和隱喻都是對比的手法，不過兩者並不相同。明喻使用 as 和 like 來對比兩件事，例如，strong as an ox（壯得像頭牛）和 dark like night（漆黑如夜）都是明喻。隱喻是將兩件沒有相似處的事物作對比，「The stars are diamond in the sky（星星像是高掛天空的鑽石）」和「There is a sea of sand（有一片沙海）」都是隱喻。

誇飾也是修辭的一種，是一種誇大的形式。人們說話或寫作的時候經常會誇大其詞，舉例來說，「There were a million people in the store（店裡人山人海）」和「I worked all day and all night（我日以繼夜地工作）」都屬於誇飾法。

最後，人常會賦予物體或動物一些人的特質，這就是擬人。「The wind is whispering（風在呢喃）」和「My dog is speaking to me（我的狗在對我說話）」都使用了擬人法。風和狗都不是人，但在兩個例子中，皆出現了人的特質，所以兩者都是擬人法。

填空
1 明喻和隱喻是兩種修辭手法。(figures)
2 明喻使用 like 和 as 來作對比。(simile)
3 誇飾是一種誇大的形式。(Hyperbole)
4 擬人法賦予物體或動物一些人的特質。(Personification)

Unit 27 ● Learning about Language (p.126)

A
1 sentence fragment　2 comma splice
3 direct object　4 indirect object　5 interjection
6 pronoun　7 nominative case　8 objective case
9 possessive case　10 coordinating conjunction
11 modify　12 qualify　13 replace　14 complete
15 possessive adjective　16 gender

B
1 fragment　2 indirect　3 direct　4 interjections
5 pronouns　6 objective case　7 possessive case
8 Coordinating

C
1 take　2 modify　3 reflexive　4 number

D
1 sentence fragment　2 comma splice
3 objective case　4 coordinating conjunction

E 英文常見的錯誤

英文寫作並不容易，有許多文法規則，所以必須小心謹慎。兩種常見的文法錯誤是句子片段和逗點謬誤。

句子片段是一個不完整的句子，一個句子一定要有主詞和動詞。讓我們看看以下的句子片段：
　　attend the school　　My father, who is a doctor
以上兩個例子皆不完整，前者缺乏主詞，後者缺乏動詞。完整的句子應該是：「Jane attends the school.」以及「My father, who is a doctor, is home now.」。

逗點謬誤也是很常見的錯誤，這些句子使用逗點來連接兩個獨立的子句。讓我們看看以下的逗點謬誤：
　　My brother studies hard, he's a good student.
　　I'm sorry, it was an accident.
以上兩個句子皆不正確，第一個句子要用句號或是 because：「My brother studies hard because he's a good student.」。第二個句子要用句號而非逗號：「I'm sorry. It was an accident.」

以下何者為「是」？請在空格中填入「T」或「F」。
1 英文沒有文法規則。(F)
2 句子片段是一個完整的句子。(F)
3 逗點謬誤是正確的文法。(F)
4 逗點謬誤通常應該用句點而非逗點。(T)

Unit 28 ● Renaissance Art (p.130)

A
1 Renaissance　2 rebirth　3 Humanism
4 harmony　5 perspective　6 realistic　7 enrich
8 mural　9 fresco　10 plaster　11 last　12 prosper
13 flourish　14 admire　15 fascinate　16 depict

B
1 Renaissance　2 rebirth　3 Humanism　4 harmony
5 perspective　6 Enriched　7 frescoes　8 plaster

C
1 lasted　2 prospered　3 admired　4 portrayed

D
1 Renaissance　2 mural　3 fresco　4 perspective

E 文藝復興藝術家

文藝復興期間有許多傑出的藝術家，包含拉斐爾、波提切利、喬托以及多那太羅，不過被視為最偉大的兩位是李奧納多‧達文西與米開朗基羅‧布奧納洛提。

達文西是個真正的文藝復興人，他多才多藝，不僅是工程師、科學家，也是發明家、建築師和藝術家，是史上最偉大的人物之一。身為一名藝術家，達文西創作了世界上最著名的繪畫作品之一《蒙娜麗莎》，另一幅《最後的晚餐》也是名畫，畫中呈現耶穌與其門徒一起的畫面。李奧納多尚有其他無數知名的畫作，不過這兩幅最廣為人知。

米開朗基羅是個天才雕刻家，他創造了兩座絕世的著名雕像。第一是《大衛像》，第二則是《聖殤》。《聖殤》是刻畫耶穌死後，聖母瑪利亞懷抱著祂的雕刻作品。米開朗基羅也是個偉大的畫家，他在西斯汀教堂的天花板上繪製了濕壁畫，其中最著名的一幅當屬《創造亞當》，此畫表現出上帝與亞當伸手接觸的樣貌。

回答下列問題。
1 拉斐爾與波提切利創作於什麼時代？
　(during the Renaissance)
2 達文西是什麼樣的人？
　(He was a true Renaissance man.)
3 達文西最有名的兩幅作品為？
　(the *Mona Lisa* and *The Last Supper*)
4 米開朗基羅最著名的兩座雕像為？(*David* and *Pietà*)

Unit 29 ● American Art (p.134)

A
1 genre painting　2 luminism　3 silversmith
4 patronage　5 photography　6 expressionism
7 pop art　8 self-portrait　9 watercolor
10 Hudson River School　11 engrave　12 etch
13 pose　14 idealize　15 abound　16 photograph

B
1 Genre painting　2 Luminism　3 silversmith
4 patronage　5 self-portrait　6 watercolors
7 Expressionism　8 Pop art

C
1 engraved　2 pose　3 photographed　4 abounded

D
1 genre painting　2 Hudson River School
3 self-portrait　4 luminism

E 19世紀的美國風景畫

19世紀時，美洲大部分地區尚無人定居，也沒什麼城市。鄉村人口也不多，所以有許多美景可供畫家寫生。

有一群風景畫家被稱為哈德遜河畫派。哈德遜河流經紐約，這些畫家就專畫這一帶的土地。這裡大部分是森林，也有牧場、田野和許多山脈。湯瑪斯‧科爾是第一位哈德遜河畫派的畫家，另外兩位是弗雷德里克‧艾德溫‧丘奇以及艾許‧杜蘭。哈德遜河畫派的畫家是浪漫主義者，他們會美化其所繪製的風景。他們所畫的風景是依照他們想呈現的樣貌，而非真實景色。

在同一時期，還有另一派的畫家，稱為自然主義者或寫實主義者，他們將自然的真實樣貌呈現出來，威廉‧布雷斯‧貝克就是其中一位。他同樣描繪哈德遜河一帶，不過他的作品與哈德遜河畫派截然不同。貝克的作品走寫實風格，《沒落君主》就是寫實畫派中最美麗的作品之一。

以下何者為「是」？請在空格中填入「T」或「F」。
1 美洲很少地方可以寫生。(F)
2 哈德遜河畫派在紐約市裡作畫。(F)
3 湯瑪斯‧科爾美化他的風景。(T)
4 威廉‧布雷斯‧貝克是自然主義畫家。(T)

Unit 30 ● A World of Music (p.138)

A
1 repeat sign　2 refrain　3 rondo　4 chorus
5 chord　6 monotone music　7 polyphonic music
8 a cappella　9 canon　10 spiritual　11 repeat
12 inspire　13 motivate　14 comfort/console
15 dotted note　16 decrescendo

B
1 repeat sign　2 refrain　3 rondo　4 chord
5 polyphonic　6 Monotone　7 Canon　8 spiritual

C
1 repeats　2 inspire　3 comforts　4 dotted

D
1 refrain　2 chorus　3 a cappella　4 spiritual

E 靈歌

音樂經常與宗教息息相關。在基督教中，人們唱著各式各樣的歌曲，有讚歌、聖誕頌歌、禱文及其他等等，還有一種叫作靈歌。

靈歌誕生於18世紀的美國，當時一股宗教復興風潮，促成了靈歌的創作。靈歌常是激勵人心的歌曲，內容取自《聖經》裡的故事和題材，風格屬於民間音樂或民間讚歌。

靈歌多由美國黑人演唱，但也有許多白人靈歌。由於創作這些靈歌的黑人，許多是來自非洲的奴隸，因此歌曲受非洲的影響非常大。不久，這類型的音樂又受到歐洲與美洲的影響，造就了靈歌的出現。

現今靈歌音樂又被稱為福音音樂，是一種非常虔誠的音樂形式。各種民族都會演唱並聆聽福音音樂，它不僅鼓舞人們，也撫慰了人心。

填空
1 讚歌、聖誕頌歌、禱文是與宗教有關的音樂。(religion)
2 靈歌最初出現於18世紀的美國。(eighteenth)
3 靈歌中的故事來自《聖經》。(Bible)
4 人們今日稱靈歌為福音音樂。(gospel)

Review Test 6

A
1 legend　2 epic　3 literal　4 figurative
5 sentence fragment　6 Renaissance　7 perspective
8 genre painting　9 expressionism　10 refrain
11 abduct　12 lay siege to　13 Achilles' heel
14 figure of speech　15 onomatopoeia　16 modify
17 chorus　18 prosper　19 contemporary　20 spiritual

B
1 (c)　2 (a)　3 (b)　4 (c)

C
1 *Iliad*　2 metaphor　3 rebirth　4 chord

AMERICAN SCHOOL TEXTBOOK
VOCABULARY KEY

Workbook

GRADE 5

Michael A. Putlack

FÜN學美國英語課本
各學科關鍵英單 二版

Unit 01

A Listen to the passage and fill in the blanks.

🎧 121 **The Bill of Rights**

In 1787, the states' leaders started to write the 1._____. The Constitution is the 2._____ law of the land. But many Americans were not happy. They were worried about the strength of the national government. They knew a strong government could take away their rights. So they wanted to add some 3._____ to the Constitution. These would give specific rights to the people and the states. So they wrote 10 amendments to the Constitution. Together, they were called the 4._____. The Bill of Rights was 5._____ in 1791 and then became law.

The First Amendment is about 6._____. People have freedom of speech, 7._____, and the 8._____ and the right to assemble peacefully. The Second Amendment gives people the right to have guns. The Third Amendment says the government cannot put soldiers in people's houses. The Fourth Amendment protects people from illegal searches and 9._____. The Fifth Amendment says a person cannot be tried twice for the same crime. The Sixth Amendment gives people the right to a 10._____. The Seventh Amendment gives people the right to a 11._____. The Eighth Amendment protects people from 12._____. The Ninth and Tenth amendments protect the people and states by giving them all rights not mentioned in the Constitution.

B Read the passage above and answer the following questions.

_____ 13. Which amendment would protect an American from going to trial more than once for the same crime?
- a The First Amendment.
- b The Third Amendment.
- c The Fifth Amendment.
- d The Seventh Amendment.

_____ 14. "The Constitution is the **supreme** law of the land." In this sentence, the word "supreme" means _____.
- a highest
- b best
- c most popular
- d toughest

_____ 15. The subject of this article is _____.
- a the strength of the American government
- b the creation of the Constitution
- c the ways Americans can avoid prison
- d the legal rights of Americans

Unit 02

A **Listen to the passage and fill in the blanks.**

🎧 122

The American Presidential Election System

In the United States, there are many political 1._____. But two are very powerful. They are the 2._____ and the 3._____.

About two years before the presidential election, members of both parts start 4._____ for president. They want to be their party's presidential 5._____.

They 6._____ money and travel around the country giving speeches.

Every four years, the U.S. elects a president. In an election year, every state has either a 7._____ or a 8._____. This is where they elect 9._____.

The 10._____ want to get as many delegates as possible. New Hampshire has the first primary in the country. Iowa has the first caucus. As the states hold their primaries and caucuses, unpopular politicians drop out of the race. When one candidate has enough delegates, he or she becomes the party's nominee. In July or August, both parties have 11._____. They officially nominate their presidential and vice presidential candidates there. Then, the race for president really begins. The candidates for both parties visit many states. They give speeches. They try to win 12._____. On the first Tuesday in November, the American voters decide who the next president will be.

B **Read the passage above and answer the following questions.**

_____ 13. Which statement is closest to the main idea of the passage?
   a The presidential election process has many steps.
   b The election process in the United States is unfair.
   c Most candidates for presidency aren't qualified.
   d Voting is an important right for people of the United States.

_____ 14. "As the states hold their primaries and caucuses, unpopular politicians **drop out of the race**." In this sentence, "drop out of the race" means _____.
   a to quit politics forever   b to stop running for president
   c to refuse to vote   d to start running for vice-president

_____ 15. If you wanted to become a party's nominee for presidency, you would have to _____.
   a know the current president well   b come from a wealthy family
   c have enough delegates   d be a democratic or republican

3

A Listen to the passage and fill in the blanks.

🎧 123 **What Do Historians Do?**

Historians study the past. They are 1._____ about past events and people who lived in the past. But historians do not just learn names, dates, and places. Instead, they try to 2._____ past events. They want to know why an event happened. They want to know why a person acted in a certain way. And they want to know how one event caused another to 3._____.

To do this, historians must study many 4._____. First, they use 5._____. These are sources that were 6._____ at the same time an event occurred. They could be 7._____. They could be books. They could be newspaper articles or photographs. In modern times, they could even be 8._____ recordings. Historians use primary sources to get the opinions of 9._____ to important events. They also use 10._____. These are works written by people who did not witness an event. Good historians use both primary and secondary sources in their work.

There are many kinds of history. Some historians like 11._____ history. Others study military history. Some 12._____ economics. And others prefer social or cultural history. All of them are important. And all of them help us understand the past better.

B Read the passage above and answer the following questions.

_____ 13. Another good title for this article would be _____.
     ⓐ Understanding the Past   ⓑ Primary and Secondary Sources
     ⓒ Witnessing Important Events   ⓓ Military and Economic History

_____ 14. On what kind of history do historians focus?
     ⓐ Important people.   ⓑ Cultural history.
     ⓒ All kinds of history.   ⓓ Important events.

_____ 15. "They are **concerned** about past events and people who lived in the past."
     In this sentences, the word "concerned" means _____.
     ⓐ worried   ⓑ interested   ⓒ nervous   ⓓ troubled

Unit 04

A Listen to the passage and fill in the blanks.

 124

The Anasazi

Today, there are many Native American 1._____ in North America. In the past, there were many more. However, some of them, like the Maya and Aztecs, 2._____. This happened to another tribe of Native Americans many 3._____ ago. They were the Anasazi.

The Anasazi lived in the area that is the 4._____ today. They lived in that area more than a thousand years ago. They had an 5._____ culture. They made their own unique 6._____. And some of them even lived in homes built into cliffs. However, around 1200, they suddenly disappeared. No one is sure what happened. Some people believe another tribe 7._____ the Anasazi in war. Others believe that a 8._____ killed them. But most 9._____ think there was a 10._____. The area in the Southwest where they lived gets very little rain. The Anasazi had a lot of people in their tribes. If it did not rain for a while, they would have quickly run out of water. Perhaps a drought caused them to move to another area. Today, only 11._____ and the 12._____ of Anasazi buildings remain. No one knows where the people went, though.

B Read the passage above and answer the following questions.

_____ 13. What is closest to the main point the author wants to make?
  a The Anasazi were the most powerful tribe in North America.
  b The Anasazi were more advanced than the Europeans.
  c The Anasazi were advanced but disappeared mysteriously.
  d The Anasazi built large houses into cliffs.

_____ 14. Which of the following is NOT an idea describing how the Anasazi disappeared?
  a They were defeated in a war.
  b They were destroyed in an earthquake.
  c They died of thirst from a drought.
  d They were struck down by disease.

_____ 15. "They had an **impressive** culture." The word with the opposite meaning to "impressive" is _____.
  a unimportant   b great   c strict   d serious

5

Unit 05

Listen to the passage and fill in the blanks.

🎧 125 **The Age of Exploration**

In 1453, the Ottoman Turks defeated the Byzantine Empire. They captured its 1._____ city Constantinople. Suddenly, the land 2._____ from Europe to Asia became more dangerous. At that time, many Europeans 3._____ spices from China and other Asian countries. But now they could not get them from land. So they tried to get their spices by sea.

This began the 4._____. Many Europeans began 5._____ south around Africa. At first, the 6._____ and Spanish started sailing south. But then other Europeans started to follow them.

In 1488, Bartolomeu Dias became the first European to sail to the 7._____ in Africa. This was the 8._____ point of Africa. He had 9._____ the way to India by water. In 1498, Vasco da Gama sailed across the Indian Ocean and 10._____ in India. He returned to Portugal in 1499.

By this time, the Americas had been discovered. But people did not know how big the earth was. Finally, in 1519, Ferdinand Magellan 11._____ from Spain. He sailed past the southern part of South America and into the Pacific Ocean. Magellan was later killed during a fight with the native people of the Philippines. But, in 1522, his 12._____ returned to Spain. They had sailed around the world!

B **Read the passage above and answer the following questions.**

_____ 13. _____ was/were the first to discover how big the earth was.
- a Ferdinand Magellan
- b Vasco da Gama
- c The Ottoman Turks
- d Magellan's crew

_____ 14. Another good title for this article would be _____.
- a The Victory of the Ottoman Turks
- b Magellan: His Life and Death
- c The Hunt for Spices
- d Sailing to Discover

_____ 15. Magellan might have made it all the way around the world if he hadn't stopped in _____.
- a Spain
- b the Philippines
- c the Cape of Good Hope
- d India

Unit 06

A Listen to the passage and fill in the blanks.

 126 | **The Spanish Conquer the New World**

When Christopher Columbus discovered America in 1492, there were already millions of people living in the Americas. Some of them had formed great empires. Two of these were the Aztecs and the Incas. However, after a few years, the 1._____ defeated both of them.

The Aztec Empire was in the area of 2._____ Mexico. The Aztecs were very 3._____. They had 4._____ many of their neighbors. But they did not have modern 5._____ like guns and cannons. In 1519, Hernando Cortés 6._____ the Aztec Empire. He only had about 500 soldiers. But many neighboring tribes 7._____ with him. They disliked the Aztecs very much. There were several battles as Cortés and his men 8._____ to Tenochtitlan, the Aztec capital. In 1521, Cortés 9._____ the city and conquered the empire.

The Inca Empire was in South America in the Andes Mountains. In 1531, Francisco Pizarro arrived there with 182 soldiers. At that time, the Inca Empire was already 10._____. There had just been a civil war in the empire. By 1532, Pizarro and his men had captured the Incan 11._____. The next year, they put their own emperor on the 12._____. They had succeeded in defeating the Incas.

B Read the passage above and answer the following questions.

_____ 13. What is this article's purpose?
- [a] To describe the fall of the Spanish Empire.
- [b] To describe early life in North America.
- [c] To describe the fall of the Aztecs and the Incas.
- [d] To describe Inca and Aztec culture.

_____ 14. Why was the Inca Empire so weak when the Spanish arrived in the Americas?
- [a] The Incas were at war with the Aztec Empire.
- [b] There had just been a civil war.
- [c] There had just been an earthquake.
- [d] There wasn't enough food to feed the Inca army.

_____ 15. "The Aztecs were very **warlike**." The word with the opposite meaning to "warlike" is _____.
- [a] direct
- [b] peaceful
- [c] heavy
- [d] ugly

A Listen to the passage and fill in the blanks.

🎧 127 **The *Mayflower***

In Britain, there was a group of people called 1._____. They were different from most people there. They had certain religious 2._____ that others did not share. So they wanted to leave Britain and go to the 3._____. They hired a ship called the *Mayflower* to take them to America.

They left in 1620 and landed in America after two months of sailing. They were supposed to go to the Hudson River area. But they landed at a place called 4._____. It was in modern-day Massachusetts on 5._____. Still, the Pilgrims decided to 6._____ there.

The first winter was hard. Many Pilgrims died. But the Native Americans there 7._____ them. Their leader was Samoset. He brought Squanto to stay with the Pilgrims. Squanto and other Native Americans taught the Pilgrims how to 8._____ the land properly. That year, the Pilgrims 9._____ many 10._____. They had a big three-day 11._____ with the Native Americans. That was the first Thanksgiving.

Every year, the Pilgrim colony became stronger and stronger. More 12._____ came from Britain. So the colony became very successful.

B Read the passage above and answer the following questions.

_____ 13. According to the article, where was the "New World"?
   a Britain.   b The Hudson River area.
   c America.   d Massachusetts.

_____ 14. This article is mainly about _____.
   a a ship called The *Mayflower*
   b a group of British people who moved to America
   c Native Americans who moved to America
   d the first Thanksgiving celebrated

_____ 15. Which of the following sentences is TRUE?
   a The pilgrims were supposed to travel to the Hudson River area.
   b The pilgrims decided to live in the Hudson River area.
   c The pilgrims originally wanted to live in Plymouth Rock.
   d The pilgrims wanted to sail to modern-day Cape Cod.

Unit 08

A Listen to the passage and fill in the blanks.

🎧 128

The French and Indian War Leads to Revolution

In the eighteenth century, countries in Europe often fought wars against each other. They usually fought in Europe. But sometimes they fought in other places. One of these other places was in America. In the 1750s and 1760s, the British and French fought a war in North America. Some people called it the 1._____. Others called it the Seven Years' War. Basically, the British and American colonists were 2._____. The French and Native Americans were on the other side.

The British won the war. So the French left most of North America. They had to give many of their 3._____ to the British. But the war was very expensive for the British. So King George III of Britain wanted to 4._____ taxes in the colonies. He said the British had 5._____ the colonies. So they should pay higher taxes.

The British 6._____ many taxes. These included the 7._____ and the 8._____. There were many others, though. The Americans hated the taxes and thought they were 9._____. They called them the 10._____. Eventually, Britain's actions 11._____ war in the colonies. The Americans 12._____. And then they gained their freedom from Britain.

B Read the passage above and answer the following questions.

_____ 13. This article is mainly about _____.
   a why Americans revolted against the British
   b tax increases in the United States
   c the war between the Indians and the French
   d the wars of the 18th century

_____ 14. According to the article, why did Britain increase the taxes for the British living in America?
   a Because they had lost the war.
   b Because they won the war.
   c Because they had protected the colonies.
   d Because they had more money.

_____ 15. "The Americans hated the taxes and thought they were **unfair**." A word that means the opposite of "unfair" is _____.
   a reasonable   b special   c cruel   d wrong

Unit 09

A Listen to the passage and fill in the blanks.

🎧 129　**The Roaring Twenties and the Great Depression**

In the 1920s, the American economy was very strong, and life was good. World War I had just ended. So people were interested in peace, not war. They had jobs and were making a lot of money. There were new technologies being created, and people could 1._____ to buy them. They began moving to the 2._____ and living in houses. People had 3._____ time, so they could go out and enjoy themselves.

Then, on October 24, 1929, the 4._____ crashed. Suddenly, life changed for millions of people. Instantly, people lost 5._____ of dollars in stock. Companies went 6._____. As they went out of business, millions of people lost their jobs. The 7._____ rate climbed. The president at the time, Herbert Hoover, was 8._____ for the economic problems. In 1932, Franklin Roosevelt was elected the new president of the United States.

Roosevelt had a plan to end the 9._____. His plan was called the 10._____. He increased the 11._____ of the government on the economy. He tried to have the government give people jobs. During the 1930s, life in the U.S. was very difficult. It was only when World War II began in 1941 that the Great Depression ended. Then, the U.S. economy began to 12._____.

B Read the passage above and answer the following questions.

_____ 13. Which of the following statements is TRUE?
   a The stock market crashed in the 1940's.
   b The Great Depression started in the fifties.
   c President Roosevelt was blamed for the Great Depression.
   d The economy was good after World War I.

_____ 14. What is the main point discussed in the article?
   a New technology changed the way people communicated.
   b President Herbert Hoover saved the economy from crashing.
   c The Great Depression was a difficult time for Americans.
   d Life for Americans was great after the economy was saved.

_____ 15. "The unemployment rate **climbed**." In this sentence, the word "climbed" means _____.
   a increased　　b went up a hill　　c lowered　　d remained the same

10

Unit 10

A Listen to the passage and fill in the blanks.

🎧 130 **The Cold War**

World War II lasted from 1939 to 1945. When it ended, another war immediately began. It was between the United States and the 1._____. But this was a different kind of war. It was called the 2._____. The U.S. was for freedom and 3._____. The Soviet Union was for 4._____ and 5._____. So they battled around the world in different places.

There were many events in the Cold War, but few involved actual fighting. The 6._____ of 1948 and 1949 was one incident. So was the 7._____ of the Berlin Wall in 1961. Of course, there were some wars. Both the Korean War and the 8._____ War were part of the Cold War since the U.S. and the Soviet Union both supported 9._____ sides. Even the Space Race in the 1950s and 1960s was part of the Cold War. And so was the nuclear race. Both countries had thousands of 10._____, but they never used them.

Eventually, the Cold War ended in the 1980s. Thanks to U.S. President Ronald Reagan, the Soviet Union began to 11._____. In 1989, the Berlin Wall 12._____. The countries of Eastern Europe started becoming free. And, in 1991, the Soviet Union ended. The Cold War was over.

B Read the passage above and answer the following questions.

_____ 13. "The Berlin Blockage of 1948 and 1949 was one **incident**." A similar word to "incident" is _____.
    a accident   b event   c celebration   d problem

_____ 14. "There were many events of the Cold War, but few involved **actual** fighting." In this sentence, "actual" means _____.
    a dangerous   b fair   c factual   d real

_____ 15. What is the main purpose of this article?
    a It took many people to tear down the Berlin Wall.
    b The Cold War was a long war with many events.
    c The U.S and the Soviet Union supported the same sides.
    d The Cold War ended in the 1950s.

Unit 11

 131   **Kingdoms**

There are many organic creatures on Earth. Some are very different from others. But many have some similarities. So scientists have 1._____ organisms into five separate 2._____. These kingdoms are animals, plants, 3._____, 4._____, and 5._____. All of the creatures in each kingdom are similar in some way.

The animal kingdom is the biggest. It has over 800,000 6._____. Most animals are either 7._____ or 8._____. Animals include mammals, reptiles, birds, amphibians, and insects.

The second largest kingdom is the plant kingdom. Plants include trees, bushes, flowers, vines, and grasses. The third kingdom is the protists. They are animals that have only one 9._____. They include 10._____, algae, and diatoms. The fourth kingdom is the fungi. Most fungi are mushrooms. But there are also certain 11._____, yeasts, and lichen, too. The final kingdom is the bacteria. These are some kinds of bacteria and various 12._____, such as viruses.

B Read the passage above and answer the following questions.

_____ 13. Which of the following sentences is TRUE?
   a Protists like algae have multiple cells.
   b Most animals are vertebrates or invertebrates.
   c The largest kingdom is the plant kingdom.
   d Bacteria, molds, and viruses are types of fungi.

_____ 14. Which sentence is closest to the main idea of the article?
   a Organisms belong to one of five kingdoms.
   b The largest kingdom is the animal kingdom.
   c All the creatures in each kingdom are similar.
   d There are many different creatures on Earth.

_____ 15. "All of the **creatures** in each kingdom are similar in some way." The word "creatures" has a similar meaning to _____.
   a plants   b living things   c cells   d mammals

Unit 12

A Listen to the passage and fill in the blanks.

🎧 132 **Roots, Stems, and Leaves**

Plants are made up of many parts. Three of the most important are their roots, stems, and leaves. All three of them have various 1._____.

The roots are found at the bottom of the plant. Roots grow 2._____. They help 3._____ the plant to the ground. This keeps the plant from being 4._____ by rain or blown away by the wind. Also, a plant's roots help it 5._____ nutrients from the ground. These nutrients include water and various minerals.

The stems have several important responsibilities. First, they move water and 6._____ from the roots to the leaves. They also store some nutrients and water if the plant has too much of them. And they 7._____ food, such as sap, down from the leaves to the roots. Finally, they provide 8._____ for the leaves.

The leaves have a very important role. They contain 9._____. These let 10._____ take place. Because of this, plants can create sugar, which they use for food. And they also take 11._____ and turn it into 12._____. This lets all of the other animals on Earth breathe.

B Read the passage above and answer the following questions.

_____ 13. Which statement below best expresses the main idea of this article?
  a Plants were the earliest life on Earth.
  b Plants are made up of three important parts.
  c Plants need sunlight to survive.
  d Plants turn carbon dioxide into oxygen.

_____ 14. Which of the following allows plants to create sugar that is used for food?
  a Roots.   b Photosynthesis.
  c Nutrients.   d Oxygen.

_____ 15. The leaves of a plant take carbon dioxide and turn it into _____.
  a sugar   b water
  c nutrients   d oxygen

13

Unit 13

A Listen to the passage and fill in the blanks.

🎧 133 **Sexual and Asexual Reproduction**

All plants need to 1._____ in order to create new plants. There are two ways they can reproduce. The first is 2._____. The second is 3._____.

Sexual reproduction involves a male and female of the same species. Plants that reproduce this way have flowers. Flowers are where their 4._____ organs and seeds are. The male reproductive organ is the 5._____. It has 6._____ that needs to be carried to the female part of the plant. The female part is the 7._____. When the pollen gets 8._____, the plant has been 9._____. This causes seeds to grow in the flower. Soon, the seeds 10._____, which means they are growing into young plants.

The second method is asexual reproduction. In this method, there is only one 11._____ plant. Asexual reproduction can happen in many ways. For example, a new plant may simply start growing from an old plant. Other plants reproduce from 12._____. Onions and potatoes are both bulbs. Parts of these plants can simply begin growing roots, and thus they become new plants. In the case of asexual reproduction, there is no pollen, and there are no male and female plants. New plants simply grow from old ones.

B Read the passage above and answer the following questions.

_____ 13. The male reproductive part of a plant is called a _____.

     a stamen   b pistil   c seed   d bulb

_____ 14. This passage is mostly about _____.

     a sex organs in plants
     b two types of reproduction in plants
     c how potatoes and onions grow
     d the germination process

_____ 15. In the case of asexual reproduction, new plants _____.

     a germinate from pollen   b sprout from seeds
     c grow from old plants   d develop pistils

A Listen to the passage and fill in the blanks.

🎧 134 | **Pollination and Fertilization**

Plants that reproduce 1._____ have both male and female parts. A plant must be 2._____ in order to reproduce. Pollen from the 3._____ – the male part – must reach the 4._____ – the female part. There are two major ways this happens. The first is the wind. Sometimes, the wind carries pollen from one plant to another. However, this is not a very effective method.

Fortunately, many animals help pollinate plants. Usually, the animals are insects, such as bees and butterflies. Plants' flowers often produce 5._____, which insects like. As the insects collect a plant's nectar, they 6._____ pollen. As the insects go from plant to plant, the pollen on them 7._____ the pistils of other plants. This pollinates the plants.

Now that the pollen has been transferred, the plant must be 8._____. The 9._____ of a plant has a pollen 10._____. At least one grain of pollen must go down that tube. This is not easy because the tube is so small, so plants often need many grains of pollen to ensure that one will go down the tube. Once that happens, then the male and female cells can 11._____. This results in the 12._____ of the plant. And it can now reproduce.

B Read the passage above and answer the following questions.

_____ 13. According to the article, the most effective way for a plant to be pollinated is with the help of _____.
a the wind   b gardeners   c itself   d animals

_____ 14. What is the main idea of the article?
a Without animals like insects, there would be no plants.
b People should help plants become pollinated.
c Plants need to be pollinated and fertilized to reproduce.
d Plant reproduction is difficult and takes a long time.

_____ 15. "Now that the pollen has been **transferred**, the plant must be fertilized."
In this sentence, the word "transferred" means _____.
a reassigned   b turned over   c removed   d relocated

Unit 15

Listen to the passage and fill in the blanks.

🎧 135 | **Tropisms**

People know that animals often 1._____ to their environment. This is called 2._____. It can take place over a very long time. And it can change animals very much. Plants can also adapt. Their adaptations are called 3._____.

Tropisms are the reactions of plants to external 4._____. These stimuli can be light, 5._____, or 6._____. Tropisms are 7._____, but they help plants survive.

Plants need light in order to live. Without light, they cannot 8._____ 9._____. So plants will always grow toward light. If they are in shadows or dark places, they will bend toward the light that they need to survive.

The same is true of moisture. Without water, plants will die. Plants' roots will grow toward the parts of the ground that have moisture. Plants' leaves will adapt so that they can 10._____ as much moisture as possible.

Gravity is another force which causes tropisms. Stems will always move against gravity. This means that they will move in an 11._____ direction. However, roots move with gravity. This means that they move 12._____.

B **Read the passage above and answer the following questions.**

_____ 13. Evolution is when animals _____ to their environments.
- a move
- b adapt
- c walk
- d bend

_____ 14. "Tropisms are **involuntary**, but they help plants survive." A word that has a similar meaning to "involuntary" is _____.
- a automatic
- b controlled
- c regular
- d forced

_____ 15. Another good title for this article is _____.
- a How Plants Survive
- b The Survival of Plants and Animals
- c Time for Evolution
- d Moving Toward the Light

Unit 16

Listen to the passage and fill in the blanks.

🎧 136 **The Development of a Baby**

When a woman becomes 1._____, a baby starts to grow in her body. For the next nine months, she will have another life inside her. Until the baby is born, the baby is called a 2._____. The fetus 3._____ several 4._____ of development over nine months.

At first, the new life is just an 5._____. It starts growing 6._____ and becoming larger. After three weeks, the body's 7._____ begin to develop, and it takes a human 8._____. After two months, most of the organs are completely developed. Only the 9._____ and 10._____ are not.

In the ninth week, the embryo is now said to be a fetus. The fetus starts to develop more quickly now. By week fourteen, doctors can determine if it is a male or a female. And after about four or five months of 11._____, the mother can feel her baby moving around inside her. By the sixth month, the fetus is able to survive outside the 12._____. The fetus still needs about three more months to develop inside the mother. Finally, during the ninth month, most babies are born.

B Read the passage above and answer the following questions.

_____ 13. What is the subject of the article?
- a How a woman's body changes during pregnancy.
- b How a baby develops during pregnancy.
- c How women need to stay healthy during pregnancy.
- d How a woman becomes pregnant with a baby.

_____ 14. "By week fourteen, doctors can **determine** if it is a male or a female."
Another way to say "determine" is _____.
- a find out
- b diagnose
- c prescribe
- d test

_____ 15. Which of the following statements is TRUE?
- a Most of a baby's organs are formed after two months.
- b A baby's spine and brain have developed by the first month.
- c All babies are born in the ninth month of pregnancy.
- d A woman can feel her baby move inside her after three weeks.

Unit 17

A Listen to the passage and fill in the blanks.

🎧 137 | **How Ecosystems Change**

Many ecosystems are 1._____ communities that are full of life. However, many of them were once empty and were 2._____ lands. But they changed to become places with many kinds of organisms.

The first step is called 3._____. This happens in a place that has never had life on it. Soil must be made first. Then 4._____ come to the land. These are 5._____ organisms like 6._____ and mosses. Over time, the soil starts to be able to support more complicated organisms. These are various grasses. Once there is some minor 7._____, animals like insects and birds move in. Eventually, bushes and trees start to grow. Finally, even larger animals move in to the land.

Eventually, the ecosystem will grow enough that a 8._____ will be formed. This means that the ecosystem is fairly 9._____. The ecosystem will not change anymore unless something from outside 10._____ it. It could be an 11._____. Or it could be a 12._____. But unless something affects the ecosystem, it will never change.

B Read the passage above and answer the following questions.

_____ 13. What is the main idea of the article?
  a New ecosystems develop over time in stages.
  b Many ecosystems were once empty, barren lands.
  c The first stage of ecosystem growth is primary succession.
  d Most ecosystems in the world are fairly stable.

_____ 14. "Then **pioneer species** come to the land." In this sentence, what does "pioneer species" mean?
  a The first species to arrive and grow in a certain location.
  b Strong, healthy plants that grow in a new location.
  c Large plants growing in an ecosystem for the first time.
  d Plants from other countries grown for food.

_____ 15. "Many ecosystems are **thriving** communities that are full of life." A word that means the opposite of "thriving" is _____.
  a living   b old   c failing   d dangerous

18

A Listen to the passage and fill in the blanks.

🎧 138 | **Earthquakes**

Sometimes, the ground suddenly begins to 1._____. Buildings and bridges move 2._____. They might even fall down. Places in the ground begin to 3._____. This is an 4._____. Earthquakes happen all the time all around the earth. Most of the time, they are so small that we cannot even feel them. But sometimes there are very large earthquakes. These can cause great 5._____, kill many people, and even change the way the earth looks.

The earth's 6._____ is its top part. The crust is formed of many 7._____. These are called 8._____ plates. There are seven large plates and around twelve smaller ones. These plates are enormous. But they also move really slowly. Sometimes they move back and forth against each other. This causes earthquakes.

The 9._____ scale measures the power of earthquakes. A level 2 10._____ is ten times as powerful as a level 1 quake. For each whole number increase, the power of the earthquake increases 11._____. Levels 1 to 4 are weak earthquakes. Level 5 earthquakes can cause some damage. Levels 6 and 7 can be dangerous. Levels 8 and 9 can cause huge amounts of death and 12._____.

B Read the passage above and answer the following questions.

_____ 13. Which of the following sentences is TRUE?
   a Tectonic plates can move very quickly.
   b There are a total of 17 tectonic plates.
   c Some earthquakes are so small that they can't be felt.
   d Level-one earthquakes can destroy buildings.

_____ 14. According to the article, what causes earthquakes?
   a The levels of the Richter scale.   b Plates moving against each other.
   c The thickness of Earth's crust.   d Too many buildings and bridges.

_____ 15. What is this article mainly about?
   a The causes and measurement of earthquakes.
   b The Richter scale levels of earthquakes.
   c The types of destruction caused by earthquakes.
   d The power of earthquakes around the world.

A **Listen to the passage and fill in the blanks.**

🎧 139 **Elements**

The entire universe is made of 1._____. And matter is made of either individual 2._____ or 3._____. Compounds are combinations of two or more elements. What is an element? It is matter made of only one type of 4._____. There are 117 elements. Most are natural. So they appear in nature. But scientists have made a few elements. They only appear in 5._____.

All elements have a similar structure. They have a 6._____. This is the element's core. Inside the nucleus are 7._____ and 8._____. Elements have different numbers of them. For example, hydrogen has 1 proton and 0 neutrons. Helium has 2 protons and 2 neutrons. Oxygen has 8 protons and 8 neutrons. Gold has 79 protons and 118 neutrons.

Outside the nucleus are 9._____. They 10._____ the nucleus. Electrons have 11._____ charges. But protons have 12._____ charges. Also, an element usually has the same number of protons and electrons. But they can sometimes be different.

B **Read the passage above and answer the following questions.**

_____ 13. "Outside the nucleus are electrons. They **orbit** the nucleus." The word "orbit" is similar in meaning to _____.
   a circle   b protect   c feed   d attack

_____ 14. This article is mainly about _____.
   a the characteristics of elements
   b the number of elements
   c the invention of elements
   d the discovery of elements

_____ 15. Which of the following statements is FALSE?
   a Electrons have negative charges.
   b All elements have an atom.
   c There are more than 1,000 elements.
   d Most elements are natural.

Unit 20

A Listen to the passage and fill in the blanks.

 140

Are We Alone?

For thousands of years, men have looked at the stars and asked, "Are we alone?" Men are 1._____ by the stars and the possibility of there being life on other 2._____. Myths in many cultures tell stories about 3._____ coming to Earth. But no one knows if there really are aliens or not.

Nowadays, scientists are searching for life on other planets. Some believe there could be life on 4._____. Others think the 5._____ Europa or Io could have life. And others are looking at other star systems. They are trying to find 6._____ planets.

What does life need to survive on other planets? Life on Earth is all 7._____ based. That kind of life needs a 8._____ to provide heat and light. It needs an 9._____ with 10._____. It needs water.

Of course, other forms of life could be 11._____ different elements. We don't know what they would need to survive. But we do know one thing: Men will continue looking for 12._____ life until we find it.

B Read the passage above and answer the following questions.

_____ 13. What is the main idea of this article?
  a Scientists are searching for life on other planets.
  b Scientists are looking for stories about aliens.
  c Scientists are trying to prove only Earth has life.
  d Scientists are afraid that we are not alone.

_____ 14. Which of the following statements is TRUE?
  a There is definitely life on other planets.
  b All scientists believe there are aliens.
  c Women aren't interested in extraterrestrial life.
  d Some people believe there could be life on Mars.

_____ 15. "Life on Earth is all carbon **based**." A word with a similar meaning to "based" as it is used in this sentence is _____.
  a rooted   b researched   c examined   d fed

Unit 21

A **Listen to the passage and fill in the blanks.**

🎧 141 | **Roman Numerals**

We count with numbers today. The 1._____ we use is very easy. But not every culture has counted the same way. Many systems are different. In ancient Rome, the Romans used 2._____. But these were not actually numerals. Instead, they were 3._____.

The Romans used the letters I, V, X, L, C, D, and M to 4._____ certain 5._____. For example, I was 1, V was 5, X was 10, L was 50, C was 100, D was 500, and M was 1,000. To make larger numbers, they just 6._____ more letters. So 2 was II, and 3 was III. 6 was VI, and 7 was VII. However, the number 4 was not IIII. Instead, it was IV. Why did they do that? When a letter was going to change to one with a greater 7._____, the Romans put the smaller letter in front of the bigger letter. That meant they should 8._____ that 9._____, not add to it. So 9 was IX. 40 was XL. 90 was XC. And 900 was CM.

Doing that was not difficult. But Romans could not count very high since it was hard to write large numbers. For example, what was 3,867? In Roman numerals, it was MMMDCCCLXVII. How about doing 10._____, subtraction, 11._____, or division? Can you imagine 12._____ MMCCXII by CCLXIV?

B **Read the passage above and answer the following questions.**

_____ 13. According to the passage, which of the following statements is TRUE?
   a Roman numbers are actually letters instead of numerals.
   b The Romans invented multiplication, division, addition, and subtraction.
   c People nowadays use Roman numerals to calculate difficult math problems.
   d It isn't difficult to write large numbers such as 3,867 using Roman numerals.

_____ 14. What is this article mainly about?
   a How the Romans developed Roman numerals.
   b How the decimal system became more popular than Roman numerals.
   c How the Roman numeral system works.
   d How most people use Roman numerals to solve math problems.

_____ 15. "The Romans used the letters I, V, X, L, C, D, and M to **stand for** certain quantities." Another way to say "stand for" is _____.
   a represent   b replace   c remind   d request

Unit 22

142

A Listen to the passage and fill in the blanks.

The Order of Operations

In math, some problems are easy to 1._____. For example, this problem: 2+3=5. That is a simple problem. But sometimes there are more 2._____ problems. For example, how about this problem: 2+3×4? How do you solve this? Do you do the 3._____ or the multiplication first? Is the answer 14 or 20?

In math, there is something called the 4._____. These tell the order in which you should solve a math problem. There are three simple 5._____: 1) Do the 6._____ inside 7._____ first. 2) Moving from 8._____, solve all multiplication and 9._____ problems first. 3) Moving from left to right, solve all addition and 10._____ problems next.

Let's look at the problem above one more time: 2+3×4. How do we solve it? First, we must 11._____ 3×4. That's 12. Then we add 2+12. That's 14. So the correct answer is 14.

How about a more complicated problem? Look at this problem: 3×(3+4)−1. First, we must solve the problem in parentheses. So 3+4 is 7. Next, we do the 12._____ problem. So 3×7 is 21. Last, we do the subtraction problem. So 21−1 is 20. The answer is 20.

B Read the passage above and answer the following questions.

_____ 13. Which of the following sentences about complicated math problems is TRUE?
- a From right to left, solve the division and multiplication problems.
- b Always solve subtraction problems before division problems.
- c Complete the calculations found in parentheses first.
- d From left to right, solve the addition problems before multiplication.

_____ 14. "But sometimes there are more **complicated** problems." A word with a similar meaning to "complicated" is _____.
- a impossible
- b simple
- c frustrating
- d complex

_____ 15. This article is mainly about _____.
- a tricks to help you multiply quickly
- b completing problems in parentheses
- c creating difficult math problems
- d solving complicated math problems

23

A Listen to the passage and fill in the blanks.

🎧 143 | **Percentages, Ratios, and Probabilities**

The weatherman may say, "There is a 70% 1._____ of rain." He is telling you the 2._____ of rain. At 70%, this means that, in the current weather conditions, it will rain 70 times 3._____ 100. Weather forecasts often use 4._____. So do sports. An announcer may say, "The basketball player shoots 52%." This means that for every 100 shots he takes, he 5._____ 52.

Ratios are a way to 6._____ two things to one another. For example, a classroom has 20 children. There are 12 boys and 8 girls. You can say, "The 7._____ of boys to girls is 12 to 8." Or you can write the ratio 8._____ 12:8 or $\frac{12}{8}$. Perhaps there are 5 cats and 8 dogs. You can say the ratio of cats to dogs is 5 to 8, 5:8, or $\frac{5}{8}$. All three ways express ratios.

Probability expresses the 9._____, or chances, of something happening. If you 10._____ a coin, there is a 1 in 2 chance of a certain side showing because a coin has two sides. If you roll a 11._____, there is a 1 in 6 chance of the number 4 appearing. Perhaps there are 10 cookies. Three are oatmeal cookies. If you grab one cookie at 12._____, there is a 3 in 10 chance you will get an oatmeal cookie.

B Read the passage above and answer the following questions.

_____ 13. According to the article, percentages are often used for _____.
- [a] describing ratios
- [b] comparing boys and girls
- [c] describing weather
- [d] comparing dogs and cats

_____ 14. "Probability **expresses** the odds, or chances, of something happening."
The word "expresses" is similar in meaning to _____.
- [a] states
- [b] speeds
- [c] guesses
- [d] prepares

_____ 15. According to the article, probability can be expressed in _____.
- [a] ratios and percentages
- [b] probability and ratios
- [c] odds and ratios
- [d] percentages and chances

Unit 24

Listen to the passage and fill in the blanks.

🎧 144 | **Solid Figures in Real Life**

Solid figures include cubes, 1._____, 2._____, 3._____, cones, and spheres. Everywhere you look, you can see solid figures. Many buildings are 4._____ prisms. A door is one, too. So are the 5._____ board in your classroom and this book you are reading right now.

Pyramids are not very common. But some of them are really famous. Think about Egypt for a minute. What comes to 6._____? The pyramids, right? There are huge pyramids all over Egypt.

Cones are among people's favorite 7._____. Why is that? The reason is that ice cream cones are solid figures. There are often many cones in areas where there is road 8._____, too. Construction workers put 9._____ on the street to show people where they can and cannot drive.

Of course, 10._____ are everywhere. People would not be able to play most sports without them. They need 11._____ balls, baseballs, basketballs, tennis balls, and many other spheres. Oranges, grapefruit, peaches, plums, and cherries are fruits that are 12._____ like spheres, too.

B Read the passage above and answer the following questions.

_____ 13. What is the main point discussed in the passage?
- a Shapes are things that have no practical purpose.
- b Shapes are things that mathematicians have yet to figure out.
- c Shapes are things we only read about in books.
- d Shapes are things we encounter in the real world.

_____ 14. According to the passage, among all the solid figures, which one is people's favorite?
- a Cones.   b Pyramids.   c Spheres.   d Prisms.

_____ 15. "There are often many cones in areas where there is road **construction**, too." Which of the follow means almost the same as "construction"?
- a Direction.   b Block.   c Development.   d Broadcast.

Unit 25

Listen to the passage and fill in the blanks.

🎧 145 | **The *Iliad* and the *Odyssey***

Two of the greatest works of literature are also very old. They are the 1._____ poems the 2._____ and the 3._____. Both were told by 4._____ and tell stories about the ancient Greeks.

The *Iliad* is about the 5._____. Paris 6._____ Helen and took her to Troy. Helen was the most beautiful woman in the world. So all of the Greeks joined together to fight the Trojans. There were many great Greek warriors. There were Agamemnon, Menelaus, 7._____, and Ajax. But 8._____ was the greatest warrior of all. The war lasted for ten years. Many people died. Finally, thanks to Odysseus, the Greeks used the 9._____ to win. The Greeks pretended to leave. They left behind a giant horse. The Trojans took the horse into their city. But many Greek warriors were hiding inside it. At night, the Greeks came out of the horse. Inside the city, they managed to capture and defeat Troy.

The *Odyssey* tells the tale of Odysseus's return home after the war. It took him ten years to get home. He had many strange 10._____. He had to fight a fearsome 11._____. He met 12._____ women like Circe and Calypso. And all of his men died. Finally, though, with help from the gods, Odysseus arrived home.

Read the passage above and answer the following questions.

_____ 13. Another good title for this article is _____.
    a Two Important Poems by Homer   b The Greatest Warrior of All Time
    c How the Greeks Defeated Troy   d Odysseus's Journey Home

_____ 14. "Paris **abducted** Helen and took her to Troy." A word with a similar meaning to "abducted" is _____.
    a punished   b injured   c fooled   d kidnapped

_____ 15. According to the article, which of the following sentences is TRUE?
    a The *Iliad* is about Odysseus's return home.
    b The Trojan War lasted a total of 20 years.
    c Achilles was the greatest warrior of all.
    d Odysseus had to fight Circe and Calypso.

Unit 26

A **Listen to the passage and fill in the blanks.**

🎧 146 | **Figures of Speech**

Writers can be 1._____. To do this, they can use 2._____.
There are many of these. Four are 3._____, 4._____, 5._____,
and 6._____.

Similes and metaphors are both 7._____. But they are not the same. Similes
use "as" or "like" to compare two things. For example, "strong as an ox" and "dark
like night" are similes. Metaphors are comparisons between two unlike things that
seem to have nothing 8._____. "The stars are diamonds in the sky" and
"There is a sea of sand" are metaphors.

Hyperbole is also a figure of speech. It is a form of 9._____. People
often 10._____ when they speak or write. For instance, "There were a
million people in the store" is hyperbole. "I worked all day and all night" is, too.

Finally, people often give objects and animals human 11._____. This
is personification. "The wind is 12._____" is one example. So is "My dog
is speaking to me." The wind and a dog are not humans. But in both cases, they
have human characteristics. So they are examples of personification.

B **Read the passage above and answer the following questions.**

_____ 13. What is the main idea of the article?

     a Writers use comparisons when writing creatively.

     b Writers typically use metaphors and personification.

     c Writers should always use figures of speech in their writing.

     d Writers can use figures of speech when writing creatively.

_____ 14. "The stars are diamonds in the sky" is an example of the use of _____.

     a metaphor   b hyperbole   c simile   d exaggeration

_____ 15. Which of the following statements is TRUE?

     a Personification gives animals and objects human characteristics.

     b Metaphors are comparisons between two things that are alike.

     c Hyperbole compares two things without using "like" or "as."

     d Similes are exaggerations people use when they speak or write.

Unit 27

Listen to the passage and fill in the blanks.

🎧 147 | **Common Mistakes in English**

Writing in English is not easy. There are many 1._____. So you have to be very careful. Two common mistakes are 2._____ and 3._____.

A sentence fragment is an 4._____ sentence. A sentence must always have a 5._____ and a 6._____. Look at the following sentence fragments:

attends the school   My father, who is a doctor

Neither of these is 7._____. The first fragment needs a subject. The second fragment needs a verb. Make them complete sentences like this: "Jane attends the school." "My father, who is a doctor, is home now."

Comma splices are also common mistakes. These are sentences that use a comma to connect two 8._____ 9._____. Look at the following comma splices:

My brother studies hard, he's a good student.   I'm sorry, it was an accident.

Neither of these is correct. The first sentence either needs a 10._____ or the word 11._____: "My brother studies hard because he's a good student." The second sentence needs a period, not a 12._____: "I'm sorry. It was an accident."

B **Read the passage above and answer the following questions.**

_____ 13. What is closest to the main point the author wants to make?
- a Comma splices are when two clauses are separated by a comma.
- b Comma splices and sentence fragments are two common errors.
- c Sentence fragments are when a sentence is missing something.
- d English is one of the hardest languages in the world to learn.

_____ 14. According to the article, a sentence fragment is _____.
- a a sentence asking a question
- b an important sentence
- c a sentence with five words
- d an incomplete sentence

_____ 15. "There are many **grammar** rules." The word "grammar" means _____.
- a a set of rules for how to draw properly
- b a set of rules for how to study history
- c a set of rules for how to make sentences
- d a set of rules for how to dress

Unit 28

A Listen to the passage and fill in the blanks.

🎧 148

Renaissance Artists

During the 1._____, there were many brilliant artists. These included Raphael, Botticelli, Giotto, and Donatello. But two are considered greater than the others. One is 2._____ da Vinci. The other is 3._____ Buonarroti.

Leonardo da Vinci was a true Renaissance man. He could do many things well. He was an engineer and scientist. He was an inventor, 4._____, and artist. He was one of the greatest men in history. As an artist, he painted one of the world's most famous pictures: the *Mona Lisa*. Another famous painting is *The Last 5._____*. It shows Jesus and his 6._____ together. Leonardo made many other famous works. But those two are the most well known.

Michelangelo was an incredible 7._____. He created two of the most famous 8._____ of all time. The first was *David*. The second was *Pietà*. Pietà is a 9._____ of Mary holding the body of Jesus after he died. Michelangelo was also a great painter. He painted the 10._____ on the 11._____ of the Sistine 12._____. The most famous of these frescoes is the *Creation of Adam*. It shows God and Adam reaching out to one another.

B Read the passage above and answer the following questions.

_____ 13. What is the main idea of the article?
- [a] Michelangelo and Leonardo da Vinci are two of the greatest Renaissance artists.
- [b] There weren't many great sculptors and painters during the Renaissance period.
- [c] Most people prefer the art of Michelangelo to that of Leonardo da Vinci.
- [d] *The Last Supper* and the *Mona Lisa* are the best paintings in history.

_____ 14. "During the Renaissance, there were many **brilliant** artists." A word with a similar meaning to "brilliant" is _____.
- [a] focused　　[b] sparkling　　[c] talented　　[d] hardworking

_____ 15. According to the article, Leonardo da Vinci was not just an artist; he was also _____.
- [a] a teacher, a traveler, and a public speaker
- [b] an engineer, scientist, inventor, and architect
- [c] a Renaissance man and a skilled doctor
- [d] a good friend and colleague of Michelangelo

Unit 29

Listen to the passage and fill in the blanks.

 149 | **Nineteenth Century American Landscapes**

In the nineteenth century, much of America was not settled. So there were few cities. Not many people lived in the countryside. So there were many beautiful places for artists to paint 1._____.

One group of landscape artists was called the 2._____.
The Hudson River flows through New York. These artists painted the land in this area. Much of it was forest. But there were also farms, 3._____, and many mountains. Thomas Cole was the first Hudson River School artist. Frederic Edwin Church and Asher Durand were two others. The Hudson River School artists were 4._____. So they 5._____ the landscapes they painted. They painted the 6._____ the way they wanted the land to look, not the way that it actually looked.

Around the same time, there was another 7._____ of artists. They were called 8._____, or 9._____. They painted nature as it 10._____.
William Bliss Baker was one of these artists. He also painted in the Hudson River area. But his paintings look very different from the Hudson River School artists' paintings. Baker's works are 11._____. His painting *Fallen* 12._____ is one of the most beautiful of the Naturalist paintings.

B **Read the passage above and answer the following questions.**

_____ 13. Hudson River School artists were considered to be _____.
      a Realists   b Modernists   c Romantics   d Naturalists

_____ 14. This article is mainly about _____.
      a two types of American painters in the nineteenth century
      b Naturalists and Realists from the Hudson River area
      c students attending two art schools in nineteenth-century America
      d the natural beauty of America before it was settled

_____ 15. "Around the same time, there was another **school** of artists." In this sentence, the word "school" means _____.
      a college   b group   c location   d education

Unit 30

A Listen to the passage and fill in the blanks.

🎧 150 **Spirituals**

Music is often 1._____ with religion. In Christianity, there are many kinds of songs people sing. There are 2._____, carols, 3._____, and others. Another type of music is the 4._____.

Spirituals were first written in the eighteenth century in the United States. They were written because there was a 5._____ of interest in religion in the U.S. then. Spirituals were often very inspiring songs. They were about stories and 6._____ from the Bible. In style, they were a kind of 7._____ music or folk hymn.

Spirituals were often sung by black Americans. Yet there were also many white spirituals, too. Many of the blacks who made these spirituals were 8._____ from Africa. So spirituals had a strong African 9._____. They later combined with European and American influences. The result was spirituals.

Nowadays, spiritual music is called 10._____ music. It is a form of music that is very 11._____. All kinds of people sing and listen to gospel music. It inspires people and gives them 12._____ as well.

B Read the passage above and answer the following questions.

_____ 13. What is the main idea of this passage?
- a Only African people can sing spirituals.
- b Spirituals are inspiring religious songs.
- c The United States is a very religious country.
- d In the Bible, there are many hymns and carols.

_____ 14. "They were written because there was a **revival** of interest in religion in the U.S. then." A "revival" of interest in an idea means that it _____.
- a is popular with children
- b becomes popular again
- c has never been popular
- d is less popular than before

_____ 15. What were the first spirituals about?
- a Churches in the United States.
- b The end of slavery in Africa.
- c Stories and themes from the Bible.
- d The lives of ordinary black people.

Unit 01

1 Constitution 2 supreme 3 amendments 4 Bill of Rights
5 ratified 6 freedom 7 religion 8 press 9 arrests
10 speedy trial 11 jury trial 12 high bail 13 c 14 a 15 d

Unit 02

1 parties 2 Republican Party 3 Democratic Party
4 running 5 nominee 6 raise 7 primary 8 caucus
9 delegates 10 candidates 11 conventions 12 voters
13 a 14 b 15 c

Unit 03

1 concerned 2 interpret 3 occur 4 sources
5 primary sources 6 recorded 7 journals 8 videotaped
9 eyewitnesses 10 secondary sources 11 political
12 focus on 13 a 14 c 15 b

Unit 04

1 tribes 2 disappeared 3 centuries 4 Southwest
5 impressive 6 pottery 7 defeated 8 disease
9 archaeologists 10 drought 11 artifacts 12 ruins
13 c 14 b 15 a

Unit 05

1 capital 2 route 3 purchased 4 Age of Exploration
5 sailing 6 Portuguese 7 Cape of Good Hope
8 southernmost 9 discovered 10 landed 11 set sail
12 crew 13 d 14 d 15 b

Unit 06

1 Spanish 2 modern-day 3 warlike 4 conquered
5 weapons 6 invaded 7 allied 8 marched 9 captured
10 weak 11 emperor 12 throne 13 c 14 b 15 b

Unit 07

1 Pilgrims 2 beliefs 3 New World 4 Plymouth Rock
5 Cape Cod 6 settle 7 made peace with 8 farm
9 harvested 10 crops 11 festival 12 colonists
13 c 14 b 15 a

Unit 08

1 French and Indian War 2 on one side 3 colonies
4 raise 5 protected 6 passed 7 Stamp Act 8 Tea Act
9 unfair 10 Intolerable Acts 11 led to 12 revolted
13 a 14 c 15 a

Unit 09

1 afford 2 suburbs 3 leisure 4 stock market 5 billions
6 bankrupt 7 unemployment 8 blamed
9 Great Depression 10 New Deal 11 influence
12 recover 13 d 14 c 15 a

Unit 10

1 Soviet Union 2 Cold War 3 democracy 4 tyranny
5 communism 6 Berlin Blockade 7 construction
8 Vietnam 9 opposite 10 nuclear weapons 11 collapse
12 came down 13 b 14 d 15 b

Unit 11

1 divided 2 kingdoms 3 protists 4 fungi 5 bacteria
6 species 7 vertebrates 8 invertebrates 9 cell
10 protozoans 11 molds 12 pathogens 13 b 14 a 15 b

Unit 12

1 functions 2 underground 3 anchor 4 washed away
5 extract 6 nutrients 7 transport 8 support
9 chloroplasts 10 photosynthesis 11 carbon dioxide
12 oxygen 13 b 14 b 15 d

Unit 13

1 reproduce 2 sexual reproduction 3 asexual reproduction
4 reproductive 5 stamen 6 pollen 7 pistil 8 transferred
9 pollinated 10 germinate 11 parent 12 bulbs 13 a
14 b 15 c

Unit 14

1 sexually 2 pollinated 3 stamen 4 pistil 5 nectar
6 pick up 7 rubs off on 8 fertilized 9 stigma 10 tube
11 unite 12 fertilization 13 d 14 c 15 d

Unit 15

1 adapt 2 evolution 3 tropisms 4 stimuli 5 moisture
6 gravity 7 involuntary 8 undergo 9 photosynthesis
10 trap 11 upward 12 downward 13 b 14 a 15 a

Unit 16

1 pregnant 2 fetus 3 goes through 4 stages 5 embryo
6 cells 7 organs 8 shape 9 brain 10 spinal cord
11 pregnancy 12 womb 13 b 14 a 15 a

Unit 17

1 thriving 2 barren 3 primary succession
4 pioneer species 5 low-level 6 lichens 7 vegetation
8 climax community 9 stable 10 affects
11 invasive species 12 natural disaster 13 a 14 a 15 c

Unit 18

1 shake 2 back and forth 3 crack 4 earthquake
5 damage 6 crust 7 plates 8 tectonic 9 Richter
10 quake 11 by ten 12 destruction 13 c 14 b 15 a

Unit 19

1 matter 2 elements 3 compounds 4 atom 5 labs
6 nucleus 7 protons 8 neutrons 9 electrons 10 orbit
11 negative 12 positive 13 a 14 a 15 c

Unit 20

1 fascinated 2 planets 3 aliens 4 Mars 5 moons
6 Earth-like 7 carbon 8 star 9 atmosphere 10 oxygen
11 based on 12 extraterrestrial 13 a 14 d 15 a

Unit 21

1 decimal system 2 Roman numerals 3 letters
4 stand for 5 quantities 6 added 7 value 8 subtract
9 amount 10 addition 11 multiplication 12 dividing
13 a 14 c 15 a

Unit 22

1 solve 2 complicated 3 addition 4 order of operations
5 rules 6 calculations 7 parentheses 8 left to right
9 division 10 subtraction 11 multiply 12 multiplication
13 c 14 d 15 d

Unit 23

1 chance 2 probability 3 out of 4 percentages
5 makes 6 compare 7 ratio 8 as 9 odds 10 flip
11 die 12 random 13 c 14 a 15 d

Unit 24

1 prisms 2 pyramids 3 cylinders 4 rectangular 5 bulletin
6 mind 7 solid figures 8 construction 9 traffic cones
10 spheres 11 soccer 12 shaped 13 d 14 a 15 c

Unit 25

1 epic 2 *Iliad* 3 *Odyssey* 4 Homer 5 Trojan War
6 abducted 7 Odysseus 8 Achilles 9 Trojan Horse
10 adventures 11 Cyclops 12 magical 13 a 14 d 15 c

Unit 26

1 creative 2 figures of speech 3 similes 4 metaphors
5 hyperbole 6 personification 7 comparisons
8 in common 9 exaggeration 10 exaggerate
11 characteristics 12 whispering 13 d 14 a 15 a

Unit 27

1 grammar rules 2 sentence fragments 3 comma splices
4 incomplete 5 subject 6 verb 7 complete 8 independent
9 clauses 10 period 11 because 12 comma 13 b 14 d 15 c

Unit 28

1 Renaissance 2 Leonardo 3 Michelangelo 4 architect
5 *Supper* 6 apostles 7 sculptor 8 statues 9 sculpture
10 frescoes 11 ceiling 12 Chapel 13 a 14 c 15 b

Unit 29

1 landscapes 2 Hudson River School 3 fields 4 Romantics
5 idealized 6 scenes 7 school 8 Naturalists 9 Realists
10 appeared 11 realistic 12 *Monarchs* 13 c 14 a 15 b

Unit 30

1 associated 2 hymns 3 chants 4 spiritual 5 revival
6 themes 7 folk 8 slaves 9 influence 10 gospel
11 religious 12 comfort 13 b 14 b 15 c